# THE LOTTERY

*and Other Stories*

# THE LOTTERY

## and Other Stories

‡

## Shirley Jackson

‡

Farrar, Straus and Giroux

New York

Farrar, Straus and Giroux
18 West 18th Street, New York 10011

The author's original title for this collection was *The Lottery or,*
*The Adventures of James Harris*

Library of Congress Control Number: 2004062825
Paperback ISBN: 978-0-374-52953-6

www.fsgbooks.com
www.twitter.com/fsgbooks • www.facebook.com/fsgbooks

*For my mother and father*

# Contents

INTRODUCTION BY A. M. HOMES, ix

I

THE INTOXICATED, 3

THE DAEMON LOVER, 9

LIKE MOTHER USED TO MAKE, 29

TRIAL BY COMBAT, 41

THE VILLAGER, 49

MY LIFE WITH R. H. MACY, 57

II

THE WITCH, 63

THE RENEGADE, 69

AFTER YOU, MY DEAR ALPHONSE, 85

CHARLES, 91

AFTERNOON IN LINEN, 97

FLOWER GARDEN, 103

DOROTHY AND MY GRANDMOTHER
AND THE SAILORS, 135

III

COLLOQUY, 145

ELIZABETH, 149

A FINE OLD FIRM, 193

THE DUMMY, 199

SEVEN TYPES OF AMBIGUITY, 209

COME DANCE WITH ME IN IRELAND, 219


IV

OF COURSE, 229

PILLAR OF SALT, 235

MEN WITH THEIR BIG SHOES, 255

THE TOOTH, 265

GOT A LETTER FROM JIMMY, 287

THE LOTTERY, 291


V

EPILOGUE, 303

# INTRODUCTION
## by A. M. Homes

The world of Shirley Jackson is eerie and unforgettable. It is a place where things are not what they seem; even on a day that is sunny and clear, "with the fresh warmth of a full-summer day," there is the threat of darkness looming, of things taking a turn for the worse. Hers is the ever-observant eye, the mind's eye, bearing witness. Out of the stories rises a magical somnambulist's ether—the reader is left forever changed, the mark of the stories indelible upon the imagination, the soul.

Jackson writes with a stunning simplicity; there is a graceful economy to her prose as she charts the smallest of movements, perceptual shifts—nothing pyrotechnic here. Her stories take place in small towns, in kitchens, at cocktail parties. Her characters are trapped by the petty prejudices of people who make themselves feel good by thinking they are somehow better than us all. They live in houses that need painting, in furnished rooms, inside the lives of others—as though in a psychic halfway house, having lost their footing. They are shy, unassuming folks who, for all intents and purposes, would pass through the physical world unnoticed. They care about appearances—how they are seen by others; they possess certain kinds of respectability and a healthy dose of small-town cruelty. This is about politics on the most macro of levels. There is great concern for how one is perceived, how one moves through and does—or, more likely, does not—fit into society, for everyone here is an outsider. Throughout, things are turned inside out, the private is made public, and there is the tension, the subtle electrical hum, of madness in the offing, of perpetual drama unfolding: something is going to happen, something assumedly unpleasant. Everything is thrown into relief, lit in a Hopperesque late-afternoon glow, the one-sided illumination both revealing and casting a long shadow. I can conjure the faces of each person Jackson describes, for the wear and tear over time is evident: they become bitter, pinched, they drink too much. These stories chart intention, behavior—they are an intimate exploration of the psychopathology of everyday life, the small-town sublime. When reading Jackson, I can't help but think of the stories of Raymond Carver, who had a similar ability to create a sort of melancholy emotional mist that floats over his stories. But Jackson also had the ability to be savagely funny: at one point in her career, Desi Arnaz reportedly inquired about her interest in writing a screenplay for Lucille Ball.

The twenty-five stories in *The Lottery and Other Stories*—originally subtitled *The Adventures of James Harris*—are a generous serving of fiction. The title story, "The Lottery," is so much an icon in the history of the American short story that one could argue it has moved from the canon of American twentieth-century fiction directly into the American psyche, our collective unconscious. And whether it is the drunken guest and the smart young girl in "The Intoxicated"—for young girls always know far more than all others, and are both understanding of and perpetually disappointed at the behavior of their elders, male elders in particular—or the well-intentioned but racist Mrs. Williams in "After You, My Dear Alphonse," Jackson's stories are infused with notions of morality, of children being better souls than adults, of a world where people are often persecuted for being different. What is brilliant about these stories is that Jackson presents them to us in such a way that we, the readers, can see them with great clarity and insight, yet the author is careful to allow her characters to remain in a world of their own making, to not pop the bubble.

Jackson works with precision; she sees things as if she's zoomed in and has got life under a magnifying glass. And it's not just any glass, but one with a curved owlish lens, so that perhaps we see and know a little more than usual. Her authorial voice is as idiosyncratic and individual as a fingerprint, and has the ring of God's honest truth.

One of the complications of the critical response to Jackson's work was that most critics couldn't make sense of— or, more likely, accept—a woman writer who could produce both serious literary fiction and the far less reputable "housewife humor" that Jackson also published. Further, Jackson was not interested in being a "woman writer"; she was just a writer, neither male nor female, in a way that to this day is still not easily accommodated by the publishing industry and booksellers. And yet she managed some version of doing it all: she was a woman writer who did not compromise her vision or her talent, and she was a wife and mother of four who managed not to lose herself in some half-baked definition of what "mother" and "married" meant in a pre-feminist era. Jackson was true to her craft and her talent, and in the face of so much seeming "normality" also knew her demons, intimately, personally, but pushed on. Few women writers have been able to manage so much. Along these lines, Jackson reminds me of the late English author Angela Carter, who was also not bound by genre, who had no interest in distinguishing or separating horror, science fiction, et cetera, from "literature." Grace Paley once described the male-female writer phenomenon to me by saying, "Women have always done men the favor of reading their work, but the men have not returned the favor." There is a nether land, a crevasse, to be crossed by women writers who are not writing books for "women" but books for readers.

Mrs. Stanley Hyman—that was her married name; her husband was a literary critic who taught at Bennington; the town itself was the model for the town in "The Lottery." I love thinking of Shirley Jackson as Mrs. Stanley Hyman, the writer in disguise, as the faculty wife and mother. Mrs. Stanley Hyman, just the sound of it is so of a time, the perfect cloak from which she could peer out unnoticed, observe, take notes, work otherwise unseen. Mrs. Stanley Hyman—this one's for you.

So how does one introduce these stories—when in fact they require no introduction? They are stunning, timeless—as relevant and terrifying now as when they were first published. Her work is an absolute must for anyone aspiring to write, anyone hoping to make sense of twentieth-century American culture. Shirley Jackson is a true master.

October 2004

A. M. HOMES is the author of the novels *Music for Torching*, *The End of Alice*, *In a Country of Mothers*, and *Jack*, and the short-story collections *The Safety of Objects* and *Things You Should Know*, along with a travel memoir, *Los Angeles: People, Places, and the Castle on the Hill*. Her fiction and nonfiction appear frequently in many magazines, including *The New Yorker*, *Granta*, *McSweeney's*, *Harper's*, *Zoetrope*, *The New York Times*, and *Vanity Fair*, for which she is a contributing editor.

I

‡

# THE INTOXICATED

HE WAS JUST TIGHT ENOUGH and just familiar enough with
the house to be able to go out into the kitchen alone, apparently
to get ice, but actually to sober up a little; he was not quite
enough a friend of the family to pass out on the living-room
couch. He left the party behind without reluctance, the group
by the piano singing "Stardust," his hostess talking earnestly
to a young man with thin clean glasses and a sullen mouth;
he walked guardedly through the dining-room where a little
group of four or five people sat on the stiff chairs reasoning
something out carefully among themselves; the kitchen doors
swung abruptly to his touch, and he sat down beside a white
enamel table, clean and cold under his hand. He put his glass
on a good spot in the green pattern and looked up to find that
a young girl was regarding him speculatively from across the
table.

"Hello," he said. "You the daughter?"

"I'm Eileen," she said. "Yes."

She seemed to him baggy and ill-formed; it's the clothes
they wear now, young girls, he thought foggily; her hair was
braided down either side of her face, and she looked young
and fresh and not dressed-up; her sweater was purplish and
her hair was dark. "You sound nice and sober," he said, realizing that it was the wrong thing to say to young girls.

"I was just having a cup of coffee," she said. "May I get
you one?"

He almost laughed, thinking that she expected she was deal-
ing knowingly and competently with a rude drunk. "Thank

you," he said, "I believe I will." He made an effort to focus his eyes; the coffee was hot, and when she put a cup in front of him, saying, "I suppose you'd like it black," he put his face into the steam and let it go into his eyes, hoping to clear his head.

"It sounds like a lovely party," she said without longing, "everyone must be having a fine time."

"It is a lovely party." He began to drink the coffee, scalding hot, wanting her to know she had helped him. His head steadied, and he smiled at her. "I feel better," he said, "thanks to you."

"It must be very warm in the other room," she said soothingly.

Then he did laugh out loud and she frowned, but he could see her excusing him as she went on, "It was so hot upstairs I thought I'd like to come down for a while and sit out here."

"Were you asleep?" he asked. "Did we wake you?"

"I was doing my homework," she said.

He looked at her again, seeing her against a background of careful penmanship and themes, worn textbooks and laughter between desks. "You're in high school?"

"I'm a Senior." She seemed to wait for him to say something, and then she said, "I was out a year when I had pneumonia."

He found it difficult to think of something to say (ask her about boys? basketball?), and so he pretended he was listening to the distant noises from the front of the house. "It's a fine party," he said again, vaguely.

"I suppose you like parties," she said.

Dumbfounded, he sat staring into his empty coffee cup. He supposed he did like parties; her tone had been faintly surprised, as though next he were to declare for an arena with gladiators fighting wild beasts, or the solitary circular waltzing of a madman in a garden. I'm almost twice your age, my girl, he thought, but it's not so long since I did homework too. "Play basketball?" he asked.

"No," she said.

He felt with irritation that she had been in the kitchen first, that she lived in the house, that he must keep on talking to her. "What's your homework about?" he asked.

"I'm writing a paper on the future of the world," she said, and smiled. "It sounds silly, doesn't it? I think it's silly."

"Your party out front is talking about it. That's one reason I came out here." He could see her thinking that that was not at all the reason he came out here, and he said quickly, "What are you saying about the future of the world?"

"I don't really think it's got much future," she said, "at least the way we've got it now."

"It's an interesting time to be alive," he said, as though he were still at the party.

"Well, after all," she said, "it isn't as though we didn't *know* about it in advance."

He looked at her for a minute; she was staring absently at the toe of her saddle shoe, moving her foot softly back and forth, following it with her eyes. "It's really a frightening time when a girl sixteen has to think of things like that." In my day, he thought of saying mockingly, girls thought of nothing but cocktails and necking.

"I'm seventeen." She looked up and smiled at him again. "There's a terrible difference," she said.

"In my day," he said, overemphasizing, "girls thought of nothing but cocktails and necking."

"That's partly the trouble," she answered him seriously.

"If people had been really, honestly scared when you were young we wouldn't be so badly off today."

His voice had more of an edge than he intended ("When *I* was young!"), and he turned partly away from her as though to indicate the half-interest of an older person being gracious to a child: "I imagine we thought we were scared. I imagine all kids sixteen—seventeen—think they're scared. It's part of a stage you go through, like being boy-crazy."

"I keep figuring how it will be." She spoke very softly, very clearly, to a point just past him on the wall. "Somehow I think of the churches as going first, before even the Empire State building. And then all the big apartment houses by the river, slipping down slowly into the water with the people inside. And the schools, in the middle of Latin class maybe, while we're reading Cæsar." She brought her eyes to his face, looking at him in numb excitement. "Each time we begin a chapter in Cæsar, I wonder if this won't be the one we never finish. Maybe we in our Latin class will be the last people who ever read Cæsar."

"That would be good news," he said lightly. "I used to hate Cæsar."

"I suppose when you were young everyone hated Cæsar," she said coolly.

He waited for a minute before he said, "I think it's a little silly for you to fill your mind with all this morbid trash. Buy yourself a movie magazine and settle down."

"I'll be able to get all the movie magazines I want," she said insistently. "The subways will crash through, you know, and the little magazine stands will all be squashed. You'll be able to pick up all the candy bars you want, and magazines, and lipsticks and artificial flowers from the five-and-ten, and dresses lying in the street from all the big stores. And fur coats."

"I hope the liquor stores will break wide open," he said, beginning to feel impatient with her, "I'd walk in and help myself to a case of brandy and never worry about anything again."

"The office buildings will be just piles of broken stones," she said, her wide emphatic eyes still looking at him. "If only you could know exactly what *minute* it will come."

"I see," he said. "I go with the rest. I see."

"Things will be different afterward," she said. "Everything that makes the world like it is now will be gone. We'll have new rules and new ways of living. Maybe there'll be a law not to live in houses, so then no one can hide from anyone else, you see."

"Maybe there'll be a law to keep all seventeen-year-old girls in school learning sense," he said, standing up.

"There won't be any schools," she said flatly. "No one will learn anything. To keep from getting back where we are now."

"Well," he said, with a little laugh. "You make it sound very interesting. Sorry I won't be there to see it." He stopped, his shoulder against the swinging door into the dining-room. He wanted badly to say something adult and scathing, and yet he was afraid of showing her that he had listened to her, that when he was young people had not talked like that. "If you have any trouble with your Latin," he said finally, "I'll be glad to give you a hand."

She giggled, shocking him. "I still do my homework every night," she said.

Back in the living-room, with people moving cheerfully around him, the group by the piano now singing "Home on the Range," his hostess deep in earnest conversation with a tall, graceful man in a blue suit, he found the girl's father and said, "I've just been having a very interesting conversation with your daughter."

His host's eye moved quickly around the room. "Eileen? Where is she?"

"In the kitchen. She's doing her Latin."

" '*Gallia est omnia divisa in partes tres*,' " his host said without expression. "I know."

"A really extraordinary girl."

His host shook his head ruefully. "Kids nowadays," he said.

‡

# THE DAEMON LOVER

SHE HAD NOT SLEPT WELL; from one-thirty, when Jamie left and she went lingeringly to bed, until seven, when she at last allowed herself to get up and make coffee, she had slept fitfully, stirring awake to open her eyes and look into the half-darkness, remembering over and over, slipping again into a feverish dream. She spent almost an hour over her coffee—they were to have a real breakfast on the way—and then, unless she wanted to dress early, had nothing to do. She washed her coffee cup and made the bed, looking carefully over the clothes she planned to wear, worried unnecessarily, at the window, over whether it would be a fine day. She sat down to read, thought that she might write a letter to her sister instead, and began, in her finest handwriting, "Dearest Anne, by the time you get this I will be married. Doesn't it sound funny? I can hardly believe it myself, but when I tell you how it happened, you'll see it's even stranger than that. . . . "

Sitting, pen in hand, she hesitated over what to say next, read the lines already written, and tore up the letter. She went to the window and saw that it was undeniably a fine day. It occurred to her that perhaps she ought not to wear the blue silk dress; it was too plain, almost severe, and she wanted to be soft, feminine. Anxiously she pulled through the dresses in the closet, and hesitated over a print she had worn the summer before; it was too young for her, and it had a ruffled neck, and it was very early in the year for a print dress, but still. . . .

She hung the two dresses side by side on the outside of the closet door and opened the glass doors carefully closed upon the small closet that was her kitchenette. She turned on the burner under the coffeepot, and went to the window; it was sunny. When the coffeepot began to crackle she came back and poured herself coffee, into a clean cup. I'll have a headache if I don't get some solid food soon, she thought, all this coffee, smoking too much, no real breakfast. A headache on her wedding day; she went and got the tin box of aspirin from the bathroom closet and slipped it into her blue pocketbook. She'd have to change to a brown pocketbook if she wore the print dress, and the only brown pocketbook she had was shabby. Helplessly, she stood looking from the blue pocketbook to the print dress, and then put the pocketbook down and went and got her coffee and sat down near the window, drinking her coffee, and looking carefully around the one-room apartment. They planned to come back here tonight and everything must be correct. With sudden horror she realized that she had forgotten to put clean sheets on the bed; the laundry was freshly back and she took clean sheets and pillow cases from the top shelf of the closet and stripped the bed, working quickly to avoid thinking consciously of why she was changing the sheets. The bed was a studio bed, with a cover to make it look like a couch, and when it was finished no one would have known she had just put clean sheets on it. She took the old sheets and pillow cases into the bathroom and stuffed them down into the hamper, and put the bathroom towels in the hamper too, and clean towels on the bathroom racks. Her coffee was cold when she came back to it, but she drank it anyway.

When she looked at the clock, finally, and saw that it was after nine, she began at last to hurry. She took a bath, and used one of the clean towels, which she put into the hamper and replaced with a clean one. She dressed carefully, all her underwear fresh and most of it new; she put everything she had worn the day before, including her nightgown, into the hamper. When she was ready for her dress, she hesitated before the closet door. The blue dress was certainly decent, and clean, and fairly becoming, but she had worn it several times with Jamie, and there was nothing about it which made it special for a wedding day. The print dress was overly pretty, and new to Jamie, and yet wearing such a print this early in the year was certainly rushing the season. Finally she thought, This is my wedding day, I can dress as I please, and she took the print dress down from the hanger. When she slipped it on over her head it felt fresh and light, but when she looked at herself in the mirror she remembered that the ruffles around the neck did not show her throat to any great advantage, and the wide swinging skirt looked irresistibly made for a girl, for someone who would run freely, dance, swing it with her hips when she walked. Looking at herself in the mirror she thought with revulsion, It's as though I was trying to make myself look prettier than I am, just for him; he'll think I want to look younger because he's marrying me; and she tore the print dress off so quickly that a seam under the arm ripped. In the old blue dress she felt comfortable and familiar, but unexciting. It isn't what you're wearing that matters, she told herself firmly, and turned in dismay to the closet to see if there might be anything else. There was nothing even remotely suitable for her marrying Jamie, and for a minute she thought of going out quickly to some little shop nearby, to get a dress. Then she saw that it was close on ten, and she had no time for more than her hair and her make-up. Her hair was easy, pulled back into a knot at the nape of her neck, but her make-up was another delicate balance between looking as well as possible, and deceiving as little. She could not try to disguise the sallowness of her skin, or the lines around her eyes, today, when it might look as though she were only doing it for her wedding, and yet she could not bear the thought of Jamie's bringing to marriage anyone who looked haggard and lined. You're thirty-four years old after *all*, she told herself cruelly in the bathroom mirror. Thirty, it said on the license.

It was two minutes after ten; she was not satisfied with her clothes, her face, her apartment. She heated the coffee again and sat down in the chair by the window. Can't do anything more now, she thought, no sense trying to improve anything the last minute.

Reconciled, settled, she tried to think of Jamie and could not see his face clearly, or hear his voice. It's always that way with someone you love, she thought, and let her mind slip past today and tomorrow, into the farther future, when Jamie was established with his writing and she had given up her job, the golden house-in-the-country future they had been preparing for the last week. "I used to be a wonderful cook," she had promised Jamie, "with a little time and practice I could remember how to make angel-food cake. And fried chicken," she said, knowing how the words would stay in Jamie's mind, half-tenderly. "And Hollandaise sauce."

Ten-thirty. She stood up and went purposefully to the phone. She dialed, and waited, and the girl's metallic voice said, ". . . the time will be exactly ten-twenty-nine." Half-consciously she set her clock back a minute; she was remembering her own voice saying last night, in the doorway: "Ten o'clock then. I'll be ready. Is it really *true*?"

And Jamie laughing down the hallway.

By eleven o'clock she had sewed up the ripped seam in

the print dress and put her sewing-box away carefully in the closet. With the print dress on, she was sitting by the window drinking another cup of coffee. I could have taken more time over my dressing after all, she thought; but by now it was so late he might come any minute, and she did not dare try to repair anything without starting all over. There was nothing to eat in the apartment except the food she had carefully stocked up for their life beginning together: the unopened package of bacon, the dozen eggs in their box, the unopened bread and the unopened butter; they were for breakfast tomorrow. She thought of running downstairs to the drugstore for something to eat, leaving a note on the door. Then she decided to wait a little longer.

By eleven-thirty she was so dizzy and weak that she had to go downstairs. If Jamie had had a phone she would have called him then. Instead, she opened her desk and wrote a note: "Jamie, have gone downstairs to the drugstore. Back in five minutes." Her pen leaked onto her fingers and she went into the bathroom and washed, using a clean towel which she replaced. She tacked the note on the door, surveyed the apartment once more to make sure that everything was perfect, and closed the door without locking it, in case he should come.

In the drugstore she found that there was nothing she wanted to eat except more coffee, and she left it half-finished because she suddenly realized that Jamie was probably upstairs waiting and impatient, anxious to get started.

But upstairs everything was prepared and quiet, as she had left it, her note unread on the door, the air in the apartment a little stale from too many cigarettes. She opened the window and sat down next to it until she realized that she had been asleep and it was twenty minutes to one.

Now, suddenly, she was frightened. Waking without prep-

aration into the room of waiting and readiness, everything
clean and untouched since ten o'clock, she was frightened,
and felt an urgent need to hurry. She got up from the chair
and almost ran across the room to the bathroom, dashed cold
water on her face, and used a clean towel; this time she put
the towel carelessly back on the rack without changing it;
time enough for that later. Hatless, still in the print dress with
a coat thrown on over it, the wrong blue pocketbook with the
aspirin inside in her hand, she locked the apartment door
behind her, no note this time, and ran down the stairs. She
caught a taxi on the corner and gave the driver Jamie's
address.

It was no distance at all; she could have walked it if she
had not been so weak, but in the taxi she suddenly realized
how imprudent it would be to drive brazenly up to Jamie's
door, demanding him. She asked the driver, therefore, to let
her off at a corner near Jamie's address and, after paying him,
waited till he drove away before she started to walk down the
block. She had never been here before; the building was
pleasant and old, and Jamie's name was not on any of the
mailboxes in the vestibule, nor on the doorbells. She checked
the address; it was right, and finally she rang the bell marked
"Superintendent." After a minute or two the door buzzer rang
and she opened the door and went into the dark hall where
she hesitated until a door at the end opened and someone
said, "Yes?"

She knew at the same moment that she had no idea what to
ask, so she moved forward toward the figure waiting against
the light of the open doorway. When she was very near, the
figure said, "Yes?" again and she saw that it was a man in
his shirtsleeves, unable to see her any more clearly than she
could see him.

With sudden courage she said, "I'm trying to get in touch with someone who lives in this building and I can't find the name outside."

"What's the name you wanted?" the man asked, and she realized that she would have to answer.

"James Harris," she said. "Harris."

The man was silent for a minute and then he said, "Harris." He turned around to the room inside the lighted doorway and said, "Margie, come here a minute."

"What now?" a voice said from inside, and after a wait long enough for someone to get out of a comfortable chair a woman joined him in the doorway, regarding the dark hall. "Lady here," the man said. "Lady looking for a guy name of Harris, lives here. Anyone in the building?"

"No," the woman said. Her voice sounded amused. "No men named Harris here."

"Sorry," the man said. He started to close the door. "You got the wrong house, lady," he said, and added in a lower voice, "or the wrong guy," and he and the woman laughed.

When the door was almost shut and she was alone in the dark hall she said to the thin lighted crack still showing, "But he *does* live here; I know it."

"Look," the woman said, opening the door again a little, "it happens all the time."

"Please don't make any mistake," she said, and her voice was very dignified, with thirty-four years of accumulated pride. "I'm afraid you don't understand."

"What did he look like?" the woman said wearily, the door still only part open.

"He's rather tall, and fair. He wears a blue suit very often. He's a writer."

"No," the woman said, and then, "Could he have lived on the third floor?"

"I'm not sure."

"There was a fellow," the woman said reflectively. "He wore a blue suit a lot, lived on the third floor for a while. The Roysters lent him their apartment while they were visiting her folks upstate."

"That might be it; I thought, though. . . ."

"This one wore a blue suit mostly, but I don't know how tall he was," the woman said. "He stayed there about a month."

"A month ago is when—"

"You ask the Roysters," the woman said. "They come back this morning. Apartment 3B."

The door closed, definitely. The hall was very dark and the stairs looked darker.

On the second floor there was a little light from a skylight far above. The apartment doors lined up, four on the floor, uncommunicative and silent. There was a bottle of milk outside 2C.

On the third floor, she waited for a minute. There was the sound of music beyond the door of 3B, and she could hear voices. Finally she knocked, and knocked again. The door was opened and the music swept out at her, an early afternoon symphony broadcast. "How do you do," she said politely to this woman in the doorway. "Mrs. Royster?"

"That's right." The woman was wearing a housecoat and last night's make-up.

"I wonder if I might talk to you for a minute?"

"Sure," Mrs. Royster said, not moving.

"About Mr. Harris."

"*What* Mr. Harris?" Mrs. Royster said flatly.

"Mr. James Harris. The gentleman who borrowed your apartment."

"O Lord," Mrs. Royster said. She seemed to open her eyes for the first time. "What'd he do?"

"Nothing. I'm just trying to get in touch with him."

"O Lord," Mrs. Royster said again. Then she opened the door wider and said, "Come in," and then, "Ralph!"

Inside, the apartment was still full of music, and there were suitcases half-unpacked on the couch, on the chairs, on the floor. A table in the corner was spread with the remains of a meal, and the young man sitting there, for a minute resembling Jamie, got up and came across the room.

"What about it?" he said.

"Mr. Royster," she said. It was difficult to talk against the music. "The superintendent downstairs told me that this was where Mr. James Harris has been living."

"Sure," he said. "If that was his name."

"I thought you lent him the apartment," she said, surprised.

"*I* don't know anything about him," Mr. Royster said. "He's one of Dottie's friends."

"Not *my* friends," Mrs. Royster said. "No friend of mine." She had gone over to the table and was spreading peanut butter on a piece of bread. She took a bite and said thickly, waving the bread and peanut butter at her husband. "Not *my* friend."

"You picked him up at one of those damn meetings," Mr. Royster said. He shoved a suitcase off the chair next to the radio and sat down, picking up a magazine from the floor next to him. "I never said more'n ten words to him."

"You said it was okay to lend him the place," Mrs. Royster said before she took another bite. "You never said a word against him, after *all*."

"*I* don't say anything about *your* friends," Mr. Royster said.

"If he'd of been a friend of mine you would have said *plenty*, believe me," Mrs. Royster said darkly. She took another bite and said, "Believe me, he would have said *plenty*."

"That's all I want to hear," Mr. Royster said, over the top of the magazine. "No more, now."

"You see." Mrs. Royster pointed the bread and peanut butter at her husband. "That's the way it is, day and night."

There was silence except for the music bellowing out of the radio next to Mr. Royster, and then she said, in a voice she hardly trusted to be heard over the radio noise, "Has he gone, then?"

"Who?" Mrs. Royster demanded, looking up from the peanut butter jar.

"Mr. James Harris."

"Him? He must've left this morning, before we got back. No sign of him anywhere."

"Gone?"

"Everything was fine, though, perfectly fine. I told you," she said to Mr. Royster, "I told you he'd take care of everything fine. I can always tell."

"You were lucky," Mr. Royster said.

"Not a thing out of place," Mrs. Royster said. She waved her bread and peanut butter inclusively. "Everything just the way we left it," she said.

"Do you know where he is now?"

"Not the slightest idea," Mrs. Royster said cheerfully. "But, like I said, he left everything fine. Why?" she asked suddenly. "You looking for *him*?"

"It's very important."

"I'm sorry he's not here," Mrs. Royster said. She stepped

forward politely when she saw her visitor turn toward the door.

"Maybe the super saw him," Mr. Royster said into the magazine.

When the door was closed behind her the hall was dark again, but the sound of the radio was deadened. She was halfway down the first flight of stairs when the door was opened and Mrs. Royster shouted down the stairwell, "If I see him I'll tell him you were looking for him."

What can I do? she thought, out on the street again. It was impossible to go home, not with Jamie somewhere between here and there. She stood on the sidewalk so long that a woman, leaning out of a window across the way, turned and called to someone inside to come and see. Finally, on an impulse, she went into the small delicatessen next door to the apartment house, on the side that led to her own apartment. There was a small man reading a newspaper, leaning against the counter; when she came in he looked up and came down inside the counter to meet her.

Over the glass case of cold meats and cheese she said, timidly, "I'm trying to get in touch with a man who lived in the apartment house next door, and I just wondered if you know him."

"Whyn't you ask the people there?" the man said, his eyes narrow, inspecting her.

It's because I'm not buying anything, she thought, and she said, "I'm sorry. I asked them, but they don't know anything about him. They think he left this morning."

"I don't know what you want *me* to do," he said, moving a little back toward his newspaper. "I'm not here to keep track of guys going in and out next door."

She said quickly, "I thought you might have noticed, that's

all. He would have been coming past here, a little before ten
o'clock. He was rather tall, and he usually wore a blue suit."

"Now how many men in blue suits go past here every day,
lady?" the man demanded. "You think I got nothing to do
but—"

"I'm sorry," she said. She heard him say, "For God's sake,"
as she went out the door.

As she walked toward the corner, she thought, he must have
come this way, it's the way he'd go to get to my house, it's
the only way for him to walk. She tried to think of Jamie:
where would he have crossed the street? What sort of person
was he actually—would he cross in front of his own apartment
house, at random in the middle of the block, at the corner?

On the corner was a newsstand; they might have seen him
there. She hurried on and waited while a man bought a paper
and a woman asked directions. When the newsstand man
looked at her she said, "Can you possibly tell me if a rather
tall young man in a blue suit went past here this morning
around ten o'clock?" When the man only looked at her, his
eyes wide and his mouth a little open, she thought, he thinks
it's a joke, or a trick, and she said urgently, "It's very important, please believe me. I'm not teasing you."

"*Look*, lady," the man began, and she said eagerly, "He's
a writer. He might have bought magazines here."

"What you want him for?" the man asked. He looked at
her, smiling, and she realized that there was another man
waiting in back of her and the newsdealer's smile included
him. "Never mind," she said, but the newsdealer said, "Listen,
maybe he did come by here." His smile was knowing and his
eyes shifted over her shoulder to the man in back of her. She
was suddenly horribly aware of her over-young print dress,
and pulled her coat around her quickly. The newsdealer said,

with vast thoughtfulness, "Now I don't know for sure, mind you, but there might have been someone like your gentleman friend coming by this morning."

"About ten?"

"About ten," the newsdealer agreed. "Tall fellow, blue suit. I wouldn't be at all surprised."

"Which way did he go?" she said eagerly. "Uptown?"

"Uptown," the newsdealer said, nodding. "He went uptown. That's just exactly it. What can I do for you, sir?"

She stepped back, holding her coat around her. The man who had been standing behind her looked at her over his shoulder and then he and the newsdealer looked at one another. She wondered for a minute whether or not to tip the newsdealer but when both men began to laugh she moved hurriedly on across the street.

Uptown, she thought, that's right, and she started up the avenue, thinking: He wouldn't have to cross the avenue, just go up six blocks and turn down my street, so long as he started uptown. About a block farther on she passed a florist's shop; there was a wedding display in the window and she thought, This is my wedding day after all, he might have gotten flowers to bring me, and she went inside. The florist came out of the back of the shop, smiling and sleek, and she said, before he could speak, so that he wouldn't have a chance to think she was buying anything: "It's *terribly* important that I get in touch with a gentleman who may have stopped in here to buy flowers this morning. *Terribly* important."

She stopped for breath, and the florist said, "Yes, what sort of flowers were they?"

"I don't know," she said, surprised. "He never—" She stopped and said, "He was a rather tall young man, in a blue suit. It was about ten o'clock."

"I see," the florist said. "Well, *really*, I'm afraid. . . ."

"But it's *so* important," she said. "He may have been in a hurry," she added helpfully.

"Well," the florist said. He smiled genially, showing all his small teeth. "For a *lady*," he said. He went to a stand and opened a large book. "Where were they to be sent?" he asked.

"Why," she said, "I don't think he'd have sent them. You see, he was coming—that is, he'd *bring* them."

"Madam," the florist said; he was offended. His smile became deprecatory, and he went on, "Really, you must realize that unless I have *something* to go on. . . ."

"*Please* try to remember," she begged. "He was tall, and had a blue suit, and it was about ten this morning."

The florist closed his eyes, one finger to his mouth, and thought deeply. Then he shook his head. "I simply *can't*," he said.

"Thank you," she said despondently, and started for the door, when the florist said, in a shrill, excited voice, "Wait! Wait just a moment, madam." She turned and the florist, thinking again, said finally, "Chrysanthemums?" He looked at her inquiringly.

"Oh, *no*," she said; her voice shook a little and she waited for a minute before she went on. "Not for an occasion like this, I'm sure."

The florist tightened his lips and looked away coldly. "Well, of *course* I don't know the *occasion*," he said, "but I'm almost certain that the gentleman you were inquiring for came in this morning and purchased one dozen chrysanthemums. No delivery."

"You're *sure*?" she asked.

"Positive," the florist said emphatically. "That was abso-

lutely the man." He smiled brilliantly, and she smiled back
and said, "Well, thank you very much."

He escorted her to the door. "Nice corsage?" he said, as
they went through the shop. "Red roses? Gardenias?"

"It was very kind of you to help me," she said at the door.

"Ladies always look their best in flowers," he said, bending
his head toward her. "Orchids, perhaps?"

"No, thank you," she said, and he said, "I hope you find
your young man," and gave it a nasty sound.

Going on up the street she thought, Everyone thinks it's so
*funny*: and she pulled her coat tighter around her, so that only
the ruffle around the bottom of the print dress was showing.

There was a policeman on the corner, and she thought, Why
don't I go to the police—you go to the police for a missing
person. And then thought, What a fool I'd look like. She had
a quick picture of herself standing in a police station, saying,
"Yes, we were going to be married today, but he didn't come,"
and the policemen, three or four of them standing around
listening, looking at her, at the print dress, at her too-bright
make-up, smiling at one another. She couldn't tell them any
more than that, could not say, "Yes, it looks silly, doesn't it,
me all dressed up and trying to find the young man who
promised to marry me, but what about all of it you don't
know? I have more than this, more than you can see: talent,
perhaps, and humor of a sort, and I'm a lady and I have pride
and affection and delicacy and a certain clear view of life that
might make a man satisfied and productive and happy; there's
more than you think when you look at me."

The police were obviously impossible, leaving out Jamie and
what he might think when he heard she'd set the police after
him. "No, no," she said aloud, hurrying her steps, and someone passing stopped and looked after her.

On the coming corner—she was three blocks from her own street—was a shoeshine stand, an old man sitting almost asleep in one of the chairs. She stopped in front of him and waited, and after a minute he opened his eyes and smiled at her.

"Look," she said, the words coming before she thought of them, "I'm sorry to bother you, but I'm looking for a young man who came up this way about ten this morning, did you see him?" And she began her description, "Tall, blue suit, carrying a bunch of flowers?"

The old man began to nod before she was finished. "I saw him," he said. "Friend of yours?"

"Yes," she said, and smiled back involuntarily.

The old man blinked his eyes and said, "I remember I thought, You're going to see your girl, young fellow. They all go to see their girls," he said, and shook his head tolerantly.

"Which way did he go? Straight on up the avenue?"

"That's right," the old man said. "Got a shine, had his flowers, all dressed up, in an awful hurry. You got a girl, I thought."

"Thank you," she said, fumbling in her pocket for her loose change.

"She sure must of been glad to see him, the way he looked," the old man said.

"Thank you," she said again, and brought her hand empty from her pocket.

For the first time she was really sure he would be waiting for her, and she hurried up the three blocks, the skirt of the print dress swinging under her coat, and turned into her own block. From the corner she could not see her own windows, could not see Jamie looking out, waiting for her, and going down the block she was almost running to get to him. Her key trembled in her fingers at the downstairs door, and as she glanced into the drugstore she thought of her panic, drinking coffee there this morning, and almost laughed. At her own door she could wait no longer, but began to say, "Jamie, I'm here, I was so worried," even before the door was open.

Her own apartment was waiting for her, silent, barren, afternoon shadows lengthening from the window. For a minute she saw only the empty coffee cup, thought, He has been here waiting, before she recognized it as her own, left from the morning. She looked all over the room, into the closet, into the bathroom.

"I never saw him," the clerk in the drugstore said. "I know because I would of noticed the flowers. No one like that's been in."

The old man at the shoeshine stand woke up again to see her standing in front of him. "Hello again," he said, and smiled.

"Are you *sure*?" she demanded. "Did he go on up the avenue?"

"I watched him," the old man said, dignified against her tone. "I thought, There's a young man's got a girl, and I watched him right into the house."

"What house?" she said remotely.

"Right there," the old man said. He leaned forward to point. "The next block. With his flowers and his shine and going to see his girl. Right into her house."

"Which one?" she said.

"About the middle of the block," the old man said. He looked at her with suspicion, and said, "What you trying to do, anyway?"

She almost ran, without stopping to say "Thank you." Up

on the next block she walked quickly, searching the houses
from the outside to see if Jamie looked from a window, listening to hear his laughter somewhere inside.

A woman was sitting in front of one of the houses, pushing
a baby carriage monotonously back and forth the length of
her arm. The baby inside slept, moving back and forth.

The question was fluent, by now. "I'm sorry, but did you
see a young man go into one of these houses about ten this
morning? He was tall, wearing a blue suit, carrying a bunch
of flowers."

A boy about twelve stopped to listen, turning intently from
one to the other, occasionally glancing at the baby.

"Listen," the woman said tiredly, "the kid has his bath at
ten. Would I see strange men walking around? I ask you."

"Big bunch of flowers?" the boy asked, pulling at her coat.
"Big bunch of flowers? I seen him, missus."

She looked down and the boy grinned insolently at her.
"Which house did he go in?" she asked wearily.

"You gonna divorce him?" the boy asked insistently.

"That's not nice to ask the lady," the woman rocking the
carriage said.

"Listen," the boy said, "I seen him. He went in there." He
pointed to the house next door. "I followed him," the boy said.
"He give me a quarter." The boy dropped his voice to a growl,
and said, " 'This is a big day for me, kid,' he says. Give me a
quarter."

She gave him a dollar bill. "Where?" she said.

"Top floor," the boy said. "I followed him till he give me
the quarter. Way to the top." He backed up the sidewalk, out
of reach, with the dollar bill. "You gonna divorce him?" he
asked again.

"Was he carrying flowers?"

"Yeah," the boy said. He began to screech. "You gonna divorce him, missus? You got something on him?" He went careening down the street, howling, "She's got something on the poor guy," and the woman rocking the baby laughed.

The street door of the apartment house was unlocked; there were no bells in the outer vestibule, and no lists of names. The stairs were narrow and dirty; there were two doors on the top floor. The front one was the right one; there was a crumpled florist's paper on the floor outside the door, and a knotted paper ribbon, like a clue, like the final clue in the paper-chase.

She knocked, and thought she heard voices inside, and she thought, suddenly, with terror, What shall I say if Jamie is there, if he comes to the door? The voices seemed suddenly still. She knocked again and there was silence, except for something that might have been laughter far away. He could have seen me from the window, she thought, it's the front apartment and that little boy made a dreadful noise. She waited, and knocked again, but there was silence.

Finally she went to the other door on the floor, and knocked. The door swung open beneath her hand and she saw the empty attic room, bare lath on the walls, floorboards unpainted. She stepped just inside, looking around; the room was filled with bags of plaster, piles of old newspapers, a broken trunk. There was a noise which she suddenly realized as a rat, and then she saw it, sitting very close to her, near the wall, its evil face alert, bright eyes watching her. She stumbled in her haste to be out with the door closed, and the skirt of the print dress caught and tore.

She knew there was someone inside the other apartment,

because she was sure she could hear low voices and sometimes laughter. She came back many times, every day for the first week. She came on her way to work, in the mornings; in the evenings, on her way to dinner alone, but no matter how often or how firmly she knocked, no one ever came to the door.

‡

# LIKE MOTHER USED TO MAKE

DAVID TURNER, who did everything in small quick movements, hurried from the bus stop down the avenue toward his street. He reached the grocery on the corner and hesitated; there had been something. Butter, he remembered with relief; this morning, all the way up the avenue to his bus stop, he had been telling himself butter, don't forget butter coming home tonight, when you pass the grocery remember butter. He went into the grocery and waited his turn, examining the cans on the shelves. Canned pork sausage was back, and corned-beef hash. A tray full of rolls caught his eye, and then the woman ahead of him went out and the clerk turned to him.

"How much is butter?" David asked cautiously.

"Eighty-nine," the clerk said easily.

"Eighty-nine?" David frowned.

"That's what it is," the clerk said. He looked past David at the next customer.

"Quarter of a pound, please," David said. "And a half-dozen rolls."

Carrying his package home he thought, I really ought not to trade there any more; you'd think they'd know me well enough to be more courteous.

There was a letter from his mother in the mailbox. He stuck it into the top of the bag of rolls and went upstairs to the third floor. No light in Marcia's apartment, the only other apartment on the floor. David turned to his own door and unlocked it, snapping on the light as he came in the door.

Tonight, as every night when he came home, the apartment looked warm and friendly and good; the little foyer, with the neat small table and four careful chairs, and the bowl of little marigolds against the pale green walls David had painted himself; beyond, the kitchenette, and beyond that, the big room where David read and slept and the ceiling of which was a perpetual trouble to him; the plaster was falling in one corner and no power on earth could make it less noticeable. David consoled himself for the plaster constantly with the thought that perhaps if he had not taken an apartment in an old brownstone the plaster would not be falling, but then, too, for the money he paid he could not have a foyer and a big room and a kitchenette, anywhere else.

He put his bag down on the table and put the butter away in the refrigerator and the rolls in the breadbox. He folded the empty bag and put it in a drawer in the kitchenette. Then he hung his coat in the hall closet and went into the big room, which he called his living-room, and lighted the desk light. His word for the room, in his own mind, was "charming." He had always been partial to yellows and browns, and he had painted the desk and the bookcases and the end tables himself, had even painted the walls, and had hunted around the city for the exact tweedish tan drapes he had in mind. The room satisfied him: the rug was a rich dark brown that picked up the darkest thread in the drapes, the furniture was almost yellow, the cover on the studio couch and the lampshades were orange. The rows of plants on the window sills gave the touch of green the room needed; right now David was looking for an ornament to set on the end table, but he had his heart set on a low translucent green bowl for more marigolds, and such things cost more than he could afford, after the silverware.

He could not come into this room without feeling that it was the most comfortable home he had ever had; tonight, as always, he let his eyes move slowly around the room, from couch to drapes to bookcase, imagined the green bowl on the end table, and sighed as he turned to the desk. He took his pen from the holder, and a sheet of the neat notepaper sitting in one of the desk cubbyholes, and wrote carefully: "Dear Marcia, don't forget you're coming for dinner tonight. I'll expect you about six." He signed the note with a "D" and picked up the key to Marcia's apartment which lay in the flat pencil tray on his desk. He had a key to Marcia's apartment because she was never home when her laundryman came, or when the man came to fix the refrigerator or the telephone or the windows, and someone had to let them in because the landlord was reluctant to climb three flights of stairs with the pass key. Marcia had never suggested having a key to David's apartment, and he had never offered her one; it pleased him to have only one key to his home, and that safely in his own pocket; it had a pleasant feeling to him, solid and small, the only way into his warm fine home.

He left his front door open and went down the dark hall to the other apartment. He opened the door with his key and turned on the light. This apartment was not agreeable for him to come into; it was exactly the same as his: foyer, kitchenette, living-room, and it reminded him constantly of his first day in his own apartment, when the thought of the careful home-making to be done had left him very close to despair. Marcia's home was bare and at random; an upright piano a friend had given her recently stood crookedly, half in the foyer, because the little room was too narrow and the big room was too cluttered for it to sit comfortably anywhere; Marcia's bed was unmade and a pile of dirty laundry lay on the floor. The window had been open all day and papers had blown wildly around the floor. David closed the window, hesitated over the papers, and then moved away quickly. He put the note on the piano keys and locked the door behind him.

In his own apartment he settled down happily to making dinner. He had made a little pot roast for dinner the night before; most of it was still in the refrigerator and he sliced it in fine thin slices and arranged it on a plate with parsley. His plates were orange, almost the same color as the couch cover, and it was pleasant to him to arrange a salad, with the lettuce on the orange plate, and the thin slices of cucumber. He put coffee on to cook, and sliced potatoes to fry, and then, with his dinner cooking agreeably and the window open to lose the odor of the frying potatoes, he set lovingly to arranging his table. First, the tablecloth, pale green, of course. And the two fresh green napkins. The orange plates and the precise cup and saucer at each place. The plate of rolls in the center, and the odd salt and pepper shakers, like two green frogs. Two glasses—they came from the five-and-ten, but they had thin green bands around them—and finally, with great care, the silverware. Gradually, tenderly, David was buying himself a complete set of silverware; starting out modestly with a service for two, he had added to it until now he had well over a service for four, although not quite a service for six, lacking salad forks and soup spoons. He had chosen a sedate, pretty pattern, one that would be fine with any sort of table setting, and each morning he gloried in a breakfast that started with a shining silver spoon for his grapefruit, and had a compact butter knife for his toast and a solid heavy knife to break his egg-shell, and a fresh silver spoon for his coffee, which he sugared with a particular spoon meant only for sugar. The silverware lay in a tarnish-proof box on a high shelf all to itself, and

David lifted it down carefully to take out a service for two. It made a lavish display set out on the table—knives, forks, salad forks, more forks for the pie, a spoon to each place, and the special serving pieces—the sugar spoon, the large serving spoons for the potatoes and the salad, the fork for the meat, and the pie fork. When the table held as much silverware as two people could possibly use he put the box back on the shelf and stood back, checking everything and admiring the table, shining and clean. Then he went into his living-room to read his mother's letter and wait for Marcia.

The potatoes were done before Marcia came, and then suddenly the door burst open and Marcia arrived with a shout and fresh air and disorder. She was a tall handsome girl with a loud voice, wearing a dirty raincoat, and she said, "I didn't forget, Davie, I'm just late as usual. What's for dinner? You're not mad, are you?"

David got up and came over to take her coat. "I left a note for you," he said.

"Didn't see it," Marcia said. "Haven't been home. Something smells good."

"Fried potatoes," David said. "Everything's ready."

"Golly." Marcia fell into a chair to sit with her legs stretched out in front of her and her arms hanging. "I'm tired," she said. "It's cold out."

"It was getting colder when I came home," David said. He was putting dinner on the table, the platter of meat, the salad, the bowl of fried potatoes. He walked quietly back and forth from the kitchenette to the table, avoiding Marcia's feet. "I don't believe you've been here since I got my silverware," he said.

Marcia swung around to the table and picked up a spoon.

"It's beautiful," she said, running her finger along the pattern. "Pleasure to eat with it."

"Dinner's ready," David said. He pulled her chair out for her and waited for her to sit down.

Marcia was always hungry; she put meat and potatoes and salad on her plate without admiring the serving silver, and started to eat enthusiastically. "Everything's beautiful," she said once. "Food is wonderful, Davie."

"I'm glad you like it," David said. He liked the feel of the fork in his hand, even the sight of the fork moving up to Marcia's mouth.

Marcia waved her hand largely. "I mean everything," she said, "furniture, and nice place you have here, and dinner, and everything."

"I *like* things this way," David said.

"I know you do." Marcia's voice was mournful. "Someone should teach me, I guess."

"You *ought* to keep your home neater," David said. "You ought to get curtains at least, and keep your windows shut."

"I never remember," she said. "Davie, you are the most *wonderful* cook." She pushed her plate away, and sighed.

David blushed happily. "I'm glad you like it," he said again, and then he laughed. "I made a pie last night."

"A pie." Marcia looked at him for a minute and then she said, "Apple?"

David shook his head, and she said, "Pineapple?" and he shook his head again, and, because he could not wait to tell her, said, "Cherry."

"My *God!*" Marcia got up and followed him into the kitchen and looked over his shoulder while he took the pie carefully out of the breadbox. "Is this the first pie you ever made?"

"I've made two before," David admitted, "but this one turned out better than the others."

She watched happily while he cut large pieces of pie and put them on other orange plates, and then she carried her own plate back to the table, tasted the pie, and made wordless gestures of appreciation. David tasted his pie and said critically, "I think it's a little sour. I ran out of sugar."

"It's perfect," Marcia said. "I always loved a cherry pie really *sour*. This isn't sour enough, even."

David cleared the table and poured the coffee, and as he was setting the coffeepot back on the stove Marcia said, "My doorbell's ringing." She opened the apartment door and listened, and they could both hear the ringing in her apartment. She pressed the buzzer in David's apartment that opened the downstairs door, and far away they could hear heavy footsteps starting up the stairs. Marcia left the apartment door open and came back to her coffee. "Landlord, most likely," she said. "I didn't pay my rent again." When the footsteps reached the top of the last staircase Marcia yelled, "Hello?" leaning back in her chair to see out the door into the hall. Then she said, "Why, Mr. Harris." She got up and went to the door and held out her hand. "Come in," she said.

"I just thought I'd stop by," Mr. Harris said. He was a very large man and his eyes rested curiously on the coffee cups and empty plates on the table. "I don't want to interrupt your dinner."

"*That's* all right," Marcia said, pulling him into the room. "It's just Davie. Davie, this is Mr. Harris, he works in my office. This is Mr. Turner."

"How do you do," David said politely, and the man looked at him carefully and said, "How do you do?"

"Sit down, sit down," Marcia was saying, pushing a chair forward. "Davie, how about another cup for Mr. Harris?"

"Please don't bother," Mr. Harris said quickly, "I just thought I'd stop by."

While David was taking out another cup and saucer and getting a spoon down from the tarnish-proof silverbox, Marcia said, "You like homemade pie?"

"Say," Mr. Harris said admiringly, "I've forgotten what homemade pie *looks* like."

"Davie," Marcia called cheerfully, "how about cutting Mr. Harris a piece of that pie?"

Without answering, David took a fork out of the silverbox and got down an orange plate and put a piece of pie on it. His plans for the evening had been vague; they had involved perhaps a movie if it were not too cold out, and at least a short talk with Marcia about the state of her home; Mr. Harris was settling down in his chair and when David put the pie down silently in front of him he stared at it admiringly for a minute before he tasted it.

"Say," he said finally, "this is certainly some pie." He looked at Marcia. "This is really *good* pie," he said.

"You like it?" Marcia asked modestly. She looked up at David and smiled at him over Mr. Harris' head. "I haven't made but two, three pies before," she said.

David raised a hand to protest, but Mr. Harris turned to him and demanded, "Did you ever eat any better pie in your life?"

"I don't think Davie liked it much," Marcia said wickedly, "I think it was too sour for him."

"I *like* a sour pie," Mr. Harris said. He looked suspiciously at David. "A cherry pie's *got* to be sour."

"I'm glad you like it, anyway," Marcia said. Mr. Harris ate

the last mouthful of pie, finished his coffee, and sat back. "I'm sure glad I dropped in," he said to Marcia.

David's desire to be rid of Mr. Harris had slid imperceptibly into an urgency to be rid of them both; his clean house, his nice silver, were not meant as vehicles for the kind of fatuous banter Marcia and Mr. Harris were playing at together; almost roughly he took the coffee cup away from the arm Marcia had stretched across the table, took it out to the kitchenette and came back and put his hand on Mr. Harris' cup.

"Don't bother, Davie, honestly," Marcia said. She looked up, smiling again, as though she and David were conspirators against Mr. Harris. "I'll do them all tomorrow, honey," she said.

"Sure," Mr. Harris said. He stood up. "Let them wait. Let's go in and sit down where we can be comfortable."

Marcia got up and led him into the living-room and they sat down on the studio couch. "Come on in, Davie," Marcia called.

The sight of his pretty table covered with dirty dishes and cigarette ashes held David. He carried the plates and cups and silverware into the kitchenette and stacked them in the sink and then, because he could not endure the thought of their sitting there any longer, with the dirt gradually hardening on them, he tied an apron on and began to wash them carefully. Now and then, while he was washing them and drying them and putting them away, Marcia would call to him, sometimes, "Davie, what *are* you doing?" or, "Davie, won't you stop all that and come sit down?" Once she said, "Davie, I don't want you to wash all those dishes," and Mr. Harris said, "Let him work, he's happy."

David put the clean yellow cups and saucers back on the shelves—by now, Mr. Harris' cup was unrecognizable; you could not tell, from the clean rows of cups, which one he had used or which one had been stained with Marcia's lipstick or which one had held David's coffee which he had finished in the kitchenette—and finally, taking the tarnish-proof box down, he put the silverware away. First the forks all went together into the little grooves which held two forks each— later, when the set was complete, each groove would hold four forks—and then the spoons, stacked up neatly one on top of another in their own grooves, and the knives in even order, all facing the same way, in the special tapes in the lid of the box. Butter knives and serving spoons and the pie knife all went into their own places, and then David put the lid down on the lovely shining set and put the box back on the shelf. After wringing out the dishcloth and hanging up the dish towel and taking off his apron he was through, and he went slowly into the living-room. Marcia and Mr. Harris were sitting close together on the studio couch, talking earnestly.

"My *father's* name was James," Marcia was saying as David came in, as though she were clinching an argument. She turned around when David came in and said, "Davie, you were so nice to do all those dishes yourself."

"That's all right," David said awkwardly. Mr. Harris was looking at him impatiently.

"I should have helped you," Marcia said. There was a silence, and then Marcia said, "Sit down, Davie, won't you?"

David recognized her tone; it was the one hostesses used when they didn't know what else to say to you, or when you had come too early or stayed too late. It was the tone he had expected to use on Mr. Harris.

"James and I were just talking about. . . ." Marcia began and then stopped and laughed. "What *were* we talking about?" she asked, turning to Mr. Harris.

"Nothing much," Mr. Harris said. He was still watching David.

"Well," Marcia said, letting her voice trail off. She turned to David and smiled brightly and then said, "Well," again.

Mr. Harris picked up the ashtray from the end table and set it on the couch between himself and Marcia. He took a cigar out of his pocket and said to Marcia, "Do you mind cigars?" and when Marcia shook her head he unwrapped the cigar tenderly and bit off the end. "Cigar smoke's good for plants," he said thickly, around the cigar, as he lighted it, and Marcia laughed.

David stood up. For a minute he thought he was going to say something that might start, "Mr. Harris, I'll thank you to. . . ." but what he actually said, finally, with both Marcia and Mr. Harris looking at him, was, "Guess I better be getting along, Marcia."

Mr. Harris stood up and said heartily, "Certainly have enjoyed meeting you." He held out his hand and David shook hands limply.

"Guess I better be getting along," he said again to Marcia, and she stood up and said, "I'm sorry you have to leave so soon."

"Lots of work to do," David said, much more genially than he intended, and Marcia smiled at him again as though they were conspirators and went over to the desk and said, "Don't forget your key."

Surprised, David took the key of her apartment from her, said good night to Mr. Harris, and went to the outside door.

"Good night, Davie honey," Marcia called out, and David said "Thanks for a simply *wonderful* dinner, Marcia," and closed the door behind him.

He went down the hall and let himself into Marcia's apart-

ment; the piano was still awry, the papers were still on the
floor, the laundry scattered, the bed unmade. David sat down
on the bed and looked around. It was cold, it was dirty, and as
he thought miserably of his own warm home he heard faintly
down the hall the sound of laughter and the scrape of a chair
being moved. Then, still faintly, the sound of his radio. Wearily, David leaned over and picked up a paper from the floor,
and then he began to gather them up one by one.

‡

# TRIAL BY COMBAT

When Emily Johnson came home one evening to her furnished room and found three of her best handkerchiefs missing from the dresser drawer, she was sure who had taken them and what to do. She had lived in the furnished room for about six weeks and for the past two weeks she had been missing small things occasionally. There had been several handkerchiefs gone, and an initial pin which Emily rarely wore and which had come from the five-and-ten. And once she had missed a small bottle of perfume and one of a set of china dogs. Emily had known for some time who was taking the things, but it was only tonight that she had decided what to do. She had hesitated about complaining to the landlady because her losses were trivial and because she had felt certain that sooner or later she would know how to deal with the situation herself. It had seemed logical to her from the beginning that the one person in the rooming-house who was home all day was the most likely suspect, and then, one Sunday morning, coming downstairs from the roof, where she had been sitting in the sun, Emily had seen someone come out of her room and go down the stairs, and had recognized the visitor. Tonight, she felt, she knew just what to do. She took off her coat and hat, put her packages down, and, while a can of tamales was heating on her electric plate, she went over what she intended to say.

After her dinner, she closed and locked her door and went downstairs. She tapped softly on the door of the room directly below her own, and when she thought she heard someone say,

"Come in," she said, "Mrs. Allen?," then opened the door carefully and stepped inside.

The room, Emily noticed immediately, was almost like her own—the same narrow bed with the tan cover, the same maple dresser and armchair; the closet was on the opposite side of the room, but the window was in the same relative position. Mrs. Allen was sitting in the armchair. She was about sixty. More than twice as old as I am, Emily thought, while she stood in the doorway, and a lady still. She hesitated for a few seconds, looking at Mrs. Allen's clean white hair and her neat, dark-blue house coat, before speaking. "Mrs. Allen," she said, "I'm Emily Johnson."

Mrs. Allen put down the *Woman's Home Companion* she had been reading and stood up slowly. "I'm very happy to meet you," she said graciously. "I've seen you, of course, several times, and thought how pleasant you looked. It's so seldom one meets anyone really"—Mrs. Allen hesitated—"really nice," she went on, "in a place like this."

"I've wanted to meet you, too," Emily said.

Mrs. Allen indicated the chair she had been sitting in. "Won't you sit down?"

"Thank you," Emily said. "You stay there. I'll sit on the bed." She smiled. "I feel as if I know the furniture so well. Mine's just the same."

"It's a shame," Mrs. Allen said, sitting down in her chair again. "I've told the landlady over and over, you can't make people feel at home if you put all the same furniture in the rooms. But she maintains that this maple furniture is clean-looking and cheap."

"It's better than most," Emily said. "You've made yours look much nicer than mine."

"I've been here for three years," Mrs. Allen said. "You've only been here a month or so, haven't you?"

"Six weeks," Emily said.

"The landlady's told me about you. Your husband's in the Army."

"Yes. I have a job here in New York."

"My husband was in the Army," Mrs. Allen said. She gestured at a group of pictures on her maple dresser. "That was a long time ago, of course. He's been dead for nearly five years." Emily got up and went over to the pictures. One of them was of a tall, dignified-looking man in Army uniform. Several were of children.

"He was a very distinguished-looking man," Emily said. "Are those your children?"

"I had no children, to my sorrow," the old lady said. "Those are nephews and nieces of my husband's."

Emily stood in front of the dresser, looking around the room. "I see you have flowers, too," she said. She walked to the window and looked at the row of potted plants. "I love flowers," she said. "I bought myself a big bunch of asters tonight to brighten up my room. But they fade so quickly."

"I prefer plants just for that reason," Mrs. Allen said. "But why don't you put an aspirin in the water with your flowers? They'll last much longer."

"I'm afraid I don't know much about flowers," Emily said. "I didn't know about putting an aspirin in the water, for instance."

"I always do, with cut flowers," Mrs. Allen said. "I think flowers make a room look so friendly."

Emily stood by the window for a minute, looking out on Mrs. Allen's daily view: the fire escape opposite, an oblique slice of the street below. Then she took a deep breath and turned around. "Actually, Mrs. Allen," she said, "I had a reason for dropping in."

"Other than to make my acquaintance?" Mrs. Allen said, smiling.

"I don't know quite what to do," Emily said. "I don't like to say anything to the landlady."

"The landlady isn't much help in an emergency," Mrs. Allen said.

Emily came back and sat on the bed, looking earnestly at Mrs. Allen, seeing a nice old lady. "It's so slight," she said, "but someone has been coming into my room."

Mrs. Allen looked up.

"I've been missing things," Emily went on, "like handkerchiefs and little inexpensive jewelry. Nothing important. But someone's been coming into my room and helping themselves."

"I'm sorry to hear it," Mrs. Allen said.

"You see, I don't like to make trouble," Emily said. "It's just that someone's coming into my room. I haven't missed anything of value."

"I see," Mrs. Allen said.

"I just noticed it a few days ago. And then last Sunday I was coming down from the roof and I saw someone coming out of my room."

"Do you have any idea who it was?" Mrs. Allen asked.

"I believe I do," Emily said.

Mrs. Allen was quiet for a minute. "I can see where you wouldn't like to speak to the landlady," she said finally.

"Of course not," Emily said. "I just want it to stop."

"I don't blame you," Mrs. Allen said.

"You see, it means someone has a key to my door," Emily said pleadingly.

"All the keys in this house open all the doors," Mrs. Allen said. "They're all old-fashioned locks."

"It *has* to stop," Emily said. "If it doesn't, I'll have to do something about it."

"I can see that," Mrs. Allen said. "The whole thing is very unfortunate." She rose. "You'll have to excuse me," she went on. "I tire very easily and I must be in bed early. I'm so happy you came down to see me."

"I'm so glad to have met you at last," Emily said. She went to the door. "I hope I won't be bothered again," she said. "Good night."

"Good night," Mrs. Allen said.

The following evening, when Emily came home from work, a pair of cheap earrings was gone, along with two packages of cigarettes which had been in her dresser drawer. That evening she sat alone in her room for a long time, thinking. Then she wrote a letter to her husband and went to bed. The next morning she got up and dressed and went to the corner drugstore, where she called her office from a phone booth and said that she was sick and would not be in that day. Then she went back to her room. She sat for almost an hour with the door slightly ajar before she heard Mrs. Allen's door open and Mrs. Allen come out and go slowly down the stairs. When Mrs. Allen had had time to get out onto the street, Emily locked her door and, carrying her key in her hand, went down to Mrs. Allen's room.

She was thinking, I just want to pretend it's my own room, so that if anyone comes I can say I was mistaken about the floor. For a minute, after she had opened the door, it seemed as though she *were* in her own room. The bed was neatly made and the shade drawn down over the window. Emily left the door unlocked and went over and pulled up the shade.

Now that the room was light, she looked around. She had a sudden sense of unbearable intimacy with Mrs. Allen, and thought, This is the way she must feel in my room. Everything was neat and plain. She looked in the closet first, but there was nothing in there but Mrs. Allen's blue house coat and one or two plain dresses. Emily went to the dresser. She looked for a moment at the picture of Mrs. Allen's husband, and then opened the top drawer and looked in. Her handkerchiefs were there, in a neat, small pile, and next to them the cigarettes and the earrings. In one corner the little china dog was sitting. Everything is here, Emily thought, all put away and very orderly. She closed the drawer and opened the next two. Both were empty. She opened the top one again. Besides her things, the drawer held a pair of black cotton gloves, and under the little pile of her handkerchiefs were two plain white ones. There was a box of Kleenex and a small tin of aspirin. For her plants, Emily thought.

Emily was counting the handkerchiefs when a noise behind her made her turn around. Mrs. Allen was standing in the doorway watching her quietly. Emily dropped the handkerchiefs she was holding and stepped back. She felt herself blushing and knew her hands were trembling. Now, she was thinking, now turn around and tell her. "Listen, Mrs. Allen," she began, and stopped.

"Yes?" Mrs. Allen said gently.

Emily found that she was staring at the picture of Mrs. Allen's husband; such a thoughtful-looking man, she was thinking. They must have had such a pleasant life together, and now she has a room like mine, with only two handkerchiefs of her own in the drawer.

"Yes?" Mrs. Allen said again.

What does she want me to say, Emily thought. What could

she be waiting for with such a ladylike manner? "I came down," Emily said, and hesitated. My voice is almost ladylike, too, she thought. "I had a terrible headache and I came down to borrow some aspirin," she said quickly. "I had this awful headache and when I found you were out I thought surely you wouldn't mind if I just borrowed some aspirin."

"I'm so sorry," Mrs. Allen said. "But I'm glad you felt you knew me well enough."

"I never would have dreamed of coming in," Emily said, "except for such a bad headache."

"Of course," Mrs. Allen said. "Let's not say any more about it." She went over to the dresser and opened the drawer. Emily, standing next to her, watched her hand pass over the handkerchiefs and pick up the aspirin. "You just take two of these and go to bed for an hour," Mrs. Allen said.

"Thank you." Emily began to move toward the door. "You've been very kind."

"Let me know if there's anything more I can do."

"Thank you," Emily said again, opening the door. She waited for a minute and then turned toward the stairs to her room.

"I'll run up later today," Mrs. Allen said, "just to see how you feel."

‡

# THE VILLAGER

Miss Clarence stopped on the corner of Sixth Avenue and Eighth Street and looked at her watch. Two-fifteen; she was earlier than she thought. She went into Whelan's and sat at the counter, putting her copy of the *Villager* down on the counter next to her pocketbook and *The Charterhouse of Parma*, which she had read enthusiastically up to page fifty and only carried now for effect. She ordered a chocolate-frosted and while the clerk was making it she went over to the cigarette counter and bought a pack of Kools. Sitting again at the soda counter, she opened the pack and lit a cigarette.

Miss Clarence was about thirty-five, and had lived in Greenwich Village for twelve years. When she was twenty-three she had come to New York from a small town upstate because she wanted to be a dancer, and because everyone who wanted to study dancing or sculpture or book-binding had come to Greenwich Village then, usually with allowances from their families to live on and plans to work in Macy's or in a book-shop until they had enough money to pursue their art. Miss Clarence, fortunate in having taken a course in shorthand and typing, had gone to work as a stenographer in a coal and coke concern. Now, after twelve years, she was a private secretary in the same concern, and was making enough money to live in a good Village apartment by the park and buy herself smart clothes. She still went to an occasional dance recital with another girl from her office, and sometimes when she wrote to her old friends at home she referred to herself as a "Village die-hard." When Miss Clarence gave the matter any thought at all, she was apt to congratulate herself on her common sense in handling a good job competently and supporting herself better than she would have in her home town.

Confident that she looked very well in her gray tweed suit and the hammered copper lapel ornament from a Village jewelry store, Miss Clarence finished her frosted and looked at her watch again. She paid the cashier and went out into Sixth Avenue, and began to walk briskly uptown. She had estimated correctly; the house she was looking for was just west of Sixth Avenue, and she stopped in front of it for a minute, pleased with herself, and comparing the building with her own presentable apartment house. Miss Clarence lived in a picturesque brick and stucco modern; this house was wooden and old, with the very new front door that is deceptive until you look at the building above and see the turn-of-the-century architecture. Miss Clarence compared the address again with the ad in the *Villager*, and then opened the front door and went into the dingy hallway. She found the name Roberts and the apartment number, 4B. Miss Clarence sighed and started up the stairs.

She stopped and rested on the third landing, and lit another one of her cigarettes so as to enter the apartment effectively. At the head of the stairs on the fourth floor she found 4B, with a typed note pinned on the door. Miss Clarence pulled the note loose from the thumbtack that held it, and took it over into the light. "Miss Clarence—" she read, "I had to run out for a few minutes, but will be back about three-thirty. Please come on in and look around till I get back— all the furniture is marked with prices. Terribly sorry. Nancy Roberts."

Miss Clarence tried the door and it was unlocked. Still

holding the note, she went in and closed the door behind her. The room was in confusion: half-empty boxes of papers and books were on the floor, the curtains were down, and the furniture piled with half-packed suitcases and clothes. The first thing Miss Clarence did was go to the window; on the fourth floor, she thought, maybe they would have a view. But she could see only dirty roofs and, far off to the left, a high building crowned with flower gardens. Someday I'll live *there*, she thought, and turned back to the room.

She went into the kitchen, a tiny alcove with a two-burner stove and a refrigerator built underneath, with a small sink on one side. Don't do much cooking, Miss Clarence thought, stove's never been cleaned. In the refrigerator were a bottle of milk and three bottles of Coca Cola and a half-empty jar of peanut butter. Eat all their meals out, Miss Clarence thought. She opened the cupboard: a glass and a bottle opener. The other glass would be in the bathroom, Miss Clarence thought; no cups: she doesn't even make coffee in the morning. There was a roach inside the cupboard door; Miss Clarence closed it hurriedly and went back into the big room. She opened the bathroom door and glanced in: an old-fashioned tub with feet, no shower. The bathroom was dirty, and Miss Clarence was sure there would be roaches in there too.

Finally Miss Clarence turned to the crowded room. She lifted a suitcase and a typewriter off one of the chairs, took off her hat and coat, and sat down, lighting another one of her cigarettes. She had already decided that she could not use any of the furniture—the two chairs and the studio bed were maple; what Miss Clarence thought of as Village Modern. The small end-table bookcase was a nice piece of furniture, but there was a long scratch running across the top, and several glass stains. It was marked ten dollars, and Miss Clarence told herself she could get a dozen new ones if she wanted to pay that price. Miss Clarence, in a mild resentment of the coal and coke company, had done her quiet apartment in shades of beige and off-white, and the thought of introducing any of this shiny maple frightened her. She had a quick picture of young Village characters, frequenters of bookshops, lounging on the maple furniture and drinking rum and coke, putting their glasses down anywhere.

For a minute Miss Clarence thought of offering to buy some books, but the ones packed on top of the boxes were mostly art books and portfolios. Some of the books had "Arthur Roberts" written inside; Arthur and Nancy Roberts, Miss Clarence thought, a nice young couple. Arthur was the artist, then, and Nancy . . . Miss Clarence turned over a few of the books and came across a book of modern dance photographs; could Nancy, she wondered affectionately, be a dancer?

The phone rang and Miss Clarence, on the other side of the room, hesitated for a minute before walking over and answering it. When she said hello a man's voice said, "Nancy?"

"No, I'm sorry, she's not home," Miss Clarence said.

"Who's this?" the voice asked.

"I'm waiting to see Mrs. Roberts," Miss Clarence said.

"Well," the voice said, "this is Artie Roberts, her husband. When she comes back ask her to call me, will you?"

"Mr. Roberts," Miss Clarence said. "Maybe you can help me, then. I came to look at the furniture."

"Who are you?"

"My name is Clarence, Hilda Clarence. I was interested in buying the furniture."

"Well, Hilda," Artie Roberts said, "what do you think? Everything's in good condition."

"I can't quite make up my mind," Miss Clarence said.

"The studio bed's as good as new," Artie Roberts went on, "I've got this chance to go to Paris, you know. That's why we're selling the stuff."

"That's wonderful," Miss Clarence said.

"Nancy's going on back to her family in Chicago. We've got to sell the stuff and get everything fixed up in such a short time."

"I know," Miss Clarence said. "It's too bad."

"Well, Hilda," Artie Roberts said, "you talk to Nancy when she gets back and she'll be glad to tell you all about it. You won't go wrong on any of it. I can guarantee that it's comfortable."

"I'm sure," Miss Clarence said.

"Tell her to call me, will you?"

"I certainly will," Miss Clarence said.

She said good-bye and hung up.


She went back to her chair and looked at her watch. Three-ten. I'll wait till just three-thirty, Miss Clarence thought, and then I'll leave. She picked up the book of dance photographs, slipping the pages through her fingers until a picture caught her eye and she turned back to it. I haven't seen this in years, Miss Clarence thought—Martha Graham. A sudden picture of herself at twenty came to Miss Clarence, before she ever came to New York, practicing the dancer's pose. Miss Clarence put the book down on the floor and stood up, raising her arms. Not as easy as it used to be, she thought, it catches you in the shoulders. She was looking down at the book over her shoulder, trying to get her arms right, when there was a knock and the door was opened. A young man—about Arthur's age, Miss Clarence thought—came in and stood just inside the door, apologetically.

"It was partly open," he said, "so I came on in."

"Yes?" Miss Clarence said, dropping her arms.

"You're Mrs. Roberts?" the young man asked.

Miss Clarence, trying to walk naturally over to her chair, said nothing.

"I came about the furniture," the man said. "I thought I might look at the chairs."

"Of course," Miss Clarence said. "The price is marked on everything."

"My name's Harris. I've just moved to the city and I'm trying to furnish my place."

"It's very difficult to find things these days."

"This must be the tenth place I've been. I want a filing cabinet and a big leather chair."

"I'm afraid . . ." Miss Clarence said, gesturing at the room.

"I know," Harris said. "Anybody who has that sort of thing these days is hanging on to it. I write," he added.

"Really?"

"Or, rather, I *hope* to write," Harris said. He had a round agreeable face and when he said this he smiled very pleasantly. "Going to get a job and write nights," he said.

"I'm sure you won't have much trouble," Miss Clarence said.

"Some one here an artist?"

"Mr. Roberts," Miss Clarence said.

"Lucky guy," Harris said. He walked over to the window. "Easier to draw pictures than write any time. This place is certainly nicer than mine," he added suddenly, looking out the window. "Mine's a hole in the wall."

Miss Clarence could not think of anything to say, and he turned again to look at her curiously. "You an artist, too?"

"No," Miss Clarence said. She took a deep breath. "Dancer," she said.

He smiled again, pleasantly. "I might have known," he said. "When I came in."

Miss Clarence laughed modestly.

"It must be wonderful," he said.

"It's hard," Miss Clarence said.

"It must be. You had much luck so far?"

"Not much," Miss Clarence said.

"I guess that's the way everything is," he said. He wandered over and opened the bathroom door; when he glanced in Miss Clarence winced. He closed the door again without saying anything and opened the kitchen door.

Miss Clarence got up and walked over to stand next to him and look into the kitchen with him. "I don't cook a lot," she said.

"Don't blame you, so many restaurants." He closed the door again and Miss Clarence went back to her chair. "I can't eat breakfasts out, though. That's one thing I can't do," he said.

"Do you make your own?"

"I try to," he said. "I'm the worst cook in the world. But it's better than going out. What I need is a wife." He smiled again and started for the door. "I'm sorry about the furniture," he said. "Wish I could have found something."

"That's all right."

"You people giving up housekeeping?"

"We have to get rid of everything," Miss Clarence said. She hesitated. "Artie's going to Paris," she said finally.

"Wish I was." He sighed. "Well, good luck to both of you."

"You, too," Miss Clarence said, and closed the door behind him slowly. She listened for the sound of his steps going down the stairs and then looked at her watch. Three-twenty-five.

Suddenly in a hurry, she found the note Nancy Roberts had left for her and wrote on the back with a pencil taken from one of the boxes: "My dear Mrs. Roberts—I waited until three-thirty. I'm afraid the furniture is out of the question for me. Hilda Clarence." Pencil in hand, she thought for a minute. Then she added: "P.S. Your husband called, and wants you to call him back."

She collected her pocketbook, *The Charterhouse of Parma*, and the *Villager*, and closed the door. The thumbtack was still there, and she pried it loose and tacked her note up with it. Then she turned and went back down the stairs, home to her own apartment. Her shoulders ached.

‡

# MY LIFE WITH R. H. MACY

AND THE FIRST THING THEY DID was segregate me. They segregated me from the only person in the place I had even a
speaking acquaintance with; that was a girl I had met going
down the hall who said to me: "Are you as scared as I am?"
And when I said, "Yes," she said, "I'm in lingerie, what are
you in?" and I thought for a while and then said, "Spun
glass," which was as good an answer as I could think of, and
she said, "Oh. Well, I'll meet you here in a sec." And she
went away and was segregated and I never saw her again.

Then they kept calling my name and I kept trotting over
to wherever they called it and they would say ("They" all
this time being startlingly beautiful young women in tailored
suits and with short-clipped hair), "Go with Miss Cooper,
here. She'll tell you what to do." All the women I met my first
day were named Miss Cooper. And Miss Cooper would say to
me: "What are you in?" and I had learned by that time to
say, "Books," and she would say, "Oh, well, then, you be-
long with Miss Cooper here," and then she would call "Miss
Cooper?" and another young woman would come and the
first one would say, "13-3138 here belongs with you," and
Miss Cooper would say, "What is she in?" and Miss Cooper
would answer, "Books," and I would go away and be segregated again.

Then they taught me. They finally got me segregated into
a classroom, and I sat there for a while all by myself (that's
how far segregated I was) and then a few other girls came
in, all wearing tailored suits (I was wearing a red velvet after-

noon frock) and we sat down and they taught us. They gave us each a big book with R. H. Macy written on it, and inside this book were pads of little sheets saying (from left to right) : "Comp. keep for ref. cust. d.a. no. or c.t. no. salesbook no. salescheck no. clerk no. dept. date M." After M there was a long line for Mr. or Mrs. and the name, and then it began again with "No. item. class. at price. total." And down at the bottom was written Original and then again, "Comp. keep for ref., and "Paste yellow gift stamp here." I read all this very carefully. Pretty soon a Miss Cooper came, who talked for a little while on the advantages we had in working at Macy's, and she talked about the salesbooks, which it seems came apart into a sort of road map and carbons and things. I listened for a while, and when Miss Cooper wanted us to write on the little pieces of paper, I copied from the girl next to me. That was training.

Finally someone said we were going on the floor, and we descended from the sixteenth floor to the first. We were in groups of six by then, all following Miss Cooper doggedly and wearing little tags saying Book Information. I never did find out what that meant. Miss Cooper said I had to work on the special sale counter, and showed me a little book called *The Stage-Struck Seal*, which it seemed I would be selling. I had gotten about halfway through it before she came back to tell me I had to stay with my unit.

I enjoyed meeting the time clock, and spent a pleasant half-hour punching various cards standing around, and then someone came in and said I couldn't punch the clock with my hat on. So I had to leave, bowing timidly at the time clock and its prophet, and I went and found out my locker number, which was 1773, and my time-clock number, which was 712, and my cash-box number, which was 1336, and my cash-register number, which was 253, and my cash-register-drawer number, which was K, and my cash-register-drawer-key number, which was 872, and my department number, which was 13. I wrote all these numbers down. And that was my first day.

My second day was better. I was officially on the floor. I stood in a corner of a counter, with one hand possessively on *The Stage-Struck Seal*, waiting for customers. The counter head was named 13-2246, and she was very kind to me. She sent me to lunch three times, because she got me confused with 13-6454 and 13-3141. It was after lunch that a customer came. She came over and took one of my stage-struck seals, and said "How much is this?" I opened my mouth and the customer said "I have a D. A. and I will have this sent to my aunt in Ohio. Part of that D. A. I will pay for with a book dividend of 32 cents, and the rest of course will be on my account. Is this book price-fixed?" That's as near as I can remember what she said. I smiled confidently, and said "Certainly; will you wait just one moment?" I found a little piece of paper in a drawer under the counter: it had "Duplicate Triplicate" printed across the front in big letters. I took down the customer's name and address, her aunt's name and address, and wrote carefully across the front of the duplicate triplicate "1 Stg. Strk. Sl." Then I smiled at the customer again and said carelessly: "That will be seventy-five cents." She said "But I have a D. A." I told her that all D. A.'s were suspended for the Christmas rush, and she gave me seventy-five cents, which I kept. Then I rang up a "No Sale" on the cash register and I tore up the duplicate triplicate because I didn't know what else to do with it.

Later on another customer came and said "Where would I find a copy of Ann Rutherford Gwynn's *He Came Like*

*Thunder?*" and I said "In medical books, right across the way," but 13-2246 came and said "That's philosophy, isn't it?" and the customer said it was, and 13-2246 said "Right down this aisle, in dictionaries." The customer went away, and I said to 13-2246 that her guess was as good as mine, anyway, and she stared at me and explained that philosophy, social sciences and Bertrand Russell were all kept in dictionaries.

So far I haven't been back to Macy's for my third day, because that night when I started to leave the store, I fell down the stairs and tore my stockings and the doorman said that if I went to my department head Macy's would give me a new pair of stockings and I went back and I found Miss Cooper and she said, "Go to the adjuster on the seventh floor and give him this," and she handed me a little slip of pink paper and on the bottom of it was printed "Comp. keep for ref. cust. d.a. no. or c.t. no. salesbook no. salescheck no. clerk no. dept. date M." And after M, instead of a name, she had written 13-3138. I took the little pink slip and threw it away and went up to the fourth floor and bought myself a pair of stockings for $.69 and then I came down and went out the customers' entrance.

I wrote Macy's a long letter, and I signed it with all my numbers added together and divided by 11,700, which is the number of employees in Macy's. I wonder if they miss me.

# II

The ignorant *Looker-on* can't imagine what the *Limner* means by those seemingly *rude Lines* and *Scrawls*, which he intends for the *Rudiments* of a *Picture,* and the *Figures of Mathematick Operation* are *Nonsense,* and *Dashes* at a *Venture,* to one un-instructed in *Mechanicks.* We are in the Dark to *one another's* Purposes and Intendments; and there are a thousand Intrigues in our little Matters, which will not presently confess their Design, even to *sagacious Inquisitors.*

Joseph Glanvil: *Sadducismus Triumphatus*

‡

# THE WITCH

THE COACH was so nearly empty that the little boy had a seat all to himself, and his mother sat across the aisle on the seat next to the little boy's sister, a baby with a piece of toast in one hand and a rattle in the other. She was strapped securely to the seat so she could sit up and look around, and whenever she began to slip slowly sideways the strap caught her and held her halfway until her mother turned around and straightened her again. The little boy was looking out the window and eating a cookie, and the mother was reading quietly, answering the little boy's questions without looking up.

"We're on a river," the little boy said. "This is a river and we're on it."

"Fine," his mother said.

"We're on a bridge over a river," the little boy said to himself.

The few other people in the coach were sitting at the other end of the car; if any of them had occasion to come down the aisle the little boy would look around and say, "Hi," and the stranger would usually say, "Hi," back and sometimes ask the little boy if he were enjoying the train ride, or even tell him he was a fine big fellow. These comments annoyed the little boy and he would turn irritably back to the window.

"There's a cow," he would say, or, sighing, "How far do we have to go?"

"Not much longer now," his mother said, each time.

Once the baby, who was very quiet and busy with her rattle and her toast, which the mother would renew constantly, fell over too far sideways and banged her head. She began to cry, and for a minute there was noise and movement around the mother's seat. The little boy slid down from his own seat and ran across the aisle to pet his sister's feet and beg her not to cry, and finally the baby laughed and went back to her toast, and the little boy received a lollipop from his mother and went back to the window.

"I saw a witch," he said to his mother after a minute. "There was a big old ugly old bad old witch outside."

"Fine," his mother said.

"A big old ugly witch and I told her to go away and she went away," the little boy went on, in a quiet narrative to himself, "she came and said, 'I'm going to eat you up,' and I said, 'no, you're not,' and I chased her away, the bad old mean witch."

He stopped talking and looked up as the outside door of the coach opened and a man came in. He was an elderly man, with a pleasant face under white hair; his blue suit was only faintly touched by the disarray that comes from a long train trip. He was carrying a cigar, and when the little boy said, "Hi," the man gestured at him with the cigar and said, "Hello yourself, son." He stopped just beside the little boy's seat, and leaned against the back, looking down at the little boy, who craned his neck to look upward. "What you looking for out that window?" the man asked.

"Witches," the little boy said promptly. "Bad old mean witches."

"I see," the man said. "Find many?"

"My father smokes cigars," the little boy said.

"All men smoke cigars," the man said. "Someday you'll smoke a cigar, too."

"I'm a man already," the little boy said.

"How old are you?" the man asked.

The little boy, at the eternal question, looked at the man suspiciously for a minute and then said, "Twenty-six. Eight hunnerd and forty eighty."

His mother lifted her head from the book. "Four," she said, smiling fondly at the little boy.

"Is that so?" the man said politely to the little boy. "Twenty-six." He nodded his head at the mother across the aisle. "Is that your mother?"

The little boy leaned forward to look and then said, "Yes, that's her."

"What's your name?" the man asked.

The little boy looked suspicious again. "Mr. Jesus," he said.

"*Johnny*," the little boy's mother said. She caught the little boy's eye and frowned deeply.

"That's my sister over there," the little boy said to the man. "She's twelve-and-a-half."

"Do you love your sister?" the man asked. The little boy stared, and the man came around the side of the seat and sat down next to the little boy. "Listen," the man said, "shall I tell you about my little sister?"

The mother, who had looked up anxiously when the man sat down next to her little boy, went peacefully back to her book.

"Tell me about your sister," the little boy said. "Was she a witch?"

"Maybe," the man said.

The little boy laughed excitedly, and the man leaned back and puffed at his cigar. "Once upon a time," he began, "I had a little sister, just like yours." The little boy looked up at the man, nodding at every word. "My little sister," the man went on, "was so pretty and so nice that I loved her more than anything else in the world. So shall I tell you what I did?"

The little boy nodded more vehemently, and the mother lifted her eyes from her book and smiled, listening.

"I bought her a rocking-horse and a doll and a million lollipops," the man said, "and then I took her and I put my hands around her neck and I pinched her and I pinched her until she was dead."

The little boy gasped and the mother turned around, her smile fading. She opened her mouth, and then closed it again as the man went on, "And then I took and I cut her head off and I took her head—"

"Did you cut her all in pieces?" the little boy asked breathlessly.

"I cut off her head and her hands and her feet and her hair and her nose," the man said, "and I hit her with a stick and I killed her."

"Wait a minute," the mother said, but the baby fell over sideways just at that minute and by the time the mother had set her up again the man was going on.

"And I took her head and I pulled out all her hair and—"

"Your little *sister*?" the little boy prompted eagerly.

"My little sister," the man said firmly. "And I put her head in a cage with a bear and the bear ate it all up."

"Ate her *head* all up?" the little boy asked.

The mother put her book down and came across the aisle. She stood next to the man and said, "Just what do you think you're doing?" The man looked up courteously and she said, "Get out of here."

"Did I frighten you?" the man said. He looked down at the little boy and nudged him with an elbow and he and the little boy laughed.

"This man cut up his little sister," the little boy said to his mother.

"I can very easily call the conductor," the mother said to the man.

"The conductor will *eat* my mommy," the little boy said. "We'll chop her head off."

"And little sister's head, too," the man said. He stood up, and the mother stood back to let him get out of the seat. "Don't ever come back in this car," she said.

"My mommy will eat *you*," the little boy said to the man.

The man laughed, and the little boy laughed, and then the man said, "Excuse me," to the mother and went past her out of the car. When the door had closed behind him the little boy said, "How much longer do we have to stay on this old train?"

"Not much longer," the mother said. She stood looking at the little boy, wanting to say something, and finally she said, "You sit still and be a good boy. You may have another lollipop."

The little boy climbed down eagerly and followed his mother back to her seat. She took a lollipop from a bag in her pocketbook and gave it to him. "What do you say?" she asked.

"Thank you," the little boy said. "Did that man really cut his little sister up in pieces?"

"He was just teasing," the mother said, and added urgently, "Just *teasing*."

"Prob'ly," the little boy said. With his lollipop he went back to his own seat, and settled himself to look out the window again. "Prob'ly he was a witch."

‡

# THE RENEGADE

IT WAS EIGHT-TWENTY in the morning. The twins were loiter-
ing over their cereal, and Mrs. Walpole, with one eye on the
clock and the other on the kitchen window past which the
school bus would come in a matter of minutes, felt the un-
reasonable irritation that comes with being late on a school
morning, the wading-through-molasses feeling of trying to
hurry children.

"You'll have to walk," she said ominously, for perhaps the
third time. "The bus won't wait."

"I'm hurrying," Judy said. She regarded her full glass of
milk smugly. "I'm closer to through than Jack."

Jack pushed his glass across the table and they measured
meticulously, precisely. "No," he said. "Look how much more
you have than me."

"It doesn't *matter*," Mrs. Walpole said, "it doesn't *matter*.
Jack, *eat* your cereal."

"She didn't have any more than me to start with," Jack
said. "Did she have any more than me, Mom?"

The alarm clock had not gone off at seven as it should.
Mrs. Walpole heard the sound of the shower upstairs and
calculated rapidly; the coffee was slower than usual this
morning, the boiled eggs a shade too soft. She had only had
time to pour herself a glass of fruit juice and no time to drink
it. *Someone*—Judy or Jack or Mr. Walpole—was going to be
late.

"*Judy*," Mrs. Walpole said mechanically, "*Jack*."

Judy's hair was not accurately braided. Jack would get

off without his handkerchief. Mr. Walpole would certainly
be irritable.

The yellow-and-red bulk of the school bus filled the road
outside the kitchen window, and Judy and Jack streaked for
the door, cereal uneaten, books most likely forgotten. Mrs.
Walpole followed them to the kitchen door, calling, "Jack,
your milk money; come straight home at noon." She watched
them climb into the school bus and then went briskly to work
clearing their dishes from the table and setting a place for
Mr. Walpole. She would have to have breakfast herself later,
in the breathing-spell that came after nine o'clock. That meant
her wash would be late getting on the line, and if it rained
that afternoon, as it certainly might, nothing would be dry.
Mrs. Walpole made an effort, and said, "Good morning,
dear," as her husband came into the kitchen. He said, "Morning," without glancing up and Mrs. Walpole, her mind full
of unfinished sentences that began, "Don't you think other
people ever have any feelings or—" started patiently to set
his breakfast before him. The soft-boiled eggs in their dish,
the toast, the coffee. Mr. Walpole devoted himself to his
paper, and Mrs. Walpole, who wanted desperately also to
say, "I don't suppose you notice that I haven't had a chance
to eat—" set the dishes down as softly as she could.

Everything was going smoothly, although half-an-hour late,
when the telephone rang. The Walpoles were on a party line,
and Mrs. Walpole usually let the phone ring her number twice
before concluding that it was really their number; this morning, before nine o'clock, with Mr. Walpole not half-through
his breakfast, it was an unbearable intrusion, and Mrs. Walpole went reluctantly to answer it. "Hello," she said forbid-
dingly.

"Mrs. Walpole," the voice said, and Mrs. Walpole said,

"Yes?" The voice—it was a woman—said, "I'm sorry to bother you, but this is—" and gave an unrecognizable name. Mrs. Walpole said, "Yes?" again. She could hear Mr. Walpole taking the coffeepot off the stove to pour himself a second cup.

"Do you have a dog? Brown-and-black hound?" the voice continued. With the word *dog* Mrs. Walpole, in the second before she answered, "Yes," comprehended the innumerable aspects of owning a dog in the country (six dollars for spaying, the rude barking late at night, the watchful security of the dark shape sleeping on the rug beside the double-decker beds in the twins' room, the inevitability of a dog in the house, as important as a stove, or a front porch, or a subscription to the local paper; more, and above any of these things, the dog herself, known among the neighbors as Lady Walpole, on an exact par with Jack Walpole or Judy Walpole; quiet, competent, exceedingly tolerant), and found in none of them a reason for such an early morning call from a voice which she realized now was as irritable as her own.

"Yes," Mrs. Walpole said shortly, "I own a dog. Why?"

"Big brown-and-black hound?"

Lady's pretty markings, her odd face. "Yes," Mrs. Walpole said, her voice a little more impatient, "yes, that is certainly my dog. Why?"

"He's been killing my chickens." The voice sounded satisfied now; Mrs. Walpole had been cornered.

For several seconds Mrs. Walpole was quiet, so that the voice said, "Hello?"

"That's perfectly ridiculous," Mrs. Walpole said.

"This morning," the voice said with relish, "your dog was chasing our chickens. We heard the chickens at about eight o'clock, and my husband went out to see what was the matter and found two chickens dead and he saw a big brown-and-black hound down with the chickens and he took a stick and chased the dog away and then he found two more dead ones. He says," the voice went on flatly, "that it's lucky he didn't think to take his shotgun out with him because you wouldn't have any more dog. Most awful mess you ever saw," the voice said, "blood and feathers everywhere."

"What makes you think it's *my* dog?" Mrs. Walpole said weakly.

"Joe White—he's a neighbor of yours—was passing at the time and saw my husband chasing the dog. Said it was your dog."

Old man White lived in the next house but one to the Walpoles. Mrs. Walpole had always made a point of being courteous to him, inquired amiably about his health when she saw him on the porch as she passed, had regarded respectfully the pictures of his grandchildren in Albany.

"I see," Mrs. Walpole said, suddenly shifting her ground. "Well, if you're absolutely *sure.* I just can't believe it of Lady. She's so gentle."

The other voice softened, in response to Mrs. Walpole's concern. "It *is* a shame," the other woman said. "I can't tell you how sorry I am that it happened. But . . ." her voice trailed off significantly.

"Of *course* we'll take care of the damage," Mrs. Walpole said quickly.

"No, no," the woman said, almost apologetically. "Don't even *think* about it."

"But of *course*—" Mrs. Walpole began, bewildered.

"The dog," the voice said. "You'll have to do something about the dog."

A sudden unalterable terror took hold of Mrs. Walpole. Her morning had gone badly, she had not yet had her coffee, she was faced with an evil situation she had never known before, and now the voice, its tone, its inflection, had managed to frighten Mrs. Walpole with a word like "something."

"How?" Mrs. Walpole said finally. "I mean, what do you want me to do?"

There was a brief silence on the other end of the wire, and then the voice said briskly, "I'm sure I don't know, missus. I've always heard that there's no way to stop a chicken-killing dog. As I say, there was no damage to speak of. As a matter of fact, the chickens the dog killed are plucked and in the oven now."

Mrs. Walpole's throat tightened and she closed her eyes for a minute, but the voice went inflexibly on. "We wouldn't ask you to do anything except take care of the dog. Naturally, you understand that we can't have a dog killing our chickens?"

Realizing that she was expected to answer, Mrs. Walpole said, "Certainly."

"So . . ." the voice said.

Mrs. Walpole saw over the top of the phone that Mr. Walpole was passing her on his way to the door. He waved briefly to her and she nodded at him. He was late; she had intended to ask him to stop at the library in the city. Now she would have to call him later. Mrs. Walpole said sharply into the phone, "First of all, of course, I'll have to make sure it's my dog. If it *is* my dog I can promise you you'll have no more trouble."

"It's your dog all right." The voice had assumed the country flatness; if Mrs. Walpole wanted to fight, the voice implied, she had picked just the right people.

"Good-bye," Mrs. Walpole said, knowing that she was making a mistake in parting from this woman angrily; knowing that she should stay on the phone for an interminable apologetic conversation, try to beg her dog's life back from this stupid inflexible woman who cared so much for *her* stupid chickens.

Mrs. Walpole put the phone down and went out into the kitchen. She poured herself a cup of coffee and made herself some toast.

I am not going to let this bother me until after I have had my coffee, Mrs. Walpole told herself firmly. She put extra butter on her toast and tried to relax, moving her back against the chair, letting her shoulders sag. Feeling like this at nine-thirty in the morning, she thought, it's a feeling that belongs with eleven o'clock at night. The bright sun outside was not as cheerful as it might be; Mrs. Walpole decided suddenly to put her wash off until tomorrow. They had not lived in the country town long enough for Mrs. Walpole to feel the disgrace of washing on Tuesday as mortal; they were still city folk and would probably always be city folk, people who owned a chicken-killing dog, people who washed on Tuesday, people who were not able to fend for themselves against the limited world of earth and food and weather that the country folk took so much for granted. In this situation as in all such others—the disposal of rubbish, the weather strip-ping, the baking of angel-food cake—Mrs. Walpole was forced to look for advice. In the country it is extremely difficult to "get a man" to do things for you, and Mr. and Mrs. Walpole had early fallen into the habit of consulting their neighbors for information which in the city would have belonged prop-erly to the superintendent, or the janitor, or the man from the gas company. When Mrs. Walpole's glance fell on Lady's water dish under the sink, and she realized that she was in-describably depressed, she got up and put on her jacket and a scarf over her head and went next door.

Mrs. Nash, her next-door neighbor, was frying doughnuts, and she waved a fork at Mrs. Walpole at the open door and called, "Come in, can't leave the stove." Mrs. Walpole, stepping into Mrs. Nash's kitchen, was painfully aware of her own kitchen with the dirty dishes in the sink. Mrs. Nash was wearing a shockingly clean house dress and her kitchen was freshly washed; Mrs. Nash was able to fry doughnuts without making any sort of a mess.

"The men do like fresh doughnuts with their lunch," Mrs. Nash remarked without any more preamble than her nod and invitation to Mrs. Walpole. "I always try to get enough made ahead, but I never do."

"I wish I could make doughnuts," Mrs. Walpole said. Mrs. Nash waved the fork hospitably at the stack of still-warm doughnuts on the table and Mrs. Walpole helped herself to one, thinking: This will give me indigestion.

"Seems like they all get eaten by the time I finish making them," Mrs. Nash said. She surveyed the cooking doughnuts and then, satisfied that she could look away for a minute, took one herself and began to eat it standing by the stove. "What's wrong with you?" she asked. "You look sort of peaked this morning."

"To tell you the truth," Mrs. Walpole said, "it's our dog. Someone called me this morning that she's been killing chickens."

Mrs. Nash nodded. "Up to Harris'," she said. "I know."

Of course she'd know by now, Mrs. Walpole thought.

"You know," Mrs. Nash said, turning again to the doughnuts, "they do say there's nothing to do with a dog kills chickens. My brother had a dog once killed sheep, and I don't know *what* they didn't do to break that dog, but of course nothing would do it. Once they get the taste of blood." Mrs. Nash lifted a golden doughnut delicately out of the frying kettle, and set it down on a piece of brown paper to drain. "They get so's they'd rather kill than eat, hardly."

"But what can I *do*?" Mrs. Walpole asked. "Isn't there *anything*?"

"You can try, of course," Mrs. Nash said. "Best thing to do first is tie her up. Keep her tied, with a good stout chain. Then at least she won't go chasing no more chickens for a while, save you getting her killed *for* you."

Mrs. Walpole got up reluctantly and began to put her scarf on again. "I guess I'd better get a chain down at the store," she said.

"You going downstreet?"

"I want to do my shopping before the kids come home for lunch."

"Don't buy any store doughnuts," Mrs. Nash said. "I'll run up later with a dishful for you. You get a good stout chain for that dog."

"Thank you," Mrs. Walpole said. The bright sunlight across Mrs. Nash's kitchen doorway, the solid table bearing its plates of doughnuts, the pleasant smell of the frying, were all symbols somehow of Mrs. Nash's safety, her confidence in a way of life and a security that had no traffic with chicken-killing, no city fears, an assurance and cleanliness so great that she was willing to bestow its overflow on the Walpoles, bring them doughnuts and overlook Mrs. Walpole's dirty kitchen. "Thank you," Mrs. Walpole said again, inadequately.

"You tell Tom Kittredge I'll be down for a pork roast later this morning," Mrs. Nash said. "Tell him to save it for me."

"I shall." Mrs. Walpole hesitated in the doorway and Mrs. Nash waved the fork at her.

"See you later," Mrs. Nash said.

Old man White was sitting on his front porch in the sun. When he saw Mrs. Walpole he grinned broadly and shouted to her, "Guess you're not going to have any more dog."

I've got to be nice to him, Mrs. Walpole thought, he's not a traitor or a bad man by country standards; anyone would tell on a chicken-killing dog; but he doesn't have to be so pleased about it, she thought, and tried to make her voice pleasant when she said, "Good morning, Mr. White."

"Gonna have her shot?" Mr. White asked. "Your man got a gun?"

"I'm so worried about it," Mrs. Walpole said. She stood on the walk below the front porch and tried not to let her hatred show in her face as she looked up at Mr. White.

"It's too bad about a dog like that," Mr. White said.

At least he doesn't blame *me*, Mrs. Walpole thought. "Is there anything I can do?" she said.

Mr. White thought. "Believe you might be able to cure a chicken-killer," he said. "You get a dead chicken and tie it around the dog's neck, so he can't shake it loose, see?"

"Around her neck?" Mrs. Walpole asked, and Mr. White nodded, grinning toothlessly.

"See, when he can't shake it loose at first he tries to play with it and then it starts to bother him, see, and then he tries to roll it off and it won't come and then he tries to bite it off and it won't come and then when he sees it won't come he thinks he's never gonna get rid of it, see, and he gets scared. And then you'll have him coming around with his tail between his legs and this thing hanging around his neck and it gets worse and worse."

Mrs. Walpole put one hand on the porch railing to steady herself. "What do you do then?" she asked.

"Well," Mr. White said, "the way I heard it, see, the chicken gets riper and riper and the more the dog sees it and feels it and smells it, see, the more he gets to hate chicken. And he can't ever get rid of it, see?"

"But the dog," Mrs. Walpole said. "Lady, I mean. How long do we have to leave it around her neck?"

"Well," Mr. White said with enthusiasm, "I guess you leave it on until it gets ripe enough to fall off by itself. See, the head. . . ."

"I see," Mrs. Walpole said. "Would it work?"

"Can't say," Mr. White said. "Never tried it myself." His voice said that *he* had never had a chicken-killing dog.

Mrs. Walpole left him abruptly; she could not shake the feeling that if it were not for Mr. White, Lady would not have been identified as the dog killing the chickens; she wondered briefly if Mr. White had maliciously blamed Lady because they were city folk, and then thought, No, no man around here would bear false witness against a dog.

When she entered the grocery it was almost empty; there was a man at the hardware counter and another man leaning against the meat counter talking to Mr. Kittredge, the grocer. When Mr. Kittredge saw Mrs. Walpole come in he called across the store, "Morning, Mrs. Walpole. Fine day."

"Lovely," Mrs. Walpole said, and the grocer said, "Bad luck about the dog."

"I don't know what to do about it," Mrs. Walpole said, and the man talking to the grocer looked at her reflectively, and then back at the grocer.

"Killed three chickens up to Harris's this morning," the grocer said to the man and the man nodded solemnly and said, "Heard about that."

Mrs. Walpole came across to the meat counter and said,

"Mrs. Nash said would you save her a roast of pork. She'll be down later to get it."

"Going up that way," the man standing with the grocer said. "Drop it off."

"Right," the grocer said.

The man looked at Mrs. Walpole and said, "Gonna have to shoot him, I guess?"

"I hope not," Mrs. Walpole said earnestly. "We're all so fond of the dog."

The man and the grocer looked at one another for a minute, and then the grocer said reasonably, "Won't do to have a dog going around killing chickens, Mrs. Walpole."

"First thing you know," the man said, "someone'll put a load of buckshot into him, he won't come home no more." He and the grocer both laughed.

"Isn't there any way to cure the dog?" Mrs. Walpole asked.

"Sure," the man said. "Shoot him."

"Tie a dead chicken around his neck," the grocer suggested. "That might do it."

"Heard of a man did that," the other man said.

"Did it help?" Mrs. Walpole asked eagerly.

The man shook his head slowly and with determination.

"You know," the grocer said. He leaned his elbow on the meat counter; he was a great talker. "You know," he said again, "my father had a dog once used to eat eggs. Got into the chicken-house and used to break the eggs open and lick them up. Used to eat maybe half the eggs we got."

"That's a bad business," the other man said. "Dog eating eggs."

"Bad business," the grocer said in confirmation. Mrs. Walpole found herself nodding. "Last, my father couldn't stand it no more. Here half his eggs were getting eaten," the grocer said. "So he took an egg once, set it on the back of the stove for two, three days, till the egg got good and ripe, good and hot through, and that egg smelled pretty bad. Then—I was there, boy twelve, thirteen years old—he called the dog one day, and the dog come running. So I held the dog, and my daddy opened the dog's mouth and put in the egg, red-hot and smelling to heaven, and then he held the dog's mouth closed so's the dog couldn't get rid of the egg anyway except swallow it." The grocer laughed and shook his head reminiscently.

"Bet that dog never ate another egg," the man said.

"Never touched another egg," the grocer said firmly. "You put an egg down in front of that dog, he'd run's though the devil was after him."

"But how did he feel about you?" Mrs. Walpole asked. "Did he ever come near *you* again?"

The grocer and the other man both looked at her. "How do you mean?" the grocer said.

"Did he ever *like* you again?"

"Well," the grocer said, and thought. "No," he said finally, "I don't believe you could say's he ever did. Not much of a dog, though."

"There's one thing you ought to try," the other man said suddenly to Mrs. Walpole, "you really want to cure that dog, there's one thing you ought to try."

"What's that?" Mrs. Walpole said.

"You want to take that dog," the man said, leaning forward and gesturing with one hand, "take him and put him in a pen with a mother hen's got chicks to protect. Time she's through with him he won't never chase another chicken."

The grocer began to laugh and Mrs. Walpole looked, bewildered, from the grocer to the other man, who was looking

at her without a smile, his eyes wide and yellow, like a cat's.
"What would happen?" she asked uncertainly.

"Scratch his eyes out," the grocer said succinctly. "He
wouldn't ever be able to *see* another chicken."

Mrs. Walpole realized that she felt faint. Smiling over her
shoulder, in order not to seem discourteous, she moved quickly
away from the meat counter and down to the other end of
the store. The grocer continued talking to the man behind
the meat counter and after a minute Mrs. Walpole went outside, into the air. She decided that she would go home and lie
down until nearly lunchtime, and do her shopping later in the
day.

At home she found that she could not lie down until the
breakfast table was cleared and the dishes washed, and by the
time she had done that it was almost time to start lunch. She
was standing by the pantry shelves, debating, when a dark
shape crossed the sunlight in the doorway and she realized
that Lady was home. For a minute she stood still, watching
Lady. The dog came in quietly, harmlessly, as though she had
spent the morning frolicking on the grass with her friends, but
there were spots of blood on her legs and she drank her water
eagerly. Mrs. Walpole's first impulse was to scold her, to hold
her down and beat her for the deliberate, malicious pain she
had inflicted, the murderous brutality a pretty dog like Lady
could keep so well hidden in their home; then Mrs. Walpole,
watching Lady go quietly and settle down in her usual spot
by the stove, turned helplessly and took the first cans she
found from the pantry shelves and brought them to the kitchen
table.

Lady sat quietly by the stove until the children came in
noisily for lunch, and then she leaped up and jumped on them,
welcoming them as though they were the aliens and she the

native to the house. Judy, pulling Lady's ears, said, "Hello, Mom, do you know what Lady did? You're a bad bad dog," she said to Lady, "you're going to get shot."

Mrs. Walpole felt faint again and set a dish down hastily on the table. "Judy Walpole," she said.

"She *is*, Mom," Judy said. "She's going to get shot."

Children don't realize, Mrs. Walpole told herself, death is never real to them. Try to be sensible, she told herself. "Sit down to lunch, children," she said quietly.

"But, *Mother*," Judy said, and Jack said, "She *is*, Mom."

They sat down noisily, unfolding their napkins and attacking their food without looking at it, eager to talk.

"You *know* what Mr. Shepherd said, Mom?" Jack demanded, his mouth full.

"Listen," Judy said, "we'll tell you what he said."

Mr. Shepherd was a genial man who lived near the Walpoles and gave the children nickels and took the boys fishing. "He says Lady's going to get shot," Jack said.

"But the spikes," Judy said. "Tell about the spikes."

"The *spikes*," Jack said. "Listen, Mommy. He says you got to get a collar for Lady. . . ."

"A strong collar," Judy said.

"And you get big thick nails, like spikes, and you hammer them into the collar."

"All around," Judy said. "Let *me* tell it, Jack. You hammer these nails all around so's they make spikes inside the collar."

"But it's loose," Jack said. "Let *me* tell this part. It's loose and you put it around Lady's neck. . . ."

"And—" Judy put her hand on her throat and made a strangling noise.

"Not *yet*," Jack said. "Not *yet*, dopey. First you get a long long long long rope."

"A *real* long rope," Judy amplified.

"And you fasten it to the collar and then we put the collar on Lady," Jack said. Lady was sitting next to him and he leaned over and said, "Then we put this real sharp spiky collar around your neck," and kissed the top of her head while Lady regarded him affectionately.

"And then we take her where there are chickens," Judy said, "and we show her the chickens, and we turn her loose."

"And make her chase the chickens," Jack said. "And *then*, and then, when she gets right up close to the chickens, we puuuuuuull on the rope—"

"And—" Judy made her strangling noise again.

"The spikes cut her head off," Jack finished dramatically.

They both began to laugh and Lady, looking from one to the other, panted as though she were laughing too.

Mrs. Walpole looked at them, at her two children with their hard hands and their sunburned faces laughing together, their dog with blood still on her legs laughing with them. She went to the kitchen doorway to look outside at the cool green hills, the motion of the apple tree in the soft afternoon breeze.

"Cut your head right off," Jack was saying.

Everything was quiet and lovely in the sunlight, the peaceful sky, the gentle line of the hills. Mrs. Walpole closed her eyes, suddenly feeling the harsh hands pulling her down, the sharp points closing in on her throat.

‡

# AFTER YOU, MY DEAR ALPHONSE

Mrs. Wilson was just taking the gingerbread out of the oven when she heard Johnny outside talking to someone.

"Johnny," she called, "you're late. Come in and get your lunch."

"Just a minute, Mother," Johnny said. "After you, my dear Alphonse."

"After *you*, my dear Alphonse," another voice said.

"No, after *you*, my dear Alphonse," Johnny said.

Mrs. Wilson opened the door. "Johnny," she said, "you come in this minute and get your lunch. You can play after you've eaten."

Johnny came in after her, slowly. "Mother," he said, "I brought Boyd home for lunch with me."

"Boyd?" Mrs. Wilson thought for a moment. "I don't believe I've met Boyd. Bring him in, dear, since you've invited him. Lunch is ready."

"Boyd!" Johnny yelled. "Hey, Boyd, come on in!"

"I'm coming. Just got to unload this stuff."

"Well, hurry, or my mother'll be sore."

"Johnny, that's not very polite to either your friend or your mother," Mrs. Wilson said. "Come sit down, Boyd."

As she turned to show Boyd where to sit, she saw he was a Negro boy, smaller than Johnny but about the same age. His arms were loaded with split kindling wood. "Where'll I put this stuff, Johnny?" he asked.

Mrs. Wilson turned to Johnny. "Johnny," she said, "what did you make Boyd do? What is that wood?"

"Dead Japanese," Johnny said mildly. "We stand them in the ground and run over them with tanks."

"How do you do, Mrs. Wilson?" Boyd said.

"How do you do, Boyd? You shouldn't let Johnny make you carry all that wood. Sit down now and eat lunch, both of you."

"Why shouldn't he carry the wood, Mother? It's his wood. We got it at his place."

"Johnny," Mrs. Wilson said, "go on and eat your lunch."

"Sure," Johnny said. He held out the dish of scrambled eggs to Boyd. "After you, my dear Alphonse."

"After *you*, my dear Alphonse," Boyd said.

"After *you*, my dear Alphonse," Johnny said. They began to giggle.

"Are you hungry, Boyd?" Mrs. Wilson asked.

"Yes, Mrs. Wilson."

"Well, don't you let Johnny stop you. He always fusses about eating, so you just see that you get a good lunch. There's plenty of food here for you to have all you want."

"Thank you, Mrs. Wilson."

"Come on, Alphonse," Johnny said. He pushed half the scrambled eggs on to Boyd's plate. Boyd watched while Mrs. Wilson put a dish of stewed tomatoes beside his plate.

"Boyd don't eat tomatoes, do you, Boyd?" Johnny said.

"*Doesn't* eat tomatoes, Johnny. And just because you don't like them, don't say that about Boyd. Boyd will eat *anything*."

"Bet he won't," Johnny said, attacking his scrambled eggs.

"Boyd wants to grow up and be a big strong man so he can work hard," Mrs. Wilson said. "I'll bet Boyd's father eats stewed tomatoes."

"My father eats anything he wants to," Boyd said.

"So does mine," Johnny said. "Sometimes he doesn't eat hardly anything. He's a little guy, though. Wouldn't hurt a flea."

"Mine's a little guy, too," Boyd said.

"I'll bet he's strong, though," Mrs. Wilson said. She hesitated. "Does he . . . work?"

"Sure," Johnny said. "Boyd's father works in a factory."

"There, you see?" Mrs. Wilson said. "And he certainly has to be strong to do that—all that lifting and carrying at a factory."

"Boyd's father doesn't have to," Johnny said. "He's a foreman."

Mrs. Wilson felt defeated. "What does your mother do, Boyd?"

"My mother?" Boyd was surprised. "She takes care of us kids."

"Oh. She doesn't work, then?"

"Why should she?" Johnny said through a mouthful of eggs. "You don't work."

"You really don't want any stewed tomatoes, Boyd?"

"No, thank you, Mrs. Wilson," Boyd said.

"No, thank you, Mrs. Wilson, no, thank you, Mrs. Wilson, no, thank you, Mrs. Wilson," Johnny said. "Boyd's sister's going to work, though. She's going to be a teacher."

"That's a very fine attitude for her to have, Boyd." Mrs. Wilson restrained an impulse to pat Boyd on the head. "I imagine you're all very proud of her?"

"I guess so," Boyd said.

"What about all your other brothers and sisters? I guess all of you want to make just as much of yourselves as you can."

"There's only me and Jean," Boyd said. "I don't know yet what I want to be when I grow up."

"We're going to be tank drivers, Boyd and me," Johnny said. "Zoom." Mrs. Wilson caught Boyd's glass of milk as Johnny's napkin ring, suddenly transformed into a tank, plowed heavily across the table.

"Look, Johnny," Boyd said. "Here's a foxhole. I'm shooting at you."

Mrs. Wilson, with the speed born of long experience, took the gingerbread off the shelf and placed it carefully between the tank and the foxhole.

"Now eat as much as you want to, Boyd," she said. "I want to see you get filled up."

"Boyd eats a lot, but not as much as I do," Johnny said. "I'm bigger than he is."

"You're not much bigger," Boyd said. "I can beat you running."

Mrs. Wilson took a deep breath. "Boyd," she said. Both boys turned to her. "Boyd, Johnny has some suits that are a little too small for him, and a winter coat. It's not new, of course, but there's lots of wear in it still. And I have a few dresses that your mother or sister could probably use. Your mother can make them over into lots of things for all of you, and I'd be very happy to give them to you. Suppose before you leave I make up a big bundle and then you and Johnny can take it over to your mother right away . . ." Her voice trailed off as she saw Boyd's puzzled expression.

"But I have plenty of clothes, thank you," he said. "And I don't think my mother knows how to sew very well, and anyway I guess we buy about everything we need. Thank you very much, though."

"We don't have time to carry that old stuff around, Mother," Johnny said. "We got to play tanks with the kids today."

Mrs. Wilson lifted the plate of gingerbread off the table as Boyd was about to take another piece. "There are many little boys like you, Boyd, who would be very grateful for the clothes someone was kind enough to give them."

"Boyd will take them if you want him to, Mother," Johnny said.

"I didn't mean to make you mad, Mrs. Wilson," Boyd said.

"Don't think I'm angry, Boyd. I'm just disappointed in you, that's all. Now let's not say anything more about it."

She began clearing the plates off the table, and Johnny took Boyd's hand and pulled him to the door. " 'Bye, Mother," Johnny said. Boyd stood for a minute, staring at Mrs. Wilson's back.

"After you, my dear Alphonse," Johnny said, holding the door open.

"Is your mother still mad?" Mrs. Wilson heard Boyd ask in a low voice.

"I don't know," Johnny said. "She's screwy sometimes."

"So's mine," Boyd said. He hesitated. "After *you*, my dear Alphonse."

‡

# CHARLES

THE DAY MY SON LAURIE started kindergarten he renounced corduroy overalls with bibs and began wearing blue jeans with a belt; I watched him go off the first morning with the older girl next door, seeing clearly that an era of my life was ended, my sweet-voiced nursery-school tot replaced by a long-trousered, swaggering character who forgot to stop at the corner and wave good-bye to me.

He came home the same way, the front door slamming open, his cap on the floor, and the voice suddenly become raucous shouting, "Isn't anybody *here*?"

At lunch he spoke insolently to his father, spilled his baby sister's milk, and remarked that his teacher said we were not to take the name of the Lord in vain.

"How *was* school today?" I asked, elaborately casual.

"All right," he said.

"Did you learn anything?" his father asked.

Laurie regarded his father coldly. "I didn't learn nothing," he said.

"Anything," I said. "Didn't learn anything."

"The teacher spanked a boy, though," Laurie said, addressing his bread and butter. "For being fresh," he added, with his mouth full.

"What did he do?" I asked. "Who was it?"

Laurie thought. "It was Charles," he said. "He was fresh. The teacher spanked him and made him stand in a corner. He was awfully fresh."

"What did he do?" I asked again, but Laurie slid off his

chair, took a cookie, and left, while his father was still saying, "See here, young man."

The next day Laurie remarked at lunch, as soon as he sat down, "Well, Charles was bad again today." He grinned enormously and said, "Today Charles hit the teacher."

"Good heavens," I said, mindful of the Lord's name, "I suppose he got spanked again?"

"He sure did," Laurie said. "Look up," he said to his father.

"What?" his father said, looking up.

"Look down," Laurie said. "Look at my thumb. Gee, you're dumb." He began to laugh insanely.

"Why did Charles hit the teacher?" I asked quickly.

"Because she tried to make him color with red crayons," Laurie said. "Charles wanted to color with green crayons so he hit the teacher and she spanked him and said nobody play with Charles but everybody did."

The third day—it was Wednesday of the first week—Charles bounced a see-saw on to the head of a little girl and made her bleed, and the teacher made him stay inside all during recess. Thursday Charles had to stand in a corner during story-time because he kept pounding his feet on the floor. Friday Charles was deprived of blackboard privileges because he threw chalk.

On Saturday I remarked to my husband, "Do you think kindergarten is too unsettling for Laurie? All this toughness, and bad grammar, and this Charles boy sounds like such a bad influence."

"It'll be all right," my husband said reassuringly. "Bound to be people like Charles in the world. Might as well meet them now as later."

On Monday Laurie came home late, full of news. "Charles,"

he shouted as he came up the hill; I was waiting anxiously
on the front steps. "Charles," Laurie yelled all the way up
the hill, "Charles was bad again."

"Come right in," I said, as soon as he came close enough.
"Lunch is waiting."

"You know what Charles did?" he demanded, following
me through the door. "Charles yelled so in school they sent
a boy in from first grade to tell the teacher she had to make
Charles keep quiet, and so Charles had to stay after school.
And so all the children stayed to watch him."

"What did he do?" I asked.

"He just sat there," Laurie said, climbing into his chair at
the table. "Hi, Pop, y'old dust mop."

"Charles had to stay after school today," I told my husband.
"Everyone stayed with him."

"What does this Charles look like?" my husband asked
Laurie. "What's his other name?"

"He's bigger than me," Laurie said. "And he doesn't have
any rubbers and he doesn't ever wear a jacket."

Monday night was the first Parent-Teachers meeting, and
only the fact that the baby had a cold kept me from going;
I wanted passionately to meet Charles's mother. On Tuesday
Laurie remarked suddenly, "Our teacher had a friend come
to see her in school today."

"Charles's mother?" my husband and I asked simultane-
ously.

"Naaah," Laurie said scornfully. "It was a man who came
and made us do exercises, we had to touch our toes. Look."
He climbed down from his chair and squatted down and
touched his toes. "Like this," he said. He got solemnly back
into his chair and said, picking up his fork, "Charles didn't
even *do* exercises."

"That's fine," I said heartily. "Didn't Charles want to do exercises?"

"Naaah," Laurie said. "Charles was so fresh to the teacher's friend he wasn't *let* do exercises."

"Fresh again?" I said.

"He kicked the teacher's friend," Laurie said. "The teacher's friend told Charles to touch his toes like I just did and Charles kicked him."

"What are they going to do about Charles, do you suppose?" Laurie's father asked him.

Laurie shrugged elaborately. "Throw him out of school, I guess," he said.

Wednesday and Thursday were routine; Charles yelled during story hour and hit a boy in the stomach and made him cry. On Friday Charles stayed after school again and so did all the other children.

With the third week of kindergarten Charles was an institution in our family; the baby was being a Charles when she cried all afternoon; Laurie did a Charles when he filled his wagon full of mud and pulled it through the kitchen; even my husband, when he caught his elbow in the telephone cord and pulled telephone, ashtray, and a bowl of flowers off the table, said, after the first minute, "Looks like Charles."

During the third and fourth weeks it looked like a reformation in Charles; Laurie reported grimly at lunch on Thursday of the third week, "Charles was so good today the teacher gave him an apple."

"What?" I said, and my husband added warily, "You mean Charles?"

"Charles," Laurie said. "He gave the crayons around and he picked up the books afterward and the teacher said he was her helper."

"What happened?" I asked incredulously.

"He was her helper, that's all," Laurie said, and shrugged.

"Can this be true, about Charles?" I asked my husband that night. "Can something like this happen?"

"Wait and see," my husband said cynically. "When you've got a Charles to deal with, this may mean he's only plotting."

He seemed to be wrong. For over a week Charles was the teacher's helper; each day he handed things out and he picked things up; no one had to stay after school.

"The P.T.A. meeting's next week again," I told my husband one evening. "I'm going to find Charles's mother there."

"Ask her what happened to Charles," my husband said. "I'd like to know."

"I'd like to know myself," I said.

On Friday of that week things were back to normal. "You know what Charles did today?" Laurie demanded at the lunch table, in a voice slightly awed. "He told a little girl to say a word and she said it and the teacher washed her mouth out with soap and Charles laughed."

"What word?" his father asked unwisely, and Laurie said, "I'll have to whisper it to you, it's so bad." He got down off his chair and went around to his father. His father bent his head down and Laurie whispered joyfully. His father's eyes widened.

"Did Charles tell the little girl to say *that*?" he asked respectfully.

"She said it *twice*," Laurie said. "Charles told her to say it *twice*."

"What happened to Charles?" my husband asked.

"Nothing," Laurie said. "He was passing out the crayons."

Monday morning Charles abandoned the little girl and said the evil word himself three or four times, getting his mouth washed out with soap each time. He also threw chalk.

My husband came to the door with me that evening as I set out for the P.T.A. meeting. "Invite her over for a cup of tea after the meeting," he said. "I want to get a look at her."

"If only she's there," I said prayerfully.

"She'll be there," my husband said. "I don't see how they could hold a P.T.A. meeting without Charles's mother."

At the meeting I sat restlessly, scanning each comfortable matronly face, trying to determine which one hid the secret of Charles. None of them looked to me haggard enough. No one stood up in the meeting and apologized for the way her son had been acting. No one mentioned Charles.

After the meeting I identified and sought out Laurie's kindergarten teacher. She had a plate with a cup of tea and a piece of chocolate cake; I had a plate with a cup of tea and a piece of marshmallow cake. We maneuvered up to one another cautiously, and smiled.

"I've been so anxious to meet you," I said. "I'm Laurie's mother."

"We're all so interested in Laurie," she said.

"Well, he certainly likes kindergarten," I said. "He talks about it all the time."

"We had a little trouble adjusting, the first week or so," she said primly, "but now he's a fine little helper. With occasional lapses, of course."

"Laurie usually adjusts very quickly," I said. "I suppose this time it's Charles's influence."

"Charles?"

"Yes," I said, laughing, "you must have your hands full in that kindergarten, with Charles."

"Charles?" she said. "We don't have any Charles in the kindergarten."

‡

# AFTERNOON IN LINEN

IT WAS a long, cool room, comfortably furnished and happily placed, with hydrangea bushes outside the large windows and their pleasant shadows on the floor. Everyone in it was wearing linen—the little girl in the pink linen dress with a wide blue belt, Mrs. Kator in a brown linen suit and a big, yellow linen hat, Mrs. Lennon, who was the little girl's grandmother, in a white linen dress, and Mrs. Kator's little boy, Howard, in a blue linen shirt and shorts. Like in *Alice Through the Looking-Glass*, the little girl thought, looking at her grandmother; like the gentleman all dressed in white paper. I'm a gentleman all dressed in pink paper, she thought. Although Mrs. Lennon and Mrs. Kator lived on the same block and saw each other every day, this was a formal call, and so they were drinking tea.

Howard was sitting at the piano at one end of the long room, in front of the biggest window. He was playing "Humoresque" in careful, unhurried tempo. I played that last year, the little girl thought; it's in G. Mrs. Lennon and Mrs. Kator were still holding their teacups, listening to Howard and looking at him, and now and then looking at each other and smiling. I could still play that if I wanted to, the little girl thought.

When Howard had finished playing "Humoresque," he slid off the piano bench and came over and gravely sat down beside the little girl, waiting for his mother to tell him whether to play again or not. He's bigger than I am, she thought, but

I'm older. I'm ten. If they ask me to play the piano for them now, I'll say no.

"I think you play very nicely, Howard," the little girl's grandmother said. There were a few moments of leaden silence. Then Mrs. Kator said, "Howard, Mrs. Lennon spoke to you." Howard murmured and looked at his hands on his knees.

"I think he's coming along very well," Mrs. Kator said to Mrs. Lennon. "He doesn't like to practise, but I think he's coming along well."

"Harriet loves to practise," the little girl's grandmother said. "She sits at the piano for hours, making up little tunes and singing."

"She probably has a real talent for music," Mrs. Kator said. "I often wonder whether Howard is getting as much out of his music as he should."

"Harriet," Mrs. Lennon said to the little girl, "won't you play for Mrs. Kator? Play one of your own little tunes."

"I don't know any," the little girl said.

"Of course you do, dear," her grandmother said.

"I'd like very much to hear a little tune you made up yourself, Harriet," Mrs. Kator said.

"I don't know any," the little girl said.

Mrs. Lennon looked at Mrs. Kator and shrugged. Mrs. Kator nodded, mouthing "Shy," and turned to look proudly at Howard.

The little girl's grandmother set her lips firmly in a tight, sweet smile. "Harriet dear," she said, "even if we don't want to play our little tunes, I think we ought to tell Mrs. Kator that music is not our forte. I think we ought to show her our really fine achievements in another line. Harriet," she continued, turning to Mrs. Kator, "has written some poems. I'm going to ask her to recite them to you, because I feel, even though I may be prejudiced"—she laughed modestly—"even though I probably *am* prejudiced, that they show real merit."

"Well, for heaven's sake!" Mrs. Kator said. She looked at Harriet, pleased. "Why, dear, I didn't know you could do anything like that! I'd really *love* to hear them."

"Recite one of your poems for Mrs. Kator, Harriet."

The little girl looked at her grandmother, at the sweet smile, and at Mrs. Kator, leaning forward, and at Howard, sitting with his mouth open and a great delight growing in his eyes. "Don't know any," she said.

"Harriet," her grandmother said, "even if you don't remember any of your poems, you have some written down. I'm sure Mrs. Kator won't mind if you read them to her."

The huge merriment that had been gradually taking hold of Howard suddenly overwhelmed him. "Poems," he said, doubling up with laughter on the couch. "Harriet writes poems." He'll tell all the kids on the block, the little girl thought.

"I do believe Howard's jealous," Mrs. Kator said.

"Aw," Howard said. "I wouldn't write a poem. Bet you couldn't make *me* write a poem if you *tried*."

"You couldn't make me, either," the little girl said. "That's all a lie about the poems."

There was a long silence. Then "Why, Harriet!" the little girl's grandmother said in a sad voice. "What a thing to say about your grandmother!" Mrs. Kator said. "I think you'd better apologize, Harriet," the little girl's grandmother said. Mrs. Kator said, "Why, you certainly *had* better."

"I didn't do anything," the little girl muttered. "I'm sorry."

The grandmother's voice was stern. "Now bring your poems out and read them to Mrs. Kator."

"I don't have any, honestly, Grandma," the little girl said desperately. "Honestly, I don't have any of those poems."

"Well, *I* have," the grandmother said. "Bring them to me from the top desk drawer."

The little girl hesitated for a minute, watching her grandmother's straight mouth and frowning eyes.

"Howard will get them for you, Mrs. Lennon," Mrs. Kator said.

"Sure," Howard said. He jumped up and ran over to the desk, pulling open the drawer. "What do they look like?" he shouted.

"In an envelope," the grandmother said tightly. "In a brown envelope with 'Harriet's poetry' written on the front."

"Here it is," Howard said. He pulled some papers out of the envelope and studied them a moment. "Look," he said. "Harriet's poems—about stars." He ran to his mother, giggling and holding out the papers. "Look, Mother, Harriet's poetry's about stars!"

"Give them to Mrs. Lennon, dear," Howard's mother said. "It was very rude to open the envelope first."

Mrs. Lennon took the envelope and the papers and held them out to Harriet. "Will you read them or shall I?" she asked kindly. Harriet shook her head. The grandmother sighed at Mrs. Kator and took up the first sheet of paper. Mrs. Kator leaned forward eagerly and Howard settled down at her feet, hugging his knees and putting his face against his leg to keep from laughing. The grandmother cleared her throat, smiled at Harriet, and began to read.

" 'The Evening Star,' " she announced.

"When evening shadows are falling,
    And dark gathers closely around,

And all the night creatures are calling,
And the wind makes a lonesome sound,

"I wait for the first star to come out,
And look for its silvery beams,
When the blue and green twilight is all about,
And grandly a lone star gleams."

Howard could contain himself no longer. "Harriet writes poems about stars!"

"Why, it's lovely, Harriet dear!" Mrs. Kator said. "I think it's really lovely, honestly. I don't see what you're so shy about it for."

"There, you see, Harriet?" Mrs. Lennon said. "Mrs. Kator thinks your poetry is very nice. Now aren't you sorry you made such a fuss about such a little thing?"

He'll tell all the kids on the block, Harriet thought. "I didn't write it," she said.

"Why, Harriet!" Her grandmother laughed. "You don't need to be so modest, child. You write very nice poems."

"I copied it out of a book," Harriet said. "I found it in a book and I copied it and gave it to my old grandmother and said I wrote it."

"I don't believe you'd do anything like that, Harriet," Mrs. Kator said, puzzled.

"I did *so*," Harriet maintained stubbornly. "I copied it right out of a book."

"Harriet, I don't believe you," her grandmother said.

Harriet looked at Howard, who was staring at her in admiration. "I copied it out of a book," she said to him. "I found the book in the library one day."

"I can't imagine her saying she did such a thing," Mrs. Lennon said to Mrs. Kator. Mrs. Kator shook her head.

"It was a book called"—Harriet thought a moment—"called *The Home Book of Verse*," she said. "That's what it was. And I copied every single word. I didn't make up *one*."

"Harriet, is this true?" her grandmother said. She turned to Mrs. Kator. "I'm afraid I must apologize for Harriet and for reading you the poem under false pretenses. I never dreamed she'd deceive me."

"Oh, they do," Mrs. Kator said deprecatingly. "They want attention and praise and sometimes they'll do almost anything. I'm sure Harriet didn't mean to be—well, dishonest."

"I did *so*," Harriet said. "I wanted everyone to think I wrote it. I said I wrote it on purpose." She went over and took the papers out of her grandmother's unresisting hand. "And you can't look at them any more, either," she said, and held them in back of her, away from everyone.

‡

# FLOWER GARDEN

AFTER LIVING in an old Vermont manor house together for
almost eleven years, the two Mrs. Winnings, mother and
daughter-in-law, had grown to look a good deal alike, as
women will who live intimately together, and work in the
same kitchen and get things done around the house in the
same manner. Although young Mrs. Winning had been a
Talbot, and had dark hair which she wore cut short, she was
now officially a Winning, a member of the oldest family in
town and her hair was beginning to grey where her mother-
in-law's hair had greyed first, at the temples; they both had
thin sharp-featured faces and eloquent hands, and sometimes
when they were washing dishes or shelling peas or polishing
silverware together, their hands, moving so quickly and simi-
larly, communicated more easily and sympathetically than
their minds ever could. Young Mrs. Winning thought sometimes, when she sat at the breakfast table next to her mother-
in-law, with her baby girl in the high-chair close by, that they
must resemble some stylized block print for a New England
wallpaper; mother, daughter, and granddaughter, with perhaps Plymouth Rock or Concord Bridge in the background.

   On this, as on other cold mornings, they lingered over their
coffee, unwilling to leave the big kitchen with the coal stove
and the pleasant atmosphere of food and cleanliness, and they
sat together silently sometimes until the baby had long finished
her breakfast and was playing quietly in the special baby corner, where uncounted Winning children had played with almost identical toys from the same heavy wooden box.

"It seems as though spring would never come," young Mrs. Winning said. "I get so tired of the cold."

"Got to be cold some of the time," her mother-in-law said. She began to move suddenly and quickly, stacking plates, indicating that the time for sitting was over and the time for working had begun. Young Mrs. Winning, rising immediately to help, thought for the thousandth time that her mother-in-law would never relinquish the position of authority in her own house until she was too old to move before anyone else.

"And I wish someone would move into the old cottage," young Mrs. Winning added. She stopped halfway to the pantry with the table napkins and said longingly, "If only *someone* would move in before spring." Young Mrs. Winning had wanted, long ago, to buy the cottage herself, for her husband to make with his own hands into a home where they could live with their children, but now, accustomed as she was to the big old house at the top of the hill where her husband's family had lived for generations, she had only a great kindness left toward the little cottage, and a wistful anxiety to see some happy young people living there. When she heard it was sold, as all the old houses were being sold in these days when no one could seem to find a newer place to live, she had allowed herself to watch daily for a sign that someone new was coming; every morning she glanced down from the back porch to see if there was smoke coming out of the cottage chimney, and every day going down the hill on her way to the store she hesitated past the cottage, watching carefully for the least movement within. The cottage had been sold in January and now, nearly two months later, even though it seemed prettier and less worn with the snow gently covering the overgrown garden and icicles in front of the blank windows, it was still forlorn and empty, despised since the day long ago when Mrs. Winning had given up all hope of ever living there.

Mrs. Winning deposited the napkins in the pantry and turned to tear the leaf off the kitchen calendar before selecting a dish towel and joining her mother-in-law at the sink. "March already," she said despondently.

"They *did* tell me down at the store yesterday," her mother-in-law said, "that they were going to start painting the cottage this week."

"Then that *must* mean someone's coming!"

"Can't take more than a couple of weeks to paint inside that little house," old Mrs. Winning said.

It was almost April, however, before the new people moved in. The snow had almost melted and was running down the street in icy, half-solid rivers. The ground was slushy and miserable to walk on, the skies grey and dull. In another month the first amazing green would start in the trees and on the ground, but for the better part of April there would be cold rain and perhaps more snow. The cottage had been painted inside, and new paper put on the walls. The front steps had been repaired and new glass put into the broken windows. In spite of the grey sky and the patches of dirty snow the cottage looked neater and firmer, and the painters were coming back to do the outside when the weather cleared. Mrs. Winning, standing at the foot of the cottage walk, tried to picture the cottage as it stood now, against the picture of the cottage she had made years ago, when she had hoped to live there herself. She had wanted roses by the porch; that could be done, and the neat colorful garden she had planned. She would have painted the outside white, and that too might still be done. Since the cottage had been sold she had not gone inside, but she remembered the little rooms, with the windows over the garden that could be so bright with gay curtains and window boxes, the small kitchen she would have painted yellow, the two bedrooms upstairs with slanting ceilings under the eaves. Mrs. Winning looked at the cottage for a long time, standing on the wet walk, and then went slowly on down to the store.

The first news she had of the new people came, at last, from the grocer a few days later. As he was tieing the string around the three pounds of hamburger the large Winning family would consume in one meal, he asked cheerfully, "Seen your new neighbors yet?"

"Have they moved in?" Mrs. Winning asked. "The people in the cottage?"

"Lady in here this morning," the grocer said. "Lady and a little boy, seem like nice people. They say her husband's dead. Nice-looking lady."

Mrs. Winning had been born in the town and the grocer's father had given her jawbreakers and licorice in the grocery store while the present grocer was still in high school. For a while, when she was twelve and the grocer's son was twenty, Mrs. Winning had hoped secretly that he would want to marry her. He was fleshy now, and middle-aged, and although he still called her Helen and she still called him Tom, she belonged now to the Winning family and had to speak critically to him, no matter how unwillingly, if the meat were tough or the butter price too high. She knew that when he spoke of the new neighbor as a "lady" he meant something different than if he had spoken of her as a "woman" or a "person." Mrs. Winning knew that he spoke of the two Mrs. Winnings to his other customers as "ladies." She hesitated and then asked, "Have they really moved in to stay?"

"She'll have to stay for a while," the grocer said drily. "Bought a week's worth of groceries."

Going back up the hill with her package Mrs. Winning watched all the way to detect some sign of the new people in the cottage. When she reached the cottage walk she slowed down and tried to watch not too obviously. There was no smoke coming from the chimney, and no sign of furniture near the house, as there might have been if people were still moving in, but there was a middle-aged car parked in the street before the cottage and Mrs. Winning thought she could see figures moving past the windows. On a sudden irresistible impulse she turned and went up the walk to the front porch, and then, after debating for a moment, on up the steps to the door. She knocked, holding her bag of groceries in one arm, and then the door opened and she looked down on a little boy, about the same age, she thought happily, as her own son.

"Hello," Mrs. Winning said.

"Hello," the boy said. He regarded her soberly.

"Is your mother here?" Mrs. Winning asked. "I came to see if I could help her move in."

"We're all moved in," the boy said. He was about to close the door, but a woman's voice said from somewhere in the house, "Davey? Are you talking to someone?"

"That's my mommy," the little boy said. The woman came up behind him and opened the door a little wider. "Yes?" she said.

Mrs. Winning said, "I'm Helen Winning. I live about three houses up the street, and I thought perhaps I might be able to help you."

"Thank you," the woman said doubtfully. She's younger than I am, Mrs. Winning thought, she's about thirty. And pretty. For a clear minute Mrs. Winning saw why the grocer had called her a lady.

"It's so nice to have someone living in this house," Mrs. Winning said shyly. Past the other woman's head she could see the small hallway, with the larger living-room beyond and the door on the left going into the kitchen, the stairs on the right, with the delicate stair-rail newly painted; they had done the hall in light green, and Mrs. Winning smiled with friendship at the woman in the doorway, thinking, She *has* done it right; this is the way it should look after all, she knows about pretty houses.

After a minute the other woman smiled back, and said, "Will you come in?"

As she stepped back to let Mrs. Winning in, Mrs. Winning wondered with a suddenly stricken conscience if perhaps she had not been too forward, almost pushing herself in. . . . "I hope I'm not making a nuisance of myself," she said unexpectedly, turning to the other woman. "It's just that I've been wanting to live here myself for so long." Why did I say that, she wondered; it had been a very long time since young Mrs. Winning had said the first thing that came into her head.

"Come see *my* room," the little boy said urgently, and Mrs. Winning smiled down at him.

"I have a little boy just about your age," she said. "What's your name?"

"Davey," the little boy said, moving closer to his mother. "Davey William MacLane."

"My little boy," Mrs. Winning said soberly, "is named Howard Talbot Winning."

The little boy looked up at his mother uncertainly, and Mrs. Winning, who felt ill at ease and awkward in this little house she so longed for, said, "How old are you? My little boy is five."

"I'm five," the little boy said, as though realizing it for the first time. He looked again at his mother and she said graciously, "Will you come in and see what we've done to the house?"

Mrs. Winning put her bag of groceries down on the slim-legged table in the green hall, and followed Mrs. MacLane into the living-room, which was L-shaped and had the windows Mrs. Winning would have fitted with gay curtains and flower-boxes. As she stepped into the room Mrs. Winning realized, with a quick wonderful relief, that it was really going to be all right, after all. Everything, from the andirons in the fireplace to the books on the table, was exactly as Mrs. Winning might have done if she were eleven years younger; a little more informal, perhaps, nothing of quite such good quality as young Mrs. Winning might have chosen, but still richly, undeniably right. There was a picture of Davey on the mantel, flanked by a picture which Mrs. Winning supposed was Davey's father; there was a glorious blue bowl on the low coffee table, and around the corner of the L stood a row of orange plates on a shelf, and a polished maple table and chairs.

"It's lovely," Mrs. Winning said. This could have been mine, she was thinking, and she stood in the doorway and said again, "It's perfectly lovely."

Mrs. MacLane crossed over to the low armchair by the fireplace and picked up the soft blue material that lay across the arm. "I'm making curtains," she said, and touched the blue bowl with the tip of one finger. "Somehow I always make my blue bowl the center of the room," she said. "I'm having the curtains the same blue, and my rug—when it comes!—will have the same blue in the design."

"It matches Davey's eyes," Mrs. Winning said, and when Mrs. MacLane smiled again she saw that it matched Mrs. MacLane's eyes too. Helpless before so much that was magic to her, Mrs. Winning said "*Have* you painted the kitchen yellow?"

"Yes," Mrs. MacLane said, surprised. "Come and see." She led the way through the L, around past the orange plates to the kitchen, which caught the late morning sun and shone with clean paint and bright aluminum; Mrs. Winning noticed the electric coffeepot, the waffle iron, the toaster, and thought, *she* couldn't have much trouble cooking, not with just the two of them.

"When I have a garden," Mrs. MacLane said, "we'll be able to see it from almost all the windows." She gestured to the broad kitchen windows, and added, "I love gardens. I imagine I'll spend most of my time working in this one, as soon as the weather is nice."

"It's a good house for a garden," Mrs. Winning said. "I've heard that it used to be one of the prettiest gardens on the block."

"I thought so too," Mrs. MacLane said. "I'm going to have flowers on all four sides of the house. With a cottage like this you can, you know."

Oh, I know, I know, Mrs. Winning thought wistfully, remembering the neat charming garden she could have had, instead of the row of nasturtiums along the side of the Winning house, which she tended so carefully; no flowers would grow well around the Winning house, because of the heavy old maple trees which shaded all the yard and which had been tall when the house was built.

Mrs. MacLane had had the bathroom upstairs done in yellow, too, and the two small bedrooms with overhanging eaves were painted green and rose. "All garden colors," she told Mrs. Winning gaily, and Mrs. Winning, thinking of the oddly-matched, austere bedrooms in the big Winning house, sighed and admitted that. it would be wonderful to have window seats under the eaved windows. Davey's bedroom was the green one, and his small bed was close to the window. "This morning," he told Mrs. Winning solemnly, "I looked out and there were four icicles hanging by my bed."

Mrs. Winning stayed in the cottage longer than she should have; she felt certain, although Mrs. MacLane was pleasant and cordial, that her visit was extended past courtesy and into curiosity. Even so, it was only her sudden guilt about the three pounds of hamburger and dinner for the Winning men that drove her away. When she left, waving good-bye to Mrs. MacLane and Davey as they stood in the cottage doorway, she had invited Davey up to play with Howard, Mrs. MacLane up for tea, both of them to come for lunch some day, and all without the permission of her mother-in-law.

Reluctantly she came to the big house and turned past the bolted front door to go up the walk to the back door, which all the family used in the winter. Her mother-in-law looked up as she came into the kitchen and said irritably, "I called the store and Tom said you left an hour ago."

"I stopped off at the old cottage," Mrs. Winning said. She put the package of groceries down on the table and began to take things out quickly, to get the doughnuts on to a plate and the hamburger into the pan before too much time was lost. With her coat still on and her scarf over her head she moved as fast as she could while her mother-in-law, slicing bread at the kitchen table, watched her silently.

"Take your coat off," her mother-in-law said finally. "Your husband will be home in a minute."

By twelve o'clock the house was noisy and full of mud tracked across the kitchen floor. The oldest Howard, Mrs. Winning's father-in-law, came in from the farm and went silently to hang his hat and coat in the dark hall before speaking to his wife and daughter-in-law; the younger Howard, Mrs. Winning's husband, came in from the barn after putting the truck away and nodded to his wife and kissed his mother; and the youngest Howard, Mrs. Winning's son, crashed into the kitchen, home from kindergarten, shouting, "Where's dinner?"

The baby, anticipating food, banged on her high-chair with the silver cup which had first been used by the oldest Howard Winning's mother. Mrs. Winning and her mother-in-law put plates down on the table swiftly, knowing after many years the exact pause between the latest arrival and the serving of food, and with a minimum of time three generations of the Winning family were eating silently and efficiently, all anxious to be back about their work: the farm, the mill, the electric train; the dishes, the sewing, the nap. Mrs. Winning, feeding the baby, trying to anticipate her mother-in-law's gestures of serving, thought, today more poignantly than ever before, that she had at least given them another Howard, with the Winning eyes and mouth, in exchange for her food and her bed.

After dinner, after the men had gone back to work and the children were in bed, the baby for her nap and Howard resting with crayons and coloring book, Mrs. Winning sat down with her mother-in-law over their sewing and tried to describe the cottage.

"It's just perfect," she said helplessly. "Everything is so

pretty. She invited us to come down some day and see it when it's all finished, the curtains and everything."

"I was talking to Mrs. Blake," the elder Mrs. Winning said, as though in agreement. "She says the husband was killed in an automobile accident. *She* had some money in her own name and I guess she decided to settle down in the country for the boy's health. Mrs. Blake said he looked peakish."

"She loves gardens," Mrs. Winning said, her needle still in her hand for a moment. "She's going to have a big garden all around the house."

"She'll need help," the elder woman said humorlessly, "that's a mighty big garden she'll have."

"She has the *most* beautiful blue bowl, Mother Winning. You'd love it, it's almost like silver."

"Probably," the elder Mrs. Winning said after a pause, "probably her people came from around here a ways back, and *that's* why she's settled in these parts."

The next day Mrs. Winning walked slowly past the cottage, and slowly the next, and the day after, and the day after that. On the second day she saw Mrs. MacLane at the window, and waved, and on the third day she met Davey on the sidewalk. "When are you coming to visit my little boy?" she asked him, and he stared at her solemnly and said, "To-morrow."

Mrs. Burton, next-door to the MacLanes, ran over on the third day they were there with a fresh apple pie, and then told all the neighbors about the yellow kitchen and the bright electric utensils. Another neighbor, whose husband had helped Mrs. MacLane start her furnace, explained that Mrs. Mac-Lane was only very recently widowed. One or another of the townspeople called on the MacLanes almost daily, and frequently, as young Mrs. Winning passed, she saw familiar faces at the windows, measuring the blue curtains with Mrs. Mac-Lane, or she waved to acquaintances who stood chatting with Mrs. MacLane on the now firm front steps. After the Mac-Lanes had been in the cottage for about a week Mrs. Winning met them one day in the grocery and they walked up the hill together, and talked about putting Davey into the kindergarten. Mrs. MacLane wanted to keep him home as long as possible, and Mrs. Winning asked her, "Don't you feel terribly tied down, having him with you all the time?"

"I like it," Mrs. MacLane said cheerfully, "we keep each other company," and Mrs. Winning felt clumsy and ill-mannered, remembering Mrs. MacLane's widowhood.

As the weather grew warmer and the first signs of green showed on the trees and on the wet ground, Mrs. Winning and Mrs. MacLane became better friends. They met almost daily at the grocery and walked up the hill together, and twice Davey came up to play with Howard's electric train, and once Mrs. MacLane came up to get him and stayed for a cup of coffee in the great kitchen while the boys raced round and round the table and Mrs. Winning's mother-in-law was visiting a neighbor.

"It's such an old house," Mrs. MacLane said, looking up at the dark ceiling. "I love old houses; they feel so secure and warm, as though lots of people had been perfectly satisfied with them and they *knew* how useful they were. You don't get that feeling with a new house."

"This dreary old place," Mrs. Winning said. Mrs. MacLane, with a rose-colored sweater and her bright soft hair, was a spot of color in the kitchen that Mrs. Winning knew she could never duplicate. "I'd give anything in the world to live in your house," Mrs. Winning said.

"*I* love it," Mrs. MacLane said. "I don't think I've ever been so happy. Everyone around here is so nice, and the house is so pretty, and I planted a lot of bulbs yesterday." She laughed. "I used to sit in that apartment in New York and dream about planting bulbs again."

Mrs. Winning looked at the boys, thinking how Howard was half-a-head taller, and stronger, and how Davey was small and weak and loved his mother adoringly. "It's been good for Davey already," she said. "There's color in his cheeks."

"Davey loves it," Mrs. MacLane agreed. Hearing his name Davey came over and put his head in her lap and she touched his hair, bright like her own. "We'd better be getting on home, Davey boy," she said.

"Maybe our flowers have grown some since yesterday," said Davey.

Gradually the days became miraculously long and warm, and Mrs. MacLane's garden began to show colors and became an ordered thing, still very young and unsure, but promising rich brilliance for the end of the summer, and the next summer, and summers ten years from now.

"It's even better than I hoped," Mrs. MacLane said to Mrs. Winning, standing at the garden gate. "Things grow so much better here than almost anywhere else."

Davey and Howard played daily after the school was out for the summer, and Howard was free all day. Sometimes Howard stayed at Davey's house for lunch, and they planted a vegetable patch together in the MacLane back yard. Mrs. Winning stopped for Mrs. MacLane on her way to the store in the mornings and Davey and Howard frolicked ahead of them down the street. They picked up their mail together and read it walking back up the hill, and Mrs. Winning went more cheerfully back to the big Winning house after walking most of the way home with Mrs. MacLane.

One afternoon Mrs. Winning put the baby in Howard's wagon and with the two boys they went for a long walk in the country. Mrs. MacLane picked Queen Anne's lace and put it into the wagon with the baby, and the boys found a garter snake and tried to bring it home. On the way up the hill Mrs. MacLane helped pull the wagon with the baby and the Queen Anne's lace, and they stopped halfway to rest and Mrs. MacLane said, "Look, I believe you can see my garden all the way from here."

It was a spot of color almost at the top of the hill and they stood looking at it while the baby threw the Queen Anne's lace out of the wagon. Mrs. MacLane said, "I always want to stop here to look at it," and then, "Who is that *beautiful* child?"

Mrs. Winning looked, and then laughed. "He *is* attractive, isn't he," she said. "It's Billy Jones." She looked at him herself, carefully, trying to see him as Mrs. MacLane would. He was a boy about twelve, sitting quietly on a wall across the street, with his chin in his hands, silently watching Davey and Howard.

"He's like a young statue," Mrs. MacLane said. "So brown, and will you look at that face?" She started to walk again to see him more clearly, and Mrs. Winning followed her. "Do I know his mother and fath—?"

"The Jones children are half-Negro," Mrs. Winning said hastily. "But they're all beautiful children; you should see the girl. They live just outside town."

Howard's voice reached them clearly across the summer air. "Nigger," he was saying, "nigger, nigger boy."

"Nigger," Davey repeated, giggling.

Mrs. MacLane gasped, and then said, *"Davey,"* in a voice

that made Davey turn his head apprehensively; Mrs. Winning had never heard her friend use such a voice, and she too watched Mrs. MacLane.

"Davey," Mrs. MacLane said again, and Davey approached slowly. "What did I hear you say?"

"Howard," Mrs. Winning said, "leave Billy alone."

"Go tell that boy you're sorry," Mrs. MacLane said. "Go at once and tell him you're sorry."

Davey blinked tearfully at his mother and then went to the curb and called across the street, "I'm sorry."

Howard and Mrs. Winning waited uneasily, and Billy Jones across the street raised his head from his hands and looked at Davey and then, for a long time, at Mrs. MacLane. Then he put his chin on his hands again.

Suddenly Mrs. MacLane called, "Young man—Will you come here a minute, please?"

Mrs. Winning was surprised, and stared at Mrs. MacLane, but when the boy across the street did not move Mrs. Winning said sharply, "Billy! Billy Jones! Come here at once!"

The boy raised his head and looked at them, and then slid slowly down from the wall and started across the street. When he was across the street and about five feet from them he stopped, waiting.

"Hello," Mrs. MacLane said gently, "what's your name?"

The boy looked at her for a minute and then at Mrs. Winning, and Mrs. Winning said, "He's Billy Jones. Answer when you're spoken to, Billy."

"Billy," Mrs. MacLane said, "I'm sorry my little boy called you a name, but he's very little and he doesn't always know what he's saying. But he's sorry, too."

"Okay," Billy said, still watching Mrs. Winning. He was wearing an old pair of blue jeans and a torn white shirt, and he was barefoot. His skin and hair were the same color, the golden shade of a very heavy tan, and his hair curled lightly; he had the look of a garden statue.

"Billy," Mrs. MacLane said, "how would you like to come and work for me? Earn some money?"

"Sure," Billy said.

"Do you like gardening?" Mrs. MacLane asked. Billy nodded soberly. "Because," Mrs. MacLane went on enthusiastically, "I've been needing someone to help me with my garden, and it would be just the thing for you to do." She waited a minute and then said, "Do you know where I live?"

"Sure," Billy said. He turned his eyes away from Mrs. Winning and for a minute looked at Mrs. MacLane, his brown eyes expressionless. Then he looked back at Mrs. Winning, who was watching Howard up the street.

"Fine," Mrs. MacLane said. "Will you come tomorrow?"

"Sure," Billy said. He waited for a minute, looking from Mrs. MacLane to Mrs. Winning, and then ran back across the street and vaulted over the wall where he had been sitting. Mrs. MacLane watched him admiringly. Then she smiled at Mrs. Winning and gave the wagon a tug to start it up the hill again. They were nearly at the MacLane cottage before Mrs. MacLane finally spoke. "I just can't stand that," she said, "to hear children attacking people for things they can't help."

"They're strange people, the Joneses," Mrs. Winning said readily. "The father works around as a handyman; maybe you've seen him. You see—" she dropped her voice—"the mother was white, a girl from around here. A local girl," she said again, to make it more clear to a foreigner. "She left the whole litter of them when Billy was about two, and went off with a white man."

"Poor children," Mrs. MacLane said.

"*They're* all right," Mrs. Winning said. "The church takes care of them, of course, and people are always giving them things. The girl's old enough to work now, too. She's sixteen, but. . . ."

"But what?" Mrs. MacLane said, when Mrs. Winning hesitated.

"Well, people talk about her a lot, you know," Mrs. Winning said. "Think of her mother, after all. And there's another boy, couple of years older than Billy."

They stopped in front of the MacLane cottage and Mrs. MacLane touched Davey's hair. "Poor unfortunate child," she said.

"Children *will* call names," Mrs. Winning said. "There's not much you can do."

"Well . . ." Mrs. MacLane said. "Poor child."

The next day, after the dinner dishes were washed, and while Mrs. Winning and her mother-in-law were putting them away, the elder Mrs. Winning said casually, "Mrs. Blake tells me your friend Mrs. MacLane was asking around the neighbors how to get hold of the Jones boy."

"She wants someone to help in the garden, I think," Mrs. Winning said weakly. "She needs help in that big garden."

"Not *that* kind of help," the elder Mrs. Winning said. "You tell her about them?"

"She seemed to feel sorry for them," Mrs. Winning said, from the depths of the pantry. She took a long time settling the plates in even stacks in order to neaten her mind. She *shouldn't* have done it, she was thinking, but her mind refused to tell her why. She should have asked me first, though, she thought finally.

The next day Mrs. Winning stopped off at the cottage with Mrs. MacLane after coming up the hill from the store. They sat in the yellow kitchen and drank coffee, while the boys played in the back yard. While they were discussing the possibilities of hammocks between the apple trees there was a knock at the kitchen door and when Mrs. MacLane opened it she found a man standing there, so that she said, "Yes?" politely, and waited.

"Good morning," the man said. He took off his hat and nodded his head at Mrs. MacLane. "Billy told me you was looking for someone to work your garden," he said.

"Why . . ." Mrs. MacLane began, glancing sideways uneasily at Mrs. Winning.

"I'm Billy's father," the man said. He nodded his head toward the back yard and Mrs. MacLane saw Billy Jones sitting under one of the apple trees, his arms folded in front of him, his eyes on the grass at his feet.

"How do you do," Mrs. MacLane said inadequately.

"Billy told me you said for him to come work your garden," the man said. "Well, now, I think maybe a summer job's too much for a boy his age, he ought to be out playing in the good weather. And that's the kind of work I do anyway, so's I thought I'd just come over and see if you found anyone yet."

He was a big man, very much like Billy, except that where Billy's hair curled only a little, his father's hair curled tightly, with a line around his head where his hat stayed constantly and where Billy's skin was a golden tan, his father's skin was darker, almost bronze. When he moved, it was gracefully, like Billy, and his eyes were the same fathomless brown. "Like to work this garden," Mr. Jones said, looking around. "Could be a mighty nice place."

"You were very nice to come," Mrs. MacLane said. "I certainly do need help."

Mrs. Winning sat silently, not wanting to speak in front of Mr. Jones. She was thinking, I wish she'd ask me first, this is impossible . . . and Mr. Jones stood silently, listening courteously, with his dark eyes on Mrs. MacLane while she spoke. "I guess a lot of the work would be too much for a boy like Billy," she said. "There are a lot of things I can't even do myself, and I was sort of hoping I could get someone to give me a hand."

"That's fine, then," Mr. Jones said. "Guess I can manage most of it," he said, and smiled.

"Well," Mrs. MacLane said, "I guess that's all settled, then. When do you want to start?"

"How about right now?" he said.

"Grand," Mrs. MacLane said enthusiastically, and then, "Excuse me for a minute," to Mrs. Winning over her shoulder. She took down her gardening gloves and wide straw hat from the shelf by the door. "Isn't it a lovely day?" she asked Mr. Jones as she stepped out into the garden while he stood back to let her pass.

"You go along home now, Bill," Mr. Jones called as they went toward the side of the house.

"Oh, why not let him stay?" Mrs. MacLane said. Mrs. Winning heard her voice going on as they went out of sight. "He can play around the garden, and he'd probably enjoy . . ."

For a minute Mrs. Winning sat looking at the garden, at the corner around which Mr. Jones had followed Mrs. MacLane, and then Howard's face appeared around the side of the door and he said, "Hi, is it nearly time to eat?"

"Howard," Mrs. Winning said quietly, and he came in

through the door and came over to her. "It's time for you to run along home," Mrs. Winning said. "I'll be along in a minute."

Howard started to protest, but she added, "I want you to go right away. Take my bag of groceries if you think you can carry it."

Howard was impressed by her conception of his strength, and he lifted down the bag of groceries; his shoulders, already broad out of proportion, like his father's and his grandfather's, strained under the weight, and then he steadied on his feet. "Aren't I strong?" he asked exultantly.

"*Very* strong," Mrs. Winning said. "Tell Grandma I'll be right up. I'll just say good-bye to Mrs. MacLane."

Howard disappeared through the house; Mrs. Winning heard him walking heavily under the groceries, out through the open front door and down the steps. Mrs. Winning rose and was standing by the kitchen door when Mrs. MacLane came back.

"You're not ready to go?" Mrs. MacLane exclaimed when she saw Mrs. Winning with her jacket on. "Without finishing your coffee?"

"I'd better catch Howard," Mrs. Winning said. "He ran along ahead."

"I'm sorry I left you like that," Mrs. MacLane said. She stood in the doorway beside Mrs. Winning, looking out into the garden. "How *wonderful* it all is," she said, and laughed happily.

They walked together through the house; the blue curtains were up by now, and the rug with the touch of blue in the design was on the floor.

"Good-bye," Mrs. Winning said on the front steps.

Mrs. MacLane was smiling, and following her look Mrs.

Winning turned and saw Mr. Jones, his shirt off and his strong back shining in the sun as he bent with a scythe over the long grass at the side of the house. Billy lay nearby, under the shade of the bushes; he was playing with a grey kitten. "I'm going to have the finest garden in town," Mrs. MacLane said proudly.

"You won't have him working here past today, will you?" Mrs. Winning asked. "Of course you won't have him any longer than just today?"

"But surely—" Mrs. MacLane began, with a tolerant smile, and Mrs. Winning, after looking at her for an incredulous minute, turned and started, indignant and embarrassed, up the hill.

Howard had brought the groceries safely home and her mother-in-law was already setting the table.

"Howard says you sent him home from MacLane's," her mother-in-law said, and Mrs. Winning answered briefly, "I thought it was getting late."

The next morning when Mrs. Winning reached the cottage on her way down to the store she saw Mr. Jones swinging the scythe expertly against the side of the house, and Billy Jones and Davey sitting on the front steps watching him. "Good morning, Davey," Mrs. Winning called, "is your mother ready to go downstreet?"

"Where's Howard?" Davey asked, not moving.

"He stayed home with his grandma today," Mrs. Winning said brightly. "Is your mother ready?"

"She's making lemonade for Billy and me," Davey said. "We're going to have it in the garden."

"Then tell her," Mrs. Winning said quickly, "tell her that I said I was in a hurry and that I had to go on ahead. I'll see her later." She hurried on down the hill.

In the store she met Mrs. Harris, a lady whose mother had worked for the elder Mrs. Winning nearly forty years before. "Helen," Mrs. Harris said, "you get greyer every year. You ought to stop all this running around."

Mrs. Winning, in the store without Mrs. MacLane for the first time in weeks, smiled shyly and said that she guessed she needed a vacation.

"Vacation!" Mrs. Harris said. "Let that husband of yours do the housework for a change. He doesn't have nuthin' else to do."

She laughed richly, and shook her head. "Nuthin' else to do," she said. "The Winnings!"

Before Mrs. Winning could step away Mrs. Harris added, her laughter penetrated by a sudden sharp curiosity: "Where's that dressed-up friend of yours get to? Usually downstreet together, ain't you?"

Mrs. Winning smiled courteously, and Mrs. Harris said, laughing again, "Just couldn't believe those shoes of hers, first time I seen them. Them shoes!"

While she was laughing again Mrs. Winning escaped to the meat counter and began to discuss the potentialities of pork shoulder earnestly with the grocer. Mrs. Harris only says what everyone else says, she was thinking, are they talking like that about Mrs. MacLane? Are they laughing at her? When she thought of Mrs. MacLane she thought of the quiet house, the soft colors, the mother and son in the garden; Mrs. MacLane's shoes were green and yellow platform sandals, odd-looking certainly next to Mrs. Winning's solid white oxfords, but so inevitably right for Mrs. MacLane's house, and her garden. . . . Mrs. Harris came up behind her and said, laughing again, "What's she got, that Jones fellow working for her now?"

When Mrs. Winning reached home, after hurrying up the hill past the cottage, where she saw no one, her mother-in-law was waiting for her in front of the house, watching her come the last few yards. "Early enough today," her mother-in-law said. "MacLane out of town?"

Resentful, Mrs.. Winning said only, "Mrs. Harris nearly drove me out of the store, with her jokes."

"Nothing wrong with Lucy Harris getting away from that man of hers wouldn't cure," the elder Mrs. Winning said. Together, they began to walk around the house to the back door. Mrs. Winning, as they walked, noticed that the grass under the trees had greened up nicely, and that the nasturtiums beside the house were bright.

"I've got something to say to you, Helen," the elder Mrs. Winning said finally.

"Yes?" her daughter-in-law said.

"It's the MacLane girl, about her, I mean. You know her so well, you ought to talk to her about that colored man working there."

"I suppose so," Mrs. Winning said.

"You *sure* you told her? You told her about those people?"

"I told her," Mrs. Winning said.

"He's there every blessed day," her mother-in-law said. "And working out there without his shirt on. He goes in the house."

And that evening Mr. Burton, next-door neighbor to Mrs. MacLane, dropped in to see the Howard Winnings about getting a new lot of shingles at the mill; he turned, suddenly, to Mrs. Winning, who was sitting sewing next to her mother-in-law at the table in the front room, and raised his voice a little when he said, "Helen, I wish you'd tell your friend Mrs. MacLane to keep that kid of hers out of my vegetables."

"Davey?" Mrs. Winning said involuntarily.

"No," Mr. Burton said, while all the Winnings looked at the younger Mrs. Winning, "no, the other one, the colored boy. He's been running loose through our back yard. Makes me sort of mad, that kid coming in spoiling other people's property. You know," he added, turning to the Howard Winnings, "you know, that does make a person mad." There was a silence, and then Mr. Burton added, rising heavily, "Guess I'll say good-night to you people."

They all attended him to the door and came back to their work in silence. I've got to do something, Mrs. Winning was thinking, pretty soon they'll stop coming to me first, they'll tell someone else to speak to *me*. She looked up, found her mother-in-law looking at her, and they both looked down quickly.

Consequently Mrs. Winning went to the store the next morning earlier than usual, and she and Howard crossed the street just above the MacLane house, and went down the hill on the other side.

"Aren't we going to see Davey?" Howard asked once, and Mrs. Winning said carelessly, "Not today, Howard. Maybe your father will take you out to the mill this afternoon."

She avoided looking across the street at the MacLane house, and hurried to keep up with Howard.

Mrs. Winning met Mrs. MacLane occasionally after that at the store or the post office, and they spoke pleasantly. When Mrs. Winning passed the cottage after the first week or so, she was no longer embarrassed about going by, and even looked at it frankly once or twice. The garden was going beautifully; Mr. Jones's broad back was usually visible through the bushes, and Billy Jones sat on the steps or lay on the grass with Davey.

One morning on her way down the hill Mrs. Winning heard a conversation between Davey MacLane and Billy Jones; they were in the bushes together and she heard Davey's high familiar voice saying, "Billy, you want to build a house with me today?"

"Okay," Billy said. Mrs. Winning slowed her steps a little to hear.

"We'll build a big house out of branches," Davey said excitedly, "and when it's finished we'll ask my mommy if we can have lunch out there."

"You can't build a house just out of branches," Billy said. "You ought to have wood, and boards."

"And chairs and tables and dishes," Davey agreed. "And walls."

"Ask your mommy can we have two chairs out here," Billy said. "Then we can pretend the whole garden is our house."

"And I'll get us some cookies, too," Davey said. "And we'll ask my mommy and your daddy to come in our house." Mrs. Winning heard them shouting as she went down along the sidewalk.

You have to admit, she told herself as though she were being strictly just, you have to admit that he's doing a lot with that garden; it's the prettiest garden on the street. And Billy acts as though he had as much right there as Davey.

As the summer wore on into long hot days undistinguishable one from another, so that it was impossible to tell with any real accuracy whether the light shower had been yesterday or the day before, the Winnings moved out into their yard to sit after supper, and in the warm darkness Mrs. Winning sometimes found an opportunity of sitting next to her husband so that she could touch his arm; she was never able to teach Howard to run to her and put his head in her lap, or inspire him with other than the perfunctory Winning affection, but she consoled herself with the thought that at least they were a family, a solid respectable thing.

The hot weather kept up, and Mrs. Winning began to spend more time in the store, postponing the long aching walk up the hill in the sun. She stopped and chatted with the grocer, with other young mothers in the town, with older friends of her mother-in-law's, talking about the weather, the reluctance of the town to put in a decent swimming pool, the work that had to be done before school started in the fall, chickenpox, the P.T.A. One morning she met Mrs. Burton in the store, and they spoke of their husbands, the heat, and the hot-weather occupations of their children before Mrs. Burton said: "By the way, Johnny will be six on Saturday and he's having a birthday party; can Howard come?"

"Wonderful," Mrs. Winning said, thinking, His good white shorts, the dark blue shirt, a carefully-wrapped present.

"Just about eight children," Mrs. Burton said, with the loving carelessness mothers use in planning the birthday parties of their children. "They'll stay for supper, of course—send Howard down about three-thirty."

"That sounds so nice," Mrs. Winning said. "He'll be delighted when I tell him."

"I thought I'd have them all play outdoors most of the time," Mrs. Burton said. "In this weather. And then perhaps a few games indoors, and supper. Keep it simple—*you* know." She hesitated, running her finger around and around the top·rim of a can of coffee. "Look," she said, "I hope you won't mind me asking, but would it be all right with you if I didn't invite the MacLane boy?"

Mrs. Winning felt sick for a minute, and had to wait for her voice to even out before she said lightly, "It's all right with me if it's all right with *you;* why do you have to ask *me?*"

Mrs. Burton laughed. "I just thought you might mind if he didn't come."

Mrs. Winning was thinking. Something bad has happened, somehow people think they know something about me that they won't say, they all pretend it's nothing, but this never happened to me before; I live with the Winnings, don't I? "Really," she said, putting the weight of the old Winning house into her voice, "why in the *world* would it bother me?" Did I take it too seriously, she was wondering, did I seem too anxious, should I have let it go?

Mrs. Burton was embarrassed, and she set the can of coffee down on the shelf and began to examine the other shelves studiously. "I'm sorry I mentioned it at all," she said.

Mrs. Winning felt that she had to say something further, something to state her position with finality, so that no longer would Mrs. Burton, at least, dare to use such a tone to a Winning, presume to preface a question with "I hope you don't mind me asking." "After all," Mrs. Winning said carefully, weighing the words, "she's like a second mother to Billy."

Mrs. Burton, turning to look at Mrs. Winning for confirmation, grimaced and said, "Good Lord, Helen!"

Mrs. Winning shrugged and then smiled and Mrs. Burton smiled and then Mrs. Winning said, "I do feel so sorry for the little boy, though."

Mrs. Burton said, "Such a sweet little thing, too."

Mrs. Winning had just said, "He and Billy are together *all* the time now," when she looked up and saw Mrs. MacLane regarding her from the end of the aisle of shelves; it was impossible to tell whether she had heard them or not. For a minute Mrs. Winning looked steadily back at Mrs. MacLane, and then she said, with just the right note of cordiality, "Good morning, Mrs. MacLane. Where is your little boy this morning?"

"Good morning, Mrs. Winning," Mrs. MacLane said, and moved on past the aisle of shelves, and Mrs. Burton caught Mrs. Winning's arm and made a desperate gesture of hiding her face and, unable to help themselves, both she and Mrs. Winning began to laugh.

Soon after that, although the grass in the Winning yard under the maple trees stayed smooth and green, Mrs. Winning began to notice in her daily trips past the cottage that Mrs. MacLane's garden was suffering from the heat. The flowers wilted under the morning sun, and no longer stood up fresh and bright; the grass was browning slightly and the rose bushes Mrs. MacLane had put in so optimistically were noticeably dying. Mr. Jones seemed always cool, working steadily; sometimes bent down with his hands in the earth, sometimes tall against the side of the house, setting up a trellis or pruning a tree, but the blue curtains hung lifelessly at the windows. Mrs. MacLane still smiled at Mrs. Winning in the store, and then one day they met at the gate of Mrs. MacLane's garden and, after hesitating for a minute, Mrs. MacLane said, "Can you come in for a few minutes? I'd like to have a talk, if you have time."

"Surely," Mrs. Winning said courteously, and followed Mrs. MacLane up the walk, still luxuriously bordered with flowering bushes, but somehow disenchanted, as though the summer heat had baked away the vivacity from the ground. In the familiar living-room Mrs. Winning sat down on a straight chair, holding herself politely stiff, while Mrs. MacLane sat as usual in her armchair.

"How is Davey?" Mrs. Winning asked finally, since Mrs. MacLane did not seem disposed to start any conversation.

"He's very well," Mrs. MacLane said, and smiled as she always did when speaking of Davey. "He's out back with Billy."

There was a quiet minute, and then Mrs. MacLane said, staring at the blue bowl on the coffee table, "What I wanted to ask you is, what on earth is gone wrong?"

Mrs. Winning had been holding herself stiff in readiness for some such question, and when she said, "I don't know what you mean," she thought, I sound exactly like Mother Winning, and realized, I'm enjoying this, just as *she* would; and no matter what she thought of herself she was unable to keep from adding, "*Is* something wrong?"

"Of course," Mrs. MacLane said. She stared at the blue bowl, and said slowly, "When I first came, everyone was so nice, and they seemed to like Davey and me and want to help us."

That's wrong, Mrs. Winning was thinking, you mustn't ever talk about whether people like you, that's bad taste.

"And the garden was going so well," Mrs. MacLane said helplessly. "And now, no one ever does more than just speak to us—I used to say 'Good morning' over the fence to Mrs. Burton, and she'd come to the fence and we'd talk about the garden, and now she just says 'Morning' and goes in the house —and no one ever smiles, or anything."

This is dreadful, Mrs. Winning thought, this is childish, this is complaining. People treat you as you treat them, she thought; she wanted desperately to go over and take Mrs.

MacLane's hand and ask her to come back and be one of the nice people again; but she only sat straighter in the chair and said, "I'm sure you must be mistaken. I've never heard anyone speak of it."

"*Are* you sure?" Mrs. MacLane turned and looked at her. "Are you sure it isn't because of Mr. Jones working here?"

Mrs. Winning lifted her chin a little higher and said, "Why on earth would anyone around here be rude to you because of Jones?"

Mrs. MacLane came with her to the door, both of them planning vigorously for the days some time next week, when they would all go swimming, when they would have a picnic, and Mrs. Winning went down the hill thinking, The nerve of her, trying to blame the colored folks.

Toward the end of the summer there was a bad thunderstorm, breaking up the prolonged hot spell. It raged with heavy wind and rain over the town all night, sweeping without pity through the trees, pulling up young bushes and flowers ruthlessly; a barn was struck on one side of town, the wires pulled down on another. In the morning Mrs. Winning opened the back door to find the Winning yard littered with small branches from the maples, the grass bent almost flat to the ground.

Her mother-in-law came to the door behind her. "Quite a storm," she said, "did it wake you?"

"I woke up once and went to look at the children," Mrs. Winning said. "It must have been about three o'clock."

"I was up later," her mother-in-law said. "I looked at the children too; they were both asleep."

They turned together and went in to start breakfast.

Later in the day Mrs. Winning started down to the store; she had almost reached the MacLane cottage when she saw Mrs. MacLane standing in the front garden with Mr. Jones standing beside her and Billy Jones with Davey in the shadows of the front porch. They were all looking silently at a great branch from one of the Burtons' trees that lay across the center of the garden, crushing most of the flowering bushes and pinning down what was to have been a glorious tulip bed. As Mrs. Winning stopped, watching, Mrs. Burton came out on to her front porch to survey the storm-damage, and Mrs. MacLane called to her, "Good morning, Mrs. Burton, it looks like we have part of your tree over here."

"Looks so," Mrs. Burton said, and she went back into her house and closed the door flatly.

Mrs. Winning watched while Mrs. MacLane stood quietly for a minute. Then she looked up at Mr. Jones almost hopefully and she and Mr. Jones looked at one another for a long time. Then Mrs. MacLane said, her clear voice carrying lightly across the air washed clean by the storm: "Do you think I ought to give it up, Mr. Jones? Go back to the city where I'll never have to see another garden?"

Mr. Jones shook his head despondently, and Mrs. MacLane, her shoulders tired, went slowly over and sat on her front steps and Davey came and sat next to her. Mr. Jones took hold of the great branch angrily and tried to move it, shaking it and pulling until his shoulders tensed with the strength he was bringing to bear, but the branch only gave slightly and stayed, clinging to the garden.

"Leave it alone, Mr. Jones," Mrs. MacLane said finally. "Leave it for the next people to move!"

But still Mr. Jones pulled against the branch, and then

suddenly Davey stood up and cried out, "There's Mrs. Winning! Hi, Mrs. Winning!"

Mrs. MacLane and Mr. Jones both turned, and Mrs. MacLane waved and called out, "Hello!"

Mrs. Winning swung around without speaking and started, with great dignity, back up the hill toward the old Winning house.

‡

# DOROTHY AND MY GRANDMOTHER
# AND THE SAILORS

THERE USED TO BE a time of year in San Francisco—in late March, I believe—when there was fine long windy weather, and the air all over the city had a touch of salt and the freshness of the sea. And then, some time after the wind first started, you could look around Market Street and Van Ness and Kearney, and the fleet was in. That, of course, was some time ago, but you could look out around the Golden Gate, unbridged at that time, and there would be the battleships. There may have been aircraft carriers and destroyers, and I believe I recall one submarine, but to Dot and me then they were battleships, all of them. They would be riding out there on the water, quiet and competently grey, and the streets would be full of sailors, walking with the roll of the sea and looking in shop windows.

I never knew what the fleet came in for; my grandmother said positively that it was for refueling; but from the time the wind first started, Dot and I would become more aware, walking closer together, and dropping our voices when we talked. Although we were all of thirty miles from where the fleet lay, when we walked with our backs to the ocean we could feel the battleships riding somewhere behind and beyond us, and when we looked toward the ocean we narrowed our eyes, almost able to see across thirty miles and into a sailor's face.

It *was* the sailors, of course. My mother told us about the kind of girls who followed sailors, and my grandmother told

us about the kind of sailors who followed girls. When we told
Dot's mother the fleet was in, she would say earnestly, "Don't
go near any sailors, you two." Once, when Dot and I were
about twelve, and the fleet was in, my mother stood us up and
looked at us intensely for a minute, and then she turned
around to my grandmother and said, "I don't approve of
young girls going to the movies alone at night," and my grandmother said, "Nonsense, they won't come this far down the
peninsula; I *know* sailors."

Dot and I were permitted only one movie at night a week,
anyway, and even then they sent my ten-year-old brother
along with us. The first time the three of us started off to the
movies together my mother looked at Dot and me again and
then speculatively at my brother, who had red curly hair, and
started to say something, and then looked at my grandmother
and changed her mind.

We lived in Burlingame, which is far enough away from
San Francisco to have palm trees in the gardens, but near
enough so that Dot and I were taken into San Francisco, to
the Emporium, to get our spring coats each year. Dot's mother
usually gave Dot her coat money, which Dot handed over to
my mother, and then Dot and I got identical coats, with my
mother officiating. This was because Dot's mother was never
well enough to go into San Francisco shopping, and particularly not with Dot and me. Consequently every year, some
time after the wind started and the fleet came in, Dot and I,
in service-weight silk stockings which we kept for that occasion, and each with a cardboard pocketbook containing a
mirror, a dime for luck, and a chiffon handkerchief caught at
one side and hanging down, got into the back seat of my
mother's car with my mother and grandmother in the front,
and headed for San Francisco and the fleet.

We always got our coats in the morning, went to the Pig'n'-Whistle for lunch, and then, while Dot and I were finishing our chocolate ice cream with chocolate sauce and walnuts, my grandmother phoned my Uncle Oliver and arranged to meet him at the launch which took us out to the fleet.

My Uncle Oliver was taken along partly because he was a man and partly because in the previous war he had been a radio operator on a battleship and partly because another uncle of mine, an Uncle Paul, was still with the Navy (my grandmother thought he had something to do with a battleship named the *Santa Volita*, or *Bonita*, or possibly *Carmelita*) and my Uncle Oliver was handy for asking people who looked like they might know my Uncle Paul if they did know him. As soon as we got on a boat my grandmother would say, as though she had never thought of it before, "Look, that one over there seems to be an officer; Ollie, just go over casually and ask him if he knows old Paul."

Oliver, having been one himself, didn't think that sailors were particularly dangerous to Dot and me if we had my mother and my grandmother with us, but he loved ships, and so he went with us and left us the minute we were on board; while we stepped cautiously over the clean decks eyeing the lifeboats apprehensively, my Uncle Oliver would touch the grey paint affectionately and go off in search of the radio apparatus.

When we met my Uncle Oliver at the launch he would usually buy Dot and me an ice-cream cone each and on the launch he would point out various boats around and name them for us. He usually got into a conversation with the sailor running the launch, and sooner or later he managed to say modestly, "I was to sea, back in '17," and the sailor would

nod respectfully. When it came time for us to leave the launch
and go up a stairway on to the battleship, my mother whispered to Dot and me, "Keep your skirts down," and Dot and
I climbed the ladder, holding on with one hand and with the
other wrapping our skirts tight around us into a bunch in
front which we held on to. My grandmother always preceded
us onto the battleship and my mother and Uncle Oliver followed us. When we got on board my mother took one of us
by the arm and my grandmother took the other and we
walked slowly around all of the ship they allowed us to see,
excepting only the lowest levels, which alarmed my grandmother. We looked solemnly at cabins, decks which my
grandmother said were aft, and lights which she said were
port (both sides were port to my grandmother; she believed
that starboard was up, in the sense that the highest mast
always pointed at the north star.) Usually we saw cannon—
all guns were cannon—which my Uncle Oliver, in what must
have been harmless teasing, assured my grandmother were
kept loaded all the time. "In case of mutiny," he told my
grandmother.

There were always a great many sight-seers on the battleships, and my Uncle Oliver was fond of gathering a little
group of boys and young men around him to explain how
the radio system worked. When he said he had been a radio
operator back in '17 someone was sure to ask him, "Did you
ever send out an S.O.S.?" and my Uncle Oliver would nod
heavily, and say, "But I'm still here to tell about it."

Once, while my Uncle Oliver was telling about '17 and my
mother and my grandmother and Dot were looking over the
rail at the ocean, I saw a dress that looked like my mother's
and followed it for quite a way down the battleship before
the lady turned around and I realized that it was not my

mother and I was lost. Remembering what my grandmother had told me, that I was always safe if I didn't lose my head, I stood still and looked around until I isolated a tall man in a uniform with lots of braid. That will be a captain, I thought, and he will certainly take care of me. He was very polite. I told him I was lost and thought my mother and my grandmother and my friend Dot and my Uncle Oliver were down the boat a ways but I was afraid to go back alone. He said he would help me find them, and he took my arm and led me down the boat. Before very long we met my mother and my grandmother hurrying along looking for me with Dot coming along behind them as fast as she could. When my grandmother saw me she ran forward and seized my arm, pulling me away from the captain and shaking me. "You gave us the scare of our lives," she said.

"She was just lost, that's all," the captain said.

"I'm glad we found her in time," my grandmother said, walking backward with me to my mother.

The captain bowed and went away, and my mother took my other arm and shook me. "Aren't you ashamed?" she said. Dot stared at me solemnly.

"But he was a captain—" I began.

"He might have *said* he was a captain," my grandmother said, "but he was a marine."

"A marine!" my mother said, looking over the side to see if the launch was there to take us back. "Get Oliver and tell him we've seen enough," she said to my grandmother.

Because of what happened that evening, that was the last year we were allowed to see the fleet. We dropped Uncle Oliver off at home, as usual, and my mother and my grandmother took Dot and me to the Merry-Go-Round for dinner.

We always had dinner in San Francisco after the fleet, and went to a movie and got home to Burlingame late in the evening. We always had dinner in the Merry-Go-Round, where the food came along on a moving platform and you grabbed it as it went by. We went there because Dot and I loved it, and next to the battleships it was the most dangerous place in San Francisco, because you had to pay fifteen cents for every dish you took and didn't finish, and Dot and I were expected to pay for these mistakes out of our allowances. This last evening Dot and I lost forty-five cents, mainly because of a mocha cream dessert that Dot hadn't known was full of coconut. The movie Dot and I chose was full, although the usher outside told my grandmother there were plenty of seats. My mother refused to wait in line to get our money back, so my grandmother said we had to go on in and take our chances on seats. As soon as two seats were vacant my grandmother shoved Dot and me toward them, and we sat down. The picture was well under way when the two seats next to Dot emptied, and we were looking for my grandmother and my mother when Dot looked around suddenly and then grabbed my arm. "Look," she said in a sort of groan, and there were two sailors coming along the row of seats toward the empty ones. They reached the seats just as my mother and grandmother got down to the other end of the row, and my grandmother had just time to say loudly, "You leave those girls alone," when two seats a few aisles away were vacated and they had to go sit down.

Dot moved far over in her seat next to me and clung to my arm.

"What are they doing?" I whispered.

"They're just sitting there," Dot said. "What do you think I ought to do?"

I leaned cautiously around Dot and looked. "Don't pay any attention," I said. "Maybe they'll go away."

"*You* can talk," Dot said tragically, "they're not next to *you*."

"I'm next to *you*," I said reasonably, "that's pretty close."

"What are they doing now?" Dot asked.

I leaned forward again. "They're looking at the picture," I said.

"I can't stand it," Dot said. "I want to go home."

Panic overwhelmed both of us at once, and fortunately my mother and my grandmother saw us running up the aisle and caught us outside.

"What did they say?" my grandmother demanded. "I'll tell the usher."

My mother said if Dot would calm down enough to talk she would take us into the tea room next door and get us each a hot chocolate. When we got inside and were sitting down we told my mother and my grandmother we were fine now and instead of a hot chocolate we would have a chocolate sundae apiece. Dot had even started to cheer up a little when the door of the tea room opened and two sailors walked in. With one wild bound Dot was in back of my grandmother's chair, cowering and clutching my grandmother's arm. "Don't let them get me," she wailed.

"They followed us," my mother said tautly.

My grandmother put her arms around Dot. "Poor child," she said, "you're safe with us."

Dot had to stay at my house that night. We sent my brother over to Dot's mother to tell her that Dot was staying with me and that Dot had bought a grey tweed coat with princess lines, very practical and warmly interlined. She wore it all that year.

# III

The Confession of *Margaret Jackson*, relict of *Tho. Stuart* in *Shaws*, who being examined by the Justices anent her being guilty of Witchcraft, declares . . . That forty years ago, or thereabout, she was at *Pollockshaw-croft*, with some few sticks on her back, and that the black Man came to her, and that she did give up herself unto the black Man, from the top of her head to the sole of her foot; and that this was after the Declarant's renouncing of her Baptism; and that the Spirit's name, which he designed her, was *Locas*. And that about the third or fourth of *January*, instant, or thereby, in the night-time, when she awaked, she found a Man to be in bed with her, whom she supposed to be her Husband; though her Husband had been dead twenty years, or thereby, and that the Man immediately disappeared: And declares, That this Man who disappeared was the Devil.

Joseph Glanvil: *Sadducismus Triumphatus*

‡

# COLLOQUY

THE DOCTOR was competent-looking and respectable. Mrs. Arnold felt vaguely comforted by his appearance, and her agitation lessened a little. She knew that he noticed her hand shaking when she leaned forward for him to light her cigarette, and she smiled apologetically, but he looked back at her seriously.

"You seem to be upset," he said gravely.

"I'm very much upset," Mrs. Arnold said. She tried to talk slowly and intelligently. "That's one reason I came to you instead of going to Doctor Murphy—our regular doctor, that is."

The doctor frowned slightly. "My husband," Mrs. Arnold went on. "I don't want him to know that I'm worried, and Doctor Murphy would probably feel it was necessary to tell him." The doctor nodded, not committing himself, Mrs. Arnold noted.

"What seems to be the trouble?"

Mrs. Arnold took a deep breath. "Doctor," she said, "how do people tell if they're going crazy?"

The doctor looked up.

"Isn't that silly," Mrs. Arnold said. "I hadn't meant to say it like that. It's hard enough to explain anyway, without making it so dramatic."

"Insanity is more complicated than you think," the doctor said.

"I *know* it's complicated," Mrs. Arnold said. "That's the

only thing I'm really *sure* of. Insanity is one of the things I mean."

"I beg your pardon?"

"That's my trouble, Doctor." Mrs. Arnold sat back and took her gloves out from under her pocketbook and put them carefully on top. Then she took them and put them underneath the pocketbook again.

"Suppose you just tell me all about it," the doctor said.

Mrs. Arnold sighed. "Everyone else seems to understand," she said, "and I don't. Look." She leaned forward and gestured with one hand while she spoke. "I don't understand the way people live. It all used to be so simple. When I was a little girl I used to live in a world where a lot of other people lived too and they all lived together and things went along like that with no fuss." She looked at the doctor. He was frowning again, and Mrs. Arnold went on, her voice rising slightly. "Look. Yesterday morning my husband stopped on his way to his office to buy a paper. He always buys the *Times* and he always buys it from the same dealer, and yesterday the dealer didn't have a *Times* for my husband and last night when he came home for dinner he said the fish was burned and the dessert was too sweet and he sat around all evening talking to himself."

"He could have tried to get it at another dealer," the doctor said. "Very often dealers downtown have papers later than local dealers."

"No," Mrs. Arnold said, slowly and distinctly, "I guess I'd better start over. When I was a little girl—" she said. Then she stopped. "Look," she said, "did there use to be words like psychosomatic medicine? Or international cartels? Or bureaucratic centralization?"

"Well," the doctor began.

"What do they *mean?*" Mrs. Arnold insisted.

"In a period of international crisis," the doctor said gently, "when you find, for instance, cultural patterns rapidly disintegrating . . ."

"International crisis," Mrs. Arnold said. "Patterns." She began to cry quietly. "He said the man had no *right* not to save him a *Times*," she said hysterically, fumbling in her pocket for a handkerchief, "and he started talking about social planning on the local level and surtax net income and geopolitical concepts and deflationary inflation." Mrs. Arnold's voice rose to a wail. "He really said deflationary inflation."

"Mrs. Arnold," the doctor said, coming around the desk, "we're not going to help things any this way."

"What is going to help?" Mrs. Arnold said. "Is everyone really crazy but me?"

"Mrs. Arnold," the doctor said severely, "I want you to get hold of yourself. In a disoriented world like ours today, alienation from reality frequently—"

"Disoriented," Mrs. Arnold said. She stood up. "Alienation," she said. "Reality." Before the doctor could stop her she walked to the door and opened it. "Reality," she said, and went out.

‡

# ELIZABETH

JUST BEFORE the alarm went off she was lying in a hot sunny garden, with green lawns around her and stretching as far as she could see. The bell of the clock was an annoyance, a warning which had to be reckoned with; she moved uneasily in the hot sun and knew she was awake. When she opened her eyes and it was raining and she saw the white outline of the window against the grey sky, she tried to turn over and bury her face in the green grass, but it was morning and habit was lifting her up and dragging her away into the rainy dull day.

It was definitely past eight o'clock. The clock said so, the radiator was beginning to crackle, and on the street two stories below she could hear the ugly morning noises of people stirring, getting out to work. She put her feet reluctantly out from under the blankets and on to the floor, and swung herself up to sit on the edge of the bed. By the time she was standing up and in her bathrobe the day had fallen into its routine; after the first involuntary rebellion against every day's alarm she subsided regularly into the shower, make-up, dress, breakfast schedule which would take her through the beginning of the day and out into the morning where she could forget the green grass and the hot sun and begin to look forward to dinner and the evening.

Because it was raining and the day seemed unimportant she put on the first things she came to; a grey tweed suit that she knew was shapeless and heavy on her now that she was so thin, a blue blouse that never felt comfortable. She knew her own face too well to enjoy the long careful scrutiny that went with putting on make-up; toward four o'clock in the afternoon her pale narrow cheeks would warm up and fill out, and the lipstick that looked too purple with her dark hair and eyes would take on a rosier touch in spite of the blue blouse, but this morning she thought, as she had thought nearly every morning standing in front of her mirror, I wish I'd been a blonde; never realizing quite that it was because there were thin hints of grey in her hair.

She walked quickly around her one-room apartment, with a sureness that came of habit rather than conviction; after more than four years in this one home she knew all its possibilities, how it could put on a sham appearance of warmth and welcome when she needed a place to hide in, how it stood over her in the night when she woke suddenly, how it could relax itself into a disagreeable unmade, badly-put-together state, mornings like this, anxious to drive her out and go back to sleep. The book she had read the night before lay face down on the end table, the ashtray next to it dirtied: the clothes she had taken off lay over the back of a chair, to be taken to the cleaner this morning.

With her coat and hat on, she made the bed quickly, pulling it straight on top over the wrinkles beneath, stuffed the clothes to go to the cleaner into the back of the closet, and thought, I'll dust and straighten and maybe wash the bathroom tonight, come home and take a hot bath and wash my hair and do my nails; by the time she had locked the apartment door behind her and started down the stairs, she was thinking, Maybe today I'll stop in and get some bright material for slip-covers and drapes. I could make them evenings and the place wouldn't look so dreary when I wake up mornings; yellow, I could get some yellow dishes and put them along the wall

in a row. Like in *Mademoiselle* or something, she told herself
ironically as she stopped at the front door, the brisk young
businesswoman and her one-room home. Suitable for entertaining brisk young businessmen. I wish I had something that
folded up into a bookcase on one side and a Sheraton desk on
the other and opened out into a dining-room table big enough
to seat twelve.

While she was standing just inside the door, pulling on her
gloves and hoping the rain might stop in these few seconds,
the door next to the stairway opened and a woman said,
"Who's that?"

"It's Miss Style," she said, "Mrs. Anderson?"

The door opened wide and an old woman put her head
out. "I thought it was that fellow has the apartment right
over you," she said. "I been meaning to catch him about
leaving them skis outside his door. Nearly broke my leg."

"I've been wishing I didn't have to go out. It's such a bad
day."

The old woman came out of her room and went to the
front door. She pulled aside the door curtain and looked out,
wrapping her arms around herself. She was wearing a dirty
house dress and the sight of her made Miss Style's grey
tweed suit suddenly seem clean and warm.

"I been trying to catch that fellow for two days now," the
old woman said. "He goes in and out so quiet." She giggled,
looking sideways at Miss Style. "I nearly caught that man of
yours night before last," she said. "He comes down the
stairs quiet, too. I saw who it was in time," and she giggled
again. "I guess all the men come downstairs quiet. All afraid
of something."

"Well, if I'm going to go out I might as well do it," Miss
Style said. She still stood in the doorway for a minute, hesi-

tating before walking out into the day and the rain and the people. She lived on a fairly quiet street, where later there would be children shouting at each other and on a nice day an organ-grinder, but today in the rain everything looked dirty. She hated to wear rubbers because she had graceful slim feet; on a day like this she went slowly, stepping carefully between puddles.

It was very late; there were only a few people still sitting at the counter in the corner drugstore. She sat on a stool, reconciled to the time, and waited patiently until the clerk came down the counter with her orange juice. "Hello, Tommy," she said dismally.

"Morning, Miss Style," he said, "lousy day."

"Isn't it," she said. "A fine day not to go out."

"I came in this morning," Tommy said. "I would have given my right arm to stay home in bed. There ought to be a law against rain."

Tommy was little and ugly and alert; looking at him, Miss Style thought, He has to get up and come to work in the mornings just like I do and just like everyone else in the world; the rain is just another break in the millions of lousy things, in getting up and going to work.

"I don't mind snow," Tommy was saying, "and I don't mind the hot weather, but I sure do hate rain."

He turned suddenly when someone called him, and went dancing down to the other end of the counter, bringing up with a flourish before his customer. "Lousy day, isn't it?" he said. "Sure do wish I was in Florida."

Miss Style drank her orange juice, remembering her dream. A sharp recollection of flowers and warmth came into her mind, and then was lost before the cold driving rain outside.

Tommy came back with her coffee and a plate of toast.

"Nothing like coffee to cheer you up in the morning," he said.

"Thanks, Tommy," she said, unenthusiastic. "How's your play coming, by the way?"

Tommy looked up eagerly. "Hey," he said, "I finished it, I meant to tell you. Finished the whole thing and sent it away day before yesterday."

Funny thing, she thought, a clerk in a drugstore, he gets up in the morning and eats and walks around and writes a play just like it was real, just like the rest of us, like me. "Fine," she said.

"I sent it to an agent a guy told me about, he said it was the best agent he knew."

"Tommy," she said, "why didn't you give it right to me?"

He laughed, looking down at the sugar bowl he was holding for her. "Listen," he said, "my friend said you didn't want stuff like mine, you want people, like, from out of town or something, they don't know if they're any good or not. Hell," he went on anxiously, "I'm not one of these guys fall for ads in the magazines."

"I see," she said.

Tommy leaned over the counter. "Don't get sore," he said, "You know what I mean, you know your business better than I do."

"I'm not sore," she said. She watched Tommy hurry away again, and she thought— Wait till I tell Robbie. Wait till I tell him the soda jerk thinks he's a bum.

"Listen," Tommy said to her, from halfway down the counter, "how long do you think I ought to wait? How long will they take to read it, these agents?"

"Couple of weeks, maybe," she said. "Maybe longer."

"I figured it might be," he said. "You want more coffee today?"

"No, thanks," she said. She slid down from the stool and walked across the store to pay her check. They're probably going to buy that play, she was thinking, and I'm going to start eating in the hamburg joint across the street.

She went out into the rain again to see her bus just pulling up across the street. She ran for it, against the light, and pushed into the crowd of people getting on. With a kind of fury left over from Tommy and his play she thrust her way against the people, and a woman turned to her and said, "Who do you think you're pushing?" Vengefully she put her elbow into the woman's ribs and got on the bus first. She dropped her nickel in and got to the last available seat, and heard the woman behind her. "These people who think they can shove anybody around, they think they're important." She looked around to see if anyone knew who the woman was talking about; the man beside her on the seat next to the window was staring straight ahead with the infinitely tired expression of the early-morning bus passenger; two girls in the seat in front were looking out the window after a man passing, and in the aisle next to her the woman was standing, still talking about her. "People who think their business is the only important thing in the world. Think they can just push anyone around." No one in the bus was listening: everyone was wet and uncomfortable and crowded, but the woman went on monotonously— "Think no one else has a right to ride on buses."

She stared past the man out the window until the crowds coming into the bus pushed the woman past her down the aisle. When she came to her stop she was timid for a minute about pushing her way out, and when she reached the door the woman was near it, staring at her as though wanting to remember her face. "Dried-up old maid," the woman said loudly, and the people around her in the bus laughed.

Miss Style put on an expression of contempt, stepping carefully down to the curb, looking up just as the bus pulled away to see the woman's face still watching her from the window. She walked through the rain to the old building where her office was, thinking, That woman was just waiting for anyone to cross her path this morning, I wish I'd said something back to her.

"Morning, Miss Style," the elevator operator said.

"Morning," she said. She walked into the open-work iron elevator and leaned against the back wall.

"Bad day," the operator said. He waited for a minute and then closed the door. "Fine day not to go out," he said.

"Sure is," she said. I wish I'd said something to that woman in the bus, she was thinking. I shouldn't have let her get away with it, let the day start off like that, with a nasty incident, I should have answered her back and got to feeling good and pleased with myself. Start the day off right.

"Here you are," the operator said. "You don't have to go out again for quite a while."

"Glad of that," she said. She got out of the elevator and walked down the hall to her office. There was a light on inside, making the *ROBERT SHAX, Literary Agents*, stand out against the door. Looks almost cheerful, she thought, Robbie must be in early.

She had worked for Robert Shax for nearly eleven years. When she came to New York the Christmas she was twenty, a thin dark girl with neat clothes and hair and moderate ambition, holding on to her pocketbook with both hands, afraid of subways, she answered an ad, and met Robert Shax before she had even found a room to live in. It had been one of those windfall ads, an assistant wanted in a literary agency, and there was no one around to tell Elizabeth Style, asking people timidly how to find the address, that if she got the job it wasn't worth getting. The literary agency was Robert Shax and a thin clever man who had disliked Elizabeth so violently that after two years she had taken Robert Shax away to start his own agency. Robert Shax was on the door and on all the checks, and Elizabeth Style hid away in her office, wrote the letters, kept the records, and came out occasionally to consult the files she allowed Robert Shax to keep on display.

They had spent much time in the eight years trying to make this office look like a severe environment for a flourishing business: a miserable place that its owners were too busy to pretty up more than enough to meet the purposes of its clients. The door opened into a tight little reception room, painted tan the year before, with two cheap chrome and brown chairs, a brown linoleum floor, and a framed picture of a vase of flowers over the small desk which was occupied five afternoons a week by a Miss Wilson, a colorless girl who answered the phone sniffling. Beyond Miss Wilson's desk were two doors, which did not give the effect of limitless offices, stretching on down the building, that Robert Shax had hoped they might; the one on the left had, on the door, "Robert Shax," and the one on the right had, on the door, "Elizabeth Style," and through the pebbled glass doors you could see, dimly, the shape of the narrow window each office owned, crowding close enough to the door and walls to admit that the two offices together were no wider than the reception room, and to hint darkly that all that protected the privacy of Mr. Shax and Miss Style was a beaverboard partition painted to look like the walls.

Every morning Elizabeth Style came into the office with the idea that something might be done for it still, that somehow there might be a way to make it look respectable, with Venetian blinds or paneling or an efficient-looking bookcase with sets of classics and the newest books that Robert Shax had presumably sold to their publishers. Or even an end table with expensive magazines. Miss Wilson thought it would be nice to have a radio, but Robert Shax wanted an expensive office with heavy carpeting and desks sitting solidly on the floor and a battery of secretaries.

This morning the office looked more cheerful than usual, probably because it was still raining outside, or else because the lights were already on and the radiators were going. Elizabeth Style went over to the door of her office and opened it, saying, "Morning, Robbie," because, since there was no one in the office, there was no need to pretend that the beaverboard partitions were walls.

"Morning, Liz," Robbie said, and then, "Come on in, will you?"

"I'll take my coat off," she said. There was a tiny closet in the corner of her office where she hung up her coat, squeezing in back of the desk to do it. She noticed that there was mail on her desk, four or five letters and a bulky envelope that would be a manuscript. She spread the letters out to make sure there was nothing of any particular interest, and then went out of her office and opened the door of Robbie's.

He was leaning down over his desk, in an attitude meant to show extreme concentration; the faintly bald top of his head was toward her and his heavy round shoulders cut off the lower half of the window. His office was almost exactly like hers; it had a small filing cabinet and an autographed photograph of one of the few reasonably successful writers the firm had handled. The photograph was signed "To Bob, with deepest gratitude, Jim," and Robert Shax was fond of using it as a happy example in his office conversations with eager authors. When she had closed the door Elizabeth was only a step away from the straight visitor's chair slanting at the desk; she sat down and stretched her feet out in front of her.

"I got soaked coming in this morning," she said.

"It's an awful day," Robbie said, without looking up. When he was alone with her he relaxed the heartiness that he usually stocked in his voice: he let his face look tired and worried. He was wearing his good grey suit that day, and later, with other people around, he would look like a golfer, a man who ate good rare roast beef and liked pretty girls. "It's one hell of a day," he repeated. He looked up at her. "Liz," he said, "that goddamned minister is in town again."

"No wonder you look so worried," she said. She had been ready to complain at him, to tell him about the woman on the bus, to ask him to sit up straight and behave, but there was nothing to say. "Poor old Robbie," she said.

"There's a note from him," Robbie said. "I've got to go up there this morning. He's in that goddamned rooming-house again."

"What are you planning to tell him?"

Robbie got up and turned around to the window. When he got out of his chair he had just room to turn around to get to the window of the closet or the filing cabinet; on a pleasanter day she might have an amiable remark about his weight. "I don't know what in hell I'm planning to tell him," Robbie said. "I'll promise him something."

I know you will, she thought. She had the familiar picture of Robbie's maneuvers to escape an awkward situation in the back of her mind: she could see Robbie shaking the old man's hand briskly, calling him "sir" and keeping his shoulders back, saying that the old man's poems were "fine, sir, really magnificent," promising anything, wildly, just to get away. "You'll come back in some kind of trouble," she said mildly.

Robbie laughed suddenly, happily. "But he won't bother us for a while."

"You ought to call him up or something. Write him a letter," she said.

"Why?" She could see that he was pleased with the idea of coming back in trouble, of being irresponsible and what he would call carefree; he would make the long trip uptown to the minister's rooming-house by subway and take a taxi for the last two blocks to arrive in style, and sit for a tiresome hour talking to the old man, just to be carefree and what he might call gallant.

Make him feel good, she thought. He has to go, not me. "You shouldn't be trusted to run a business by yourself," she said. "You're too silly."

He laughed again and walked around the desk to pat her head. "We get along pretty well, don't we, Liz?"

"Fine," she said.

He was beginning to think about it now; he was holding his head up and his voice was filling out. "I'll tell him someone wants one of his poems for an anthology," he said.

"Just don't give him any money," she said. "He has more than we have now."

He went back to his closet and took out his coat, his good coat today, and threw it carelessly over his arm. He put his hat on the back of his head and picked up his brief case from the desk. "Got all the old guy's poems in here," he said. "I figured I could kill some time reading them aloud to him."

"Have a nice trip," she said.

He patted her on the head again, and then reached out for the door. "You'll take care of everything here?"

"I'll try to cope with it," she said.

She followed him out the door and started into her own office. Halfway across the outer office he stopped, not turning. "Liz?" he said.

"Well?"

He thought for a minute. "Seems like there was something I wanted to tell you," he said. "It doesn't matter."

"See you for lunch?" she asked.

"I'll be back about twelve-thirty," he said.

He closed the door and she heard his footsteps going emphatically down the hall to the elevator; busy footsteps, she thought, in case anyone was listening in this fearful old building.

She sat for a minute at her desk, smoking and wishing she could paint her office walls a light green. If she wanted to stay late at night she could do it herself. It would only take one can of paint, she told herself bitterly, to do an office like this, with enough left over to do the front of the building. Then she put out her cigarette and thought, I've worked in it this long, maybe some day we'll get a million-dollar client and can move into a real office building where they have soundproof walls.

The mail on her desk was bad. A bill from her dentist, a letter from a client in Oregon, a couple of ads, a letter from her father, and the bulky envelope that was certainly a manuscript. She threw out the ads and the dentist's bill, which was marked "Please remit," set the manuscript and the other letter aside, and opened the letter from her father.

It was in his own peculiar style, beginning, "Dearest Daughter," and ending, "Yr. Afft. Father," and told her that the feed store was doing badly, that her sister in California was pregnant again, that old Mrs. Gill had asked after her the other day, and that he found himself very much alone since her mother's death. And he hoped she was well. She threw the letter into the wastebasket on top of the dentist's bill.

The letter from the client in Oregon wanted to know what had happened to a manuscript sent in three months before; the large bulky envelope contained a manuscript written in longhand, from a young man in Allentown who wanted it sold immediately and their fee taken out of the editor's check. She glanced through the manuscript carelessly, turning over the pages and reading a few words on each; halfway through she stopped and read a whole page, and then turned back a little and read more. With her eyes still on the manuscript, she leaned over and reached into the bottom drawer of her desk, stirring papers around until she found a small, ten-cent notebook, partly filled with notes. She opened the notebook to a blank page, copied out a paragraph from the manuscript, thinking, I can switch that around and make it a woman instead of a man; and she made another note, "make W., use any name but Helen," which was the name of the woman in the story. Then she put the notebook away and set the manuscript to one side of her desk in order to swing up the panel of the desk that brought the typewriter upright. She took out a sheet of notepaper labeled "ROBERT SHAX, Literary Agents, Elizabeth Style, Fiction Department," and put it into the typewriter; she was just typing the young man's name and the address: General Delivery, Allentown, when she heard the outer door open and close.

"Hello," she called, without looking up.

"Good morning."

She looked up then; it was such a high, girlish voice. The

girl who had come in was big and blonde, and walked across the little reception room as though she were prepared to be impressed no matter what happened to her there.

"Did you want to see me?" Elizabeth asked, her hands still resting on the typewriter keys. If God should have sent me a client, she thought, it won't hurt to look literary.

"I wanted Mr. Shax," the girl said. She waited in the doorway of Elizabeth's office.

"He was called out on very pressing business," Elizabeth said. "Did you have an appointment?"

The girl hesitated, as though doubting Elizabeth's authority. "Not exactly," she said finally. "I'm supposed to be working here, I guess."

Seemed like there was something he wanted to tell me, Elizabeth thought, that coward. "I see," she said. "Come in and sit down."

The girl came in shyly, although with no apparent timidity. She figured it was his business to tell me, not hers, Elizabeth thought. "Did Mr. Shax tell you to come to work here?"

"Well," the girl said, deciding it was all right to trust Elizabeth, "on Monday about five o'clock I was asking for a job in all the offices in this building and I came here and Mr. Shax showed me around the office and he said he thought I could do the work all right." She thought back over what she had said. "You weren't here," she added.

"I couldn't have been," Elizabeth agreed. He's known since Monday and I find out, she thought, what is this, Wednesday? I find out on Wednesday when she shows up for work. "I didn't ask your name."

"Daphne Hill," the girl said meekly.

Elizabeth wrote "Daphne Hill" down on her memorandum and looked at it, partly to seem as if she was coming to an important decision and partly to see what "Daphne Hill" looked like written down.

"Mr. Shax said," the girl began, and stopped. Her voice was high and when she was anxious she opened her small brown eyes wide and blinked. Except for her hair, which was a pale blonde and curled all over the top of her head, she was clumsy and awkward, all dressed up for her first day at work.

"What did Mr. Shax say?" Elizabeth asked when the girl seemed to have subsided permanently.

"He said he wasn't satisfied with the girl he had now and I was to learn her job and get to do it and I was to come today because he was going to tell her yesterday that I was coming."

"Fine," Elizabeth said. "Can you type, do you suppose?"

"I guess so," the girl said.

Elizabeth looked at the letter in the typewriter on her desk and then said, "Well, you go on outside and sit at the desk out there and if the phone rings you answer it. Read or something."

"Yes, Miss Style," the girl said.

"And please close my office door," Elizabeth said. She watched the girl go out and close the door carefully. The things she had wanted to say to the girl were waiting to be said: maybe she could rephrase some of them for Robbie at lunch.

What does this mean, she thought suddenly in panic, Miss Wilson has been here almost as long as I have. Is he trying in his own heavy-handed fashion to beautify the office? He might better buy a bookcase; who is going to teach this incredible girl to answer the phone and write letters, even as well as Miss Wilson? Me, she thought at last. I'm going to have to drag Robbie out of this last beautiful impulsive gesture like always; the things I do for a miserable little office and a chance to make money. Anyway, maybe Daphne will help me paint the walls after five some day; maybe the one thing Daphne knows how to do is paint.

She turned back to the letter in the typewriter. An encouraging letter to a new client; it fell into a simple formula in her mind and she wrote it without hesitating, typing clumsily and amateurishly, but quickly. "Dear Mr. Burton," she wrote. "We have read your story with a good deal of interest. Your plot is well thought out, and we believe that the character of—" She stopped for a minute and turned back to the manuscript, opening it at random—"Lady Montague, in particular, is of more than usual merit. Naturally, in order to appeal to the better-paying markets, the story needs touching up by a skilled professional editor, a decisive selling service we are able to offer our clients. Our rates—"

"Miss Style?"

In spite of the beaverboard partitions, Elizabeth said, "If you want to talk to me, Miss Hill, come in."

After a minute Miss Hill opened the door and came in. Elizabeth could see her pocketbook on the desk outside, the lipstick and compact sitting next to it. "When does Mr. Shax get back?"

"Probably not till this afternoon. He went out on important business with a client," Elizabeth said. "Why, did anyone call?"

"No, I just wondered," Miss Hill said. She closed the door and went heavily back to her desk. Elizabeth looked again at the letter in the typewriter and then turned her chair around to put her still-wet feet on the radiator under the window. After a minute she opened the bottom drawer of her desk again and this time took out a pocket reprint of a mystery story. With her feet on the radiator she settled down to read.

Because it was raining, and because she was depressed and out of sorts, and because Robbie had not come by quarter to one, Elizabeth treated herself to a Martini while she was waiting, sitting uncomfortably on a narrow chair in the restaurant, watching other unimpressive people go in and out. The restaurant was·crowded, the floors wet from the feet coming in from the rain, and it was dark and dismal. Elizabeth and Robbie had come here for lunch two or three times a week, ever since they had opened the office in the building near-by. The first day they had come had been in summer, and Elizabeth, in a sheer black dress—she remembered it still; she would be too thin for it now—and a small white hat and white gloves, had been excited and happy over the great new career opening out for her. She and Robbie had held hands across the table and talked enthusiastically: they were only going to stay in the old building for a year, or two at the most, and then they would have enough money to move uptown; the good clients who would come to the new Robert Shax Agency would be honest reputable writers, with large best-selling manuscripts; editors would go to lunch with them at sleek uptown restaurants, a drink before lunch would not be an extraordinary thing. The first order of stationery saying "ROBERT SHAX, Literary Agents, Elizabeth Style, Fiction Department," had not been delivered; they planned the letterhead at lunch that day.

Elizabeth thought about ordering another Martini and then she saw Robbie coming impatiently through the people in the aisles. He saw her across the room and waved at her, aware of people watching him, an executive late for a luncheon appointment, even in a dingy restaurant.

When he got to the table, his back to the room, his face

was tired and his voice was quiet. "Finally made it," he said. He looked surprised at the empty Martini glass. "I haven't even had breakfast yet," he said.

"Did you have a bad time with the minister?"

"Terrible," he said. "He wants a book of his poems published this year."

"What did you tell him?" Elizabeth tried not to let her voice sound strained. Time enough for that later, she thought, when he feels like answering me.

"I don't know," Robbie said. "How the hell do I know what I told the old fool?" He sat down heavily. "Something about we'd do our best."

That means he's really made a mess of it, Elizabeth thought. If he did well he'd tell me in detail. She was suddenly so tired that she let her shoulders droop and sat stupidly staring off at the people coming in and out of the door. What am I going to say to him, she thought, what words will Robbie understand best?

"What are you looking so glum about?" Robbie asked suddenly. "No one made you go way the hell uptown without breakfast."

"I had a tough morning anyway," Elizabeth said. Robbie looked up, waiting. "I had a new employee to break in."

Robbie still waited, his face a little flushed, squinting at her; he was waiting to see what she was going to say before he apologized, or lost his temper, or tried to pass the whole thing off as a fine joke.

Elizabeth watched him: this is Robbie, she was thinking, I know what he's going to do and what he's going to say and what tie he's going to wear every day in the week, and for eleven years I have known these things and for eleven years

I have been wondering how to say things to make him understand; and eleven years ago we sat here and held hands and he said we were going to be successful. "I was thinking of the day we had lunch here when we first started out together," she said quietly, and Robbie looked mystified. "The day we started out together," she repeated more distinctly. "Do you remember Jim Harris?" Robbie nodded, his mouth a little open. "We were going to make a lot of money because Jim was going to bring all his friends to us and then you had a fight with Jim and we haven't seen him since and none of his friends came to us and now we've got your friend the minister for a client and a beautiful picture of Jim on your office wall. Signed," she said. "Signed, with 'gratitude,' and if he was making enough money we'd be around trying to borrow from him even now."

"Elizabeth," Robbie said. He was confused between trying to look hurt and trying to see if anyone heard what she was saying.

"Even the boy in my corner drugstore." Elizabeth looked at him for a minute. "Daphne Hill," she said. "My God."

"I see," Robbie said, with a significant smile. "Daphne Hill." He turned when he saw the waitress coming. "Miss," he said loudly, and to Elizabeth, "I think you ought to have another drink. Cheer you up a little." When the waitress looked at him he said "Two Martinis," and turned back to Elizabeth, putting on the smile again. "I'm going to drink my breakfast," he said, and then he reached over and touched Elizabeth's hand. "Listen," he said, "Liz, if that's all that's bothering you. I was a dope, I thought you'd figured I'd done something wrong about the minister. Listen, Daphne's all right. I just thought we needed someone around who'd brighten the place up a little."

"You could have painted the wall," Elizabeth said tonelessly. When Robbie stared she said, "Nothing," and he went on, leaning forward seriously.

"Look," he said, "if you don't like this Daphne out she goes. There's no question about it, after all. We're in business together." He looked off into space and smiled reminiscently. "I remember those days, all right. We were going to do wonders." He lowered his voice and looked lovingly at Elizabeth. "I think we still can," he said.

Elizabeth laughed in spite of herself. "You'll have to go down the stairs more quietly," she said. "My janitor's wife thought you were the man who leaves skis out in the hall. She nearly broke a leg."

"Don't make fun of me," Robbie said. "Elizabeth, it really hurts me to see you let someone like Daphne Hill upset you."

"Of course it does," Elizabeth said. Robbie suddenly impressed her as funny. If only I could keep on feeling like this, she thought, even while she was laughing at him. "Here comes your breakfast for you to drink," she said.

"Miss," Robbie said to the waitress. "We'd like to order our lunch, please."

He handed the menu ceremoniously to Elizabeth and said to the waitress, "Chicken croquettes and French fried potatoes." Elizabeth said, "The same, please," and handed the menu back. When the waitress had gone Robbie picked up one of the Martinis and handed it to Elizabeth. "You need this, old girl," he said. He picked up the other and looked at her; then he lowered his voice to the same low affectionate tone, and said, "Here's to you, and our future success."

Elizabeth smiled at him sweetly and tasted her drink. She could see Robbie debating whether to toss his off all at once or to sip it slowly as though he didn't need it.

"If you drink it too fast you'll be sick, dear," she said. "Without your breakfast."

He tasted it delicately and then set it down. "Now let's talk seriously about Daphne," he said.

"I thought she was leaving," Elizabeth said.

He looked frightened. "Naturally, if you want it that way," he said stiffly. "Seems sort of rotten to hire a girl and fire her the same day because you're jealous."

"I'm not jealous," Elizabeth said. "I never said I was."

"If I can't have a good-looking girl in the office," Robbie said.

"You can," Elizabeth said. "I'd just like one who could type."

"Daphne can take care of the work all right."

"Robbie," Elizabeth said, and then stopped. Already, she thought, I don't want to laugh at him any more; I wish I could feel all the time like I did a minute ago, not like this. She looked at him carefully, his red face and the thin greying hair, and the heavy shoulders above the table; he was holding his head back and his chin firm because he knew she was looking at him. He thinks I'm awed, she thought, he's a man and he's cowed me. "Let her stay," Elizabeth said.

"After all," Robbie leaned back to let the waitress put his plate in front of him, "after all," he went on when the waitress had gone, "it isn't as though I didn't have the authority to hire someone for my own office."

"I know," Elizabeth said wearily.

"If you want to start a fuss about some small thing," Robbie said. The corners of his mouth were turned down and he refused to meet her eyes. "I can run my own office," he repeated.

"You're scared to death I might leave you some day," Elizabeth said. "Eat your lunch."

Robbie picked up his fork. "Naturally," he said, "I feel that it would be a shame to break up a pleasant partnership just because you were jealous."

"Never mind," Elizabeth said, "I won't go away anywhere."

"I hope not," Robbie said. He ate industriously for a minute. "I tell you what," he said suddenly, putting his fork down, "we'll try her out for a week and then if you don't think she's better than Miss Wilson she'll go."

"But I don't—" Elizabeth began. Then she said. "Fine. That way we can find out exactly how she'll suit us."

"Splendid idea," Robbie said. "Now I feel better." He reached across the table and this time patted her hand. "Good old Liz," he said.

"You know," Elizabeth said, "I feel so funny right now." She was looking at the doorway. "I thought I saw someone I knew."

Robbie turned around and looked at the doorway. "Who?"

"No one you know," Elizabeth said. "A boy from my home town. It wasn't the same person, though."

"Always think you see people you know in New York," Robbie said, turning back to his fork.

Elizabeth was thinking, it must have been talking about old times with Robbie and the two drinks I had, I haven't thought of Frank for years. She laughed out loud, and Robbie stopped eating to say, "What's the matter with you, anyway? People will think something's wrong."

"I was just thinking," Elizabeth said. Suddenly she felt that she must talk to Robbie, treat him as she would anyone else she knew well, like a husband almost. "I haven't thought about this fellow for years," she said. "It just brought a thousand things back to my mind."

"An old boy friend?" Robbie said without interest.

Elizabeth felt the same twinge of horror she might have felt fifteen years ago at the suggestion, "Oh, *no*," she said. "He took me to a dance once. My mother called up his mother and asked to have him take me."

"Chocolate ice cream with chocolate sauce," Robbie said to the waitress.

"Just coffee," Elizabeth said. "He was a wonderful boy," she said to Robbie. Why can't I stop myself? she was thinking, I haven't thought about this for years.

"Listen," Robbie said, "did you tell Daphne she could go out for lunch?"

"I didn't tell her anything," Elizabeth said.

"We better hurry then," Robbie said. "The poor kid must be starving."

Frank, Elizabeth thought. "Seriously," she said, "what did you and the minister decide?"

"I'll tell you later," Robbie said, "when I get my ideas straight. Right now I'm not so sure what we did decide."

And he'll spring it on me suddenly, Elizabeth thought, so I won't have time to think; he's just promised to publish the minister's poems at his own expense; or he's gone out of town, will I deal with it; or someone's going to sue us. Frank wouldn't have been in a place like this, anyway, if he's eating at all, it's some place where everything is quiet and they call him "sir" and the women are all beautiful. "It doesn't matter anyway," she said.

"Of course it doesn't," Robbie said. He evidently felt it was necessary to add one final clinching touch before they went back to Daphne Hill. "As long as we can fight it together, we'll come through everything fine," he said. "We work well together, Liz." He stood up and turned to get his coat and hat. His suit was wrinkled and he felt uncomfortable in it, from the way he moved his shoulders uneasily.

Elizabeth finished the last of her coffee. "You get fatter every day," she said.

He looked around at her, his eyes frightened. "You think I ought to start dieting again?" he asked.

They came up in the elevator together, standing in opposite corners, each looking off into space, through the iron grillwork of the elevator, into something private and secret. They had gone up and down in this elevator four or six or eight or ten times a day since they moved into the building, sometimes happily, sometimes coldly angry with one another, sometimes laughing or quarreling furiously with quick violent phrases; the elevator operator probably knew more about them than Elizabeth's landlady or the young couple who had the apartment across the hall from Robbie, and yet they got into the elevator daily and the elevator operator spoke to them civilly and stood with his back to them, riding up and down, entering briefly into their quarrels, possibly smiling with his back turned.

Today he said, "Weather still bad?" and Robbie said, "Worse than ever," and the operator said, "There ought to be a law against it," and let them off at their floor.

"I wonder what he thinks of us, the elevator man," Elizabeth said, following Robbie down the hall.

"Probably wishes he could get off that elevator for a while and sit down in an office," Robbie said. He opened the door of the office and said, "Miss Hill?"

Daphne Hill was sitting at the reception desk, reading the mystery Elizabeth had left to go out to lunch. "Hello, Mr. Shax," she said.

"Did you take that off my desk?" Elizabeth said, surprised for a minute into speaking at once without thinking.

"Wasn't it all right?" Daphne asked. "I didn't have anything to do."

"We'll find you plenty to do, young lady," Robbie said heartily, the brisk businessman again. "Sorry to keep you waiting for lunch."

"I went out and got something to eat," Daphne said.

"Good," Robbie said, looking sideways at Elizabeth. "We'll have to make some arrangement for the future."

"Hereafter," Elizabeth said sharply, "don't go into my office without permission."

"Sure," Daphne said, startled. "You want your book back?"

"Keep it," Elizabeth said. She went into her office and closed the door. She heard Robbie saying, "Miss Style doesn't like to have her things disturbed, Miss Hill," and then, "Come into my office, please." As though there were real partitions, Elizabeth thought. She heard Robbie go quickly into his office and Daphne pound her deliberate way after him, and the door close.

She sighed, and thought, I'll pretend they're real partitions; Robbie will. She noticed a note standing against her typewriter where she had left it with the letter to Mr. Burton still half-finished. She picked up the note and read it with heavy concentration to drown out Robbie's employer voice on the other side of the partition. The note was from Miss Wilson, and said:

"Miss Style, no one told me there was a new girl coming and since I've been working here so long I think you should have told me. I guess she can learn the work as well by herself. Please tell Mr. Shax to send me my money at home, the address is in the file as he knows. There was a call from a Mr. Robert Hunt for you, will you call him back at his hotel, the Addison House. Please tell Mr. Shax to send the money, it comes now to two weeks and an extra week for notice. Alice Wilson."

She must have been mad, Elizabeth thought, not to wait around for her money, she must have been furious, I guess Daphne was the first to tell her and she felt like I did; he'll never send her any money. She could hear Robbie's voice saying, "It's a terrible business, the most heart-breaking I know." He's talking about free-lance writing, she thought, Daphne probably wants to sell her life history.

She went out of the door of her office and around to Robbie's and knocked. If Robbie says, "Who is it?" she thought, I'll say "The elevator man, come up to sit down for a while." Then Robbie said, "Come on in, Liz, don't be silly."

"Robbie," she said, opening the door, "Miss Wilson was here and left a note."

"I forgot to tell you," Daphne said, "and I didn't get a chance yet anyway. She said to tell Mr. Shax to send her money."

"I'm sorry about this," Robbie said. "She should have been told yesterday. It's a damned shame for her to find out like this." Daphne was sitting in the one other chair in his office and he hesitated and then said, "Sit here, Elizabeth."

Elizabeth waited until he started to hoist himself up and then said, "That's all right, Robbie, I'm going back to work."

Robbie read Miss Wilson's letter carefully. "Miss Hill," he said, "make a note to send Miss Wilson her back pay and the extra week she asks for."

"I don't have anything to make a note on," Daphne said. Elizabeth took a pad and pencil off Robbie's desk and handed it to her, and Daphne made a solemn sentence on the first page of the pad.

"Who is this Hunt?" Robbie asked Elizabeth. "Your old boy friend?"

I know I shouldn't have told him, Elizabeth thought. "I think it's an old friend of my father's from home," she said.

"Better call him back," Robbie said, handing her the note.

"I shall," Elizabeth said. "Don't you think you'd better write Miss Wilson and explain what happened?"

Robbie looked dismayed, and then he said, "Miss Hill can do that this afternoon."

Elizabeth, carefully not looking at Daphne, said, "Fine idea. That will give her something to do."

She closed the door quietly when she went out and closed the door of her own office after herself to give the illusion of privacy. She knew that Robbie would listen to her talking on the phone; she had an odd picture of Robbie and Daphne, sitting silently one on either side of Robbie's desk, two heavy serious faces turned slightly to the partition, listening soberly to Elizabeth talking to her father's old friend.

She looked up the hotel number in the book, hearing Robbie say, "Tell her we're all sincerely sorry, but that circumstances beyond my control, and so on. Make it as pleasant as possible. Remember to tell her we'll consider her for the first new job we have here."

Elizabeth dialed the number, waiting for the sudden silence in Robbie's office. She asked the hotel clerk for Mr. Robert Hunt, and when he answered she made her voice low, and said, "Uncle Robert? This is Beth."

He answered enthusiastically, "Beth! It's fine hearing your voice. Mom thought you'd be too busy to call back."

"Is she with you? How nice," Elizabeth said. "How are you both? How is Dad?"

"All fine," he said. "How are you, Beth?"

She kept her voice low. "Just grand, Uncle Robert, getting along so well. How long have you been here? And how long are you staying? And when can I see you?"

He laughed. "Mom is talking at me from this end and you're talking at me from that end," he said. "And I can't hear a word either of you is saying. How are you, anyway?"

"I'm grand," she said again.

"Beth," he said, "we're very anxious to see you. Got a lot of messages from home and all."

"I'm pretty busy," she said, "but I'd love to see you. How long are you staying?"

"Tomorrow," he said. "Just came in for a couple of days."

She was figuring quickly, even while her voice was saying, "Oh, no," with heavy dismay. "*Why* didn't you let me know?" she said.

"Mom wants me to tell you everyone sends their love," he said.

"I'm just sick," she said. Guilt drove her into accenting her words violently. "I don't know *how* I'm going to get to see you. Maybe tomorrow morning somehow?"

"Well," he said slowly, "Mom sort of had her heart set on going to Long Island tomorrow to see her sister, and they'll take us right to the train. We thought maybe you'd come along with us tonight."

"Oh, Lord," Elizabeth said, "I've got a dinner appointment I can't break. A client," she said, "you know."

"Isn't that a shame," he said. "We're going to a show;

thought you might come along. Mom," he called, "what's that show we're going to?" He waited for a minute and then said, "She doesn't remember either. The hotel got tickets for us."

"I wish I could," she said, "I just wish I could." She thought in spite of herself of the extra ticket they had been careful to buy, the two old people alone for dinner pretending they were celebrating in a strange city. They saved tonight for me, she thought. "If it had been any other person in the world, I could have broken it, but this is one of our best clients and I just don't dare."

"Of course not." There was so long a silence that Elizabeth said hastily, "How is Dad, anyway?"

"Fine," he said. "Everyone's fine. I guess he sort of wishes you were home now."

"I imagine he's lonesome," Elizabeth said, careful not to let her voice commit her to anything. She was anxious to end the phone call, dissociate herself from the Hunts and her father and the nagging hints that she should go home. I live in New York now, she told herself while the old man's voice continued with a monotonous series of anecdotes about her father and people she had known long ago; I live in New York by myself and I don't have to remember any of these people; Uncle Robert should be glad I talk to him at all.

"I'm so glad you called," she said suddenly, through his voice. "I've got to get back to work."

"Of course," he said apologetically. "Well, Beth, write to all of us, won't you? Mom is telling me to give you her love."

They hang on to me, she thought; they're holding me back, with their letters and their "Yrs. afftly.," and their sending love back and forth. "Good-bye," she said.

"Come back soon for a visit," he went on.

"I will when I can. Good-bye," Elizabeth said. She hung up

on his "Good-bye," and then, "Oh, wait, Beth," when something more occurred to him. I couldn't listen any longer without being rude, she thought.

She heard Robbie's voice starting then in the next office, "And I guess you understand about things like answering the phone, and so on."

"I guess so," Daphne said.

Elizabeth went back to her letter to Mr. Burton, permanently curled from staying in the typewriter, and she heard Robbie and Daphne Hill talking for a while, about names of clients, and the two-button phone extension at the reception desk, and then she heard both of them go out to the reception desk and try the extension, two children, she thought, playing office. Occasionally she would hear Robbie's heavy laugh, and then, after a minute, Daphne laughing too, slow and surprised. In spite of all her attempts to concentrate on their rates for Mr. Burton she found herself listening, following Robbie and Daphne where they moved around the office. Once, louder than the slight murmur which had been going on between them, she heard Robbie's man-of-the-world voice saying, "Some quiet little restaurant," and then when the voice dropped back to its cautious tone she said to herself, Where they can talk. She waited, not to sound like an intruder, until she heard Daphne settle down solidly at the reception desk and Robbie start back for his own office. Then she said, "Robbie?"

There was a silence and then he came around and opened her office door. "You know I don't like you to yell in the office," he said.

She paused for a minute because she wanted to speak cordially. "We're going to have dinner together tonight?" she asked. They had dinner together four or five times a week, usually in the restaurant where they had had lunch, or in some small place near either Robbie's apartment or Elizabeth's. When she saw the corners of Robbie's mouth turn down and the faint turn of his head toward the outer office she raised her voice slightly. "I got out of seeing these fool people tonight," she said. "There's a lot I want to talk to you about."

"As a matter of fact, Liz," Robbie said, talking very quickly and in a low voice, "I'm afraid I'm going to be stuck for dinner." Not realizing that he was repeating what he had heard her say on the phone a few minutes before, he went on, putting on a look of annoyance, "I've got a dinner appointment I can't break, with a client." When Elizabeth looked surprised, he said, "The minister, I promised him this morning we'd get together again tonight. I haven't had a chance to tell you."

"Of course you can't break it," Elizabeth said easily. She waited, watching Robbie. He was sitting uneasily on the corner of her desk, playing absently with a pencil, wanting to leave and afraid to go too abruptly. What am I doing, Elizabeth thought suddenly, playing hide-and-seek? "Why don't you go to a movie or something?" she said.

Robbie laughed mournfully. "I wish I could," he said.

Elizabeth reached over and took the pencil away from him. "Poor old Robbie," she said. "You're all upset. You ought to get off somewhere and relax."

Robbie frowned anxiously. "Why should I?" he said. "Isn't this my office?"

Elizabeth made her voice tender. "You ought to get out of here for a few hours, Robbie, I'm serious. You won't be able to work this afternoon." She decided to allow herself one small spiteful dig. "Particularly if you have to see that old horror tonight," she said.

Robbie's mouth opened and closed, and then he said, "I can't think when it's such lousy weather. Rain drives me crazy."

"I know it does," Elizabeth said. She stood up. "You get your hat and coat on, and leave your brief case and everything here," she said, pushing him toward the door, "and then come back after sitting in a movie for a couple of hours and you'll feel like a million dollars to go out and out-talk the minister."

"I don't want to go out again in this weather," Robbie said.

"Stop and get a shave," Elizabeth said. She opened the door of her office and saw Daphne Hill staring at her. "Get a haircut," she said, touching the back of his head. "Miss Hill and I will get along fine without you. Won't we, Miss Hill?"

"Sure," Daphne said.

Robbie went uneasily into his office and came out a minute later carrying his wet coat and hat. "I don't know what you want me to go out for," he said.

"I don't know what you want to stay here for," Elizabeth said, escorting him to the outer door. "You're not good for anything when you feel like this." She opened the front door and he walked out. "See you later."

"See you later," Robbie said, starting down the hall.

Elizabeth watched him until he had gone into the elevator and then she closed the door behind her and turned to Daphne Hill. "Is that letter to Miss Wilson anywhere near written?" she asked.

"I was just doing it," Daphne said.

"Bring it to me when you finish." Elizabeth went into her office and closed the door and sat down at the desk. Frank, she was thinking, it couldn't have been Frank. He would have said "Hello" or something, I haven't changed that much. If it was Frank, what was he doing around here? It won't do any good, she thought, there's no way of finding him anyway.

She took the telephone book from the corner of her desk and looked for Frank's name; it wasn't there, and she turned further until she came to the H's, running her finger down the page till she found Harris, James. Pulling the phone over she dialed the number and waited. When a man answered she said, "Is this Jim Harris?"

"That's right," he said.

"This is Elizabeth Style."

"Hello," he said. "How are you?"

"I've been waiting for you to get in touch with me," she said. "It's been a long time."

"I know it has," he said. "Somehow I never seem to get around—"

"I'll tell you what I called you about," she said. "Do you remember Frank Davis?"

"I remember him," he said. "What's he doing now?"

"That's what I wanted to ask you," she said.

"Oh. Well. . . ."

She waited a minute, and then went on, "One of these days I'm going to take you up on that standing dinner date."

"I hope you do," he said. "I'll call you."

Oh, no, she thought. "It seems like such a long time since we got together. Listen." She made her voice sound like this was a sudden idea, one of those unexpectedly brilliant things, "Why don't we make it tonight?" He started to say something and she went on, "I've been dying to see you."

"You see, my kid sister's in town," he said.

"Can't she come along?" Elizabeth asked.

"Well," he said, "I guess so."

"Fine," Elizabeth said. "You come on down to my place for a drink first, and bring the kid along, and we can have a grand talk about old times."

"Suppose I call you back?" he asked.

"I'm leaving the office now," Elizabeth said flatly. "I'll be running around all afternoon. So let's make it around seven?"

"All right," he said.

"I'm so pleased we made it tonight," Elizabeth said. "I'll see you later."

After she had hung up she sat for a minute with her hand on the phone, thinking, good old Harris, he never has a chance if you talk fast; he must get stuck for every dirty job around town. She laughed, pleased, and then stopped abruptly when Daphne knocked on the door; when Elizabeth said, "Come in," Daphne opened the door cautiously and put her head in.

"I finished the letter, Miss Style," she said.

"Bring it here," Elizabeth said, and then added, "please."

Daphne came in and held the letter out at arm's length. "It isn't very good," she said. "But it's my first letter by myself."

Elizabeth glanced at the letter. "It doesn't matter," she said. "Sit down, Daphne."

Daphne sat down gingerly on the edge of the chair. "Sit back," Elizabeth said. "That's the only chair I've got and I don't want you breaking it."

Daphne sat back and opened her eyes wide.

Elizabeth carefully opened her pocketbook and took out a pack of cigarettes and hunted for a match. "Just a minute," Daphne said eagerly, "I've got some." She hurried out to the outer office and came back with a package of matches. "Keep them," she said, "I've got plenty more."

Elizabeth lit her cigarette and put the matches down on the edge of the desk. "Now," she said, and Daphne leaned forward. "Where did you work before you started here?"

"This is my first job," Daphne said. "I just came to New York."

"Where did you come from?"

"Buffalo," Daphne said.

"So you came to New York to make your fortune?" Elizabeth asked. This is where I have dear Daphne, she was thinking, I've already made my fortune.

"I don't know," Daphne said. "My father brought us down here because his brother needed him in the business. We just moved here a couple of months ago."

If I had a family to take care of me, Elizabeth thought, I wouldn't have a job with Robert Shax. "What sort of an education have you had?"

"I went to high school in Buffalo," Daphne said. "I was in business school for a while."

"You want to be a writer?"

"No," Daphne said, "I want to be an agent, like Mr. Shax. And you," she added.

"It's a fine business," Elizabeth said. "You can make a lot of money at it."

"That's what Mr. Shax said. He was very nice about it."

Daphne was getting braver. She was eyeing Elizabeth's cigarette and had settled down comfortably in her chair.

Elizabeth was suddenly very tired; there was no sport in Daphne. "Mr. Shax and I were talking about you at lunch," she said deliberately.

Daphne smiled. When she smiled, and when she was sitting down, without the appearance of that big body resting precariously on small feet, Daphne was an attractive girl. In spite of the small brown eyes, with that incredible mop of hair, Daphne was very attractive. I'm so thin, Elizabeth thought, and she said with pleasure, "I think you'd better rewrite that letter to Miss Wilson, Daphne."

"Sure," Daphne said.

"Telling her," Elizabeth went on, "to come back to work as soon as she can."

"Back here?" Daphne asked, with the smallest beginning of alarm.

"Back here," Elizabeth said. She smiled. "I'm afraid Mr. Shax didn't have courage enough to tell you," she said. "Mr. Shax and I are, besides business partners," she said, "very good friends. Frequently Mr. Shax takes advantage of our friendship and leaves the disagreeable tasks for me to do."

"Mr. Shax didn't tell me anything," Daphne said.

"I didn't think he had," Elizabeth said, "when I saw how you went right ahead as though you were staying here."

Daphne was frightened. She's too stupid to cry, Elizabeth thought, but she's going to have to have everything explained to her in detail. "Naturally," Elizabeth went on, "I don't like having to do this. Possibly I can make it easier for you by trying to help you get another job."

Daphne nodded.

"This may help you," Elizabeth said, "because Mr. Shax commented on it earlier, and it's the sort of thing men are particular about. Your appearance."

Daphne looked down at the ample front of her dress.

"Probably," Elizabeth said, "you already know this, and I'm very rude to comment on it, but I think you'd make a better impression and if you ever get a job you'd be able to work more comfortably if you wore something to the office instead of a silk dress. It makes you seem, somehow, as though you were just in from Buffalo."

"You want me to wear a suit or something?" Daphne asked. She spoke slowly and without malice.

"Something quieter, anyway," Elizabeth said.

Daphne looked Elizabeth up and down. "A suit like yours?" she asked.

"A suit would be fine," Elizabeth said. "And try to comb your hair down."

Daphne touched the top of her head tenderly.

"Try to be more orderly, in general," Elizabeth said. "You have beautiful hair, Daphne, but it would look more suitable to an office if you were to wear it more severely."

"Like yours?" Daphne asked, looking at the grey in Elizabeth's hair.

"Any way you please," Elizabeth said, "just so it doesn't look like a floor mop." She turned pointedly back to her desk, and after a minute Daphne rose. "Take this back," Elizabeth said, holding out the letter to Miss Wilson, "and rewrite it the way I told you to."

"Yes, Miss Style," Daphne said.

"You can go home as soon as you're through with the letter," Elizabeth said. "Leave it on your desk, along with your name and address, and Mr. Shax will send you your day's pay."

"I don't care whether he does or not," Daphne said abruptly.

Elizabeth looked up for a minute and regarded Daphne steadily. "Do you think you have any right to criticize Mr. Shax's decisions?" she asked.

For a few minutes Elizabeth sat at her desk waiting to see what Daphne would do; after the door had closed quietly behind Daphne and she had walked to her desk there had been a heavy silence; she's sitting at her desk there, Elizabeth thought, thinking it over. Then, finally, there was the small sound of Daphne's pocketbook, the snap of the catch opening, the movement of a hand searching against keys, papers; she's taking her compact out, Elizabeth thought, she's looking to see if what I said about her appearance is true; she's wondering if Robbie said anything, how he said it, whether I made it worse or smoothed it over for her. I should have told her he said she was a fat pig, or the ugliest thing he had ever seen; she might not even have seen through that. What's she doing now?

Daphne had said "Damn" very distinctly; Elizabeth sat forward in her chair, not wanting to let any trace of action escape. Then there was the quiet sound of the typewriter; Daphne was typing the letter to Miss Wilson. Elizabeth shook her head slowly and laughed. She lighted a cigarette with one of Daphne's matches, still on the edge of the desk, and looked blankly at the letter to Mr. Burton, still in the typewriter. Sitting with one arm hooked over the back of the chair and the cigarette in her mouth, she typed slowly, with one finger, "The hell with you, Burton," and then tore the page out of the typewriter and threw it in the wastebasket. That's every single bit of work I've done today, she told herself, and it doesn't matter after looking at Daphne's face when I told her. She looked at her desk, the letters waiting to be answered, the criticisms by a professional editor waiting to be written, the complaints to be satisfied, and thought, I'll go on home. I can take a bath and clean the place and get some stuff for Jim and the kid sister; I'll only wait till Daphne leaves.

"Daphne?" she called.

After a hesitation: "Yes, Miss Style?"

"Aren't you through yet?" Elizabeth said; she could afford to let herself speak gently now. "That letter to Miss Wilson should only take a minute."

"Just getting ready to leave," Daphne said.

"Don't forget to leave your name and address."

There was a silence from the other room, and Elizabeth said to her closed door, raising her voice again, "Did you hear me?"

"Mr. Shax knows my name and address," Daphne said. The outer door opened, and Daphne said, "Good-bye."

"Good-bye," Elizabeth said.

She got out of the taxi at her corner, and after paying the man, she had a ten-dollar bill and some change in her pocketbook; this, with twenty dollars more in her apartment, was all the money she had until she could ask Robbie for more. Figuring quickly, she decided to take ten dollars of her money at home to get her through the evening; Jim Harris would have to pay for her dinner; ten dollars, then, for taxis and emergencies; she would ask Robbie for more tomorrow. The money in her pocketbook would go for liquor and cocktail things; she stopped in the liquor store on the corner and bought a bottle of rye, a fifth, so that she would have some to offer Robbie the next time he came down. With her bottle under her arm she went into the delicatessen and bought ginger ale; hesitantly she selected a bag of potato chips and then a box of crackers and a liverwurst spread to put on them.

She was unused to entertaining; she and Robbie spent evenings quietly together, seldom seeing any people except an occasional client and, sometimes, an old friend who invited them out. Because they were not married, Robbie was reluctant to take her anywhere where he might be embarrassed by her presence. They ate their meals in small restaurants, did their rare drinking at home or in a corner bar, saw neighborhood movies. When it was necessary for Elizabeth to invite people to visit her Robbie was not there; they had once given a party in Robbie's larger apartment to celebrate some great occasion, probably a client of some sort, and the party had been so miserable and the guest so uncomfortable that they had never given another and had been invited to only one or two.

Consequently Elizabeth, although she spoke so blithely of "coming down for a drink," was almost completely at a loss when people actually came. As she climbed the stairs to her apartment, her packages braced between her arm and her chin, she was worrying over and over the progress of having a drink, the passing of crackers, the taking of coats.

The appearance of her room shocked her; she had forgotten her hurried departure this morning and the way she had left things around; also, the apartment was created and planned for Elizabeth; that is, the hurried departure every morning of a rather unhappy and desperate young woman with little or no ability to make things gracious, the lonely ugly evenings in one chair with one book and one ashtray, the nights spent dreaming of hot grass and heavy sunlight. There was no possible arrangement of these things that would permit of a casual grouping of three or four people, sitting easily around a room holding glasses, talking lightly. In the early evening, with one lamp on and the shadows in the corners, it looked warm and soft, but you had only to sit down in the one armchair, or touch a hand to the grey wood end table that looked polished, to see that the armchair was hard and cheap, the grey paint chipping.

For a minute Elizabeth stood in the doorway holding her packages, trying clearly to visualize her room as it might be smoothed out by an affectionate hand, but the noise of footsteps above coming down the stairs drove her inside with the door shut and, once in, there was no clear vision; she had her feet on the unpolished floor; there was a dirty finger-print on the inside doorknob. Robbie's, Elizabeth thought.

She opened the glass French doors that screened the kitch-enette and put her packages down; the kitchenette was part of one wall, with a tiny stove built in under a cabinet, a sink installed over a refrigerator, and, over the sink, two shelves on which stood her collection of china: two plates, two cups and saucers, four glasses. She also owned a small saucepan, a frying-pan, and a coffeepot. She had bought all her small house furnishings in a five-and-ten a few years before, plan-ning a tiny complete kitchen, where she could make miniature roasts for herself and Robbie, even bake a small pie or cookies, wearing a yellow apron and making funny mistakes at first. Although she had been a fairly competent cook when she first came to New York, capable of frying chops and potatoes, in the many years since she had been near a real stove she had lost all her knowledge except the fudge-making play in which she indulged herself occasionally. Cooking was, like every-thing else she had known, a decent honest knowledge meant to make her a capable happy woman ("the way to a man's heart," her mother used to say soberly), which, with the rest of her daily life, had sunk to a miniature useful only as a novelty on rare occasions.

She had to take down the four glasses and wash them; they were dusty from standing so long unused on the open shelf. She checked the refrigerator. For a while she had kept butter and eggs in the refrigerator, and bread and coffee in the cabi-net, but they had grown mouldy and rancid before she had been able to make more than one breakfast from them; she was so often late and so seldom inclined to take time over her own breakfast.

It was only four-thirty; she had time to straighten things

up and bathe and dress. Her first care was for the easy things in the apartment; she dusted the tables and emptied the ashtray, stopping to put her dustcloth down and pull the bedcovers even, smoothing the spread down to a regular roundness. She was tempted to take up the three small scatter rugs and shake them, and then wash the floor, but a glance at the bathroom discouraged her; they would certainly be in and out of the bathroom, and the floor and tub and even the walls badly needed washing. She used her dust cloth soaked in hot water from the tap, getting the floor clean at last; she put out clean towels from her small stock and started her bath water while she went back to finish the big room.

After all her haphazard work the room looked the same; still grey and inhospitable in the rainy afternoon light. She debated for a minute running downstairs for some bright flowers, and then decided that her money wouldn't last that far; they would only be in the room for a short while anyway, and with something to drink and something to eat any room should look friendly.

When she finished her bath it was nearly six, and dark enough to light the lamp on the end table. She walked barefoot across the room, feeling clean and freshened, conscious of the cologne she had put on, with her hair curling a little from the hot water. With the feeling of cleanness came an excitement; she would be happy tonight, she would be successful, something wonderful would happen to change her whole life. Following out this feeling she chose a dark red silk dress from the closet; it was youthfully styled and without the grey in her hair it made her look nearer twenty than over thirty. She selected a heavy gold chain to wear with it, and thought, I can wear my good black coat, even if it's raining I'll wear it to feel nice.

While she dressed she thought about her home. Considered honestly, there was no way to do anything with this apartment, no yellow drapes or pictures would help. She needed a new apartment, a pleasant open place with big windows and pale furniture, with the sun coming in all day. To get a new apartment she needed more money, she needed a new job, and Jim Harris would have to help her; tonight would be only the first of many exciting dinners together, building into a lovely friendship that would get her a job and a sunny apartment; while she was planning her new life she forgot Jim Harris, his heavy face, his thin voice; he was a stranger, a gallant dark man with knowing eyes who watched her across a room, he was someone who loved her, he was a quiet troubled man who needed sunlight, a warm garden, green lawns. . . .

‡

# A FINE OLD FIRM

Mrs. Concord and her older daughter, Helen, were sitting in their living-room, sewing and talking and trying to keep warm. Helen had just put down the stockings she had been mending and walked over to the French doors that opened out on to the garden. "I wish spring would hurry up and get here," she was saying when the doorbell rang.

"Good Lord," Mrs. Concord said, "if that's company! The rug's all covered with loose threads." She leaned over in her chair and began to gather up the odds and ends of material around her as Helen went to answer the door. She opened it and stood smiling while the woman outside held out a hand and began to talk rapidly. "You're Helen? I'm Mrs. Friedman," she said. "I hope you won't think I'm just breaking in on you, but I have been so anxious to meet you and your mother."

"How do you do?" Helen said. "Won't you come in?" She opened the door wider and Mrs. Friedman stepped in. She was small and dark and wearing a very smart leopard coat. "Is your mother home?" she asked Helen just as Mrs. Concord came out of the living room.

"I'm Mrs. Concord," Helen's mother said.

"I'm Mrs. Friedman," Mrs. Friedman said. "Bob Friedman's mother."

"Bob Friedman," Mrs. Concord repeated.

Mrs. Friedman smiled apologetically. "I thought surely your boy would have mentioned Bobby," she said.

"Of course he has," Helen said suddenly. "He's the one

Charlie's *always* writing about, Mother. It's so hard to make a connection," she said to Mrs. Friedman, "because Charlie seems so far away."

Mrs. Concord was nodding. "Of course," she said. "Won't you come in and sit down?"

Mrs. Friedman followed the Concords into the living-room and sat in one of the chairs not filled with sewing. Mrs. Concord waved her hand at the room. "It makes such a mess," she said, "but every now and then Helen and I just get to work and make things. These are kitchen curtains," she added, picking up the material she had been working on.

"They're very nice," Mrs. Friedman said politely.

"Well, tell us about your son," Mrs. Concord went on. "I'm amazed that I didn't recognize the name right away, but somehow I associate Bob Friedman with Charles and the Army, and it seemed strange to have his mother here in town."

Mrs. Friedman laughed. "That's just about the way I felt," she said. "Bobby wrote me that his friend's mother lived here only a few blocks from us, and said why didn't I drop in and say Hello."

"I'm so glad you did," Mrs. Concord said.

"I guess we know about as much about Bob as you do by now," Helen said. "Charlie's always writing about him."

Mrs. Friedman opened her purse. "I even have a letter from Charlie," she said. "I thought you'd like to take a look at it."

"Charles wrote you?" Mrs. Concord asked.

"Just a note. He likes the pipe tobacco I send Bobby," Mrs. Friedman explained, "and I put a tin of it in for him the last time I sent Bobby a package." She handed the letter to Mrs. Concord and said to Helen, "I imagine I could tell you all about yourselves, Bobby's said so much about all of you."

"Well," Helen said, "I know that Bob got you a Japanese

sword for Christmas. *That* must have looked lovely under the tree. Charlie helped him buy it from the boy that had it—did you hear about that, and how they almost had a fight with the boy?"

"*Bobby* almost had a fight," Mrs. Friedman said. "Charlie was smart and stayed out of it."

"No, we heard it that *Charlie* was the one who got in trouble," Helen said. She and Mrs. Friedman laughed.

"Maybe we shouldn't compare notes," Mrs. Friedman said. "They don't seem to stick together on their stories." She turned to Mrs. Concord, who had finished the letter and handed it to Helen. "I was just telling your daughter how many complimentary things I've heard about you."

"We've heard a lot about you, too," Mrs. Concord said.

"Charlie showed Bob a picture of you and your two daughters. The younger one's Nancy, isn't it?"

"Nancy, yes," Mrs. Concord said.

"Well, Charlie certainly thinks a lot of his family," Mrs. Friedman said. "Wasn't he nice to write me?" she asked Helen.

"That tobacco must be good," Helen said. She hesitated for a minute and handed the letter back to Mrs. Friedman, who put it in her purse.

"I'd love to meet Charlie sometime," Mrs. Friedman said. "It seems as though I know him so well."

"I'm sure he'll want to meet you when he comes back," Mrs. Concord said.

"I hope it won't be long now," Mrs. Friedman said. All three were silent for a minute, and then Mrs. Friedman went on with animation, "It seems so strange that we've been living in the same town and it took our boys so far away to introduce us."

"This is a very hard town to get acquainted in," Mrs. Concord said.

"Have you lived here long?" Mrs. Friedman smiled apologetically. "Of course I know of your husband," she added. "My sister's children are in your husband's high school and they speak so highly of him."

"Really?" Mrs. Concord said. "My husband has lived here all his life. I came here from the West when I was married."

"Then it hasn't been hard for you to get settled and make friends," Mrs. Friedman said.

"No, I never had much trouble," Mrs. Concord said. "Of course most of our friends are people who went to school with my husband."

"I'm sorry Bobby never got a chance to study under Mr. Concord," Mrs. Friedman said. "Well. . . ." She rose. "I have certainly enjoyed meeting you at last."

"I'm so glad you came over," Mrs. Concord said. "It's like having a letter from Charles."

"And I know how welcome a letter can be, the way I wait for Bobby's," Mrs. Friedman said. She and Mrs. Concord started for the door and Helen got up and followed them. "My husband is very much interested in Charlie, you know. Ever since he found out that Charlie was studying law when he went into the Army."

"Your husband is a lawyer?" Mrs. Concord asked.

"He's the Friedman of Grunewald, Friedman & White," Mrs. Friedman said. "When Charlie is ready to start out for himself, perhaps my husband could find a place for him."

"That's awfully kind of you," Mrs. Concord said. "Charles will be so sorry when I tell him. You see, it's always been sort of arranged that he'd go in with Charles Satterthwaite, my husband's oldest friend. Satterthwaite & Harris."

"I believe Mr. Friedman knows the firm," Mrs. Friedman said.

"A fine old firm," Mrs. Concord said. "Mr. Concord's grandfather used to be a partner."

"Give Bob our best regards when you write him," Helen said.

"I will," Mrs. Friedman said. "I'll tell him all about meeting you. It's been very nice," she said, holding out her hand to Mrs. Concord.

"I've enjoyed it," Mrs. Concord said.

"Tell Charlie I'll send him some more tobacco," Mrs. Friedman said to Helen.

"I certainly will," Helen said.

"Well, good-bye then," Mrs. Friedman said.

"Good-bye," Mrs. Concord said.

‡

# THE DUMMY

IT WAS a respectable, well-padded restaurant with a good chef and a group of entertainers who called themselves a floor show; the people who came there laughed quietly and dined thoroughly, appreciating the principle that the check was always a little more than the restaurant and the entertainment and the company warranted; it was a respectable, likable restaurant, and two women could go into it alone with perfect decorum and have a faintly exciting dinner. When Mrs. Wilkins and Mrs. Straw came noiselessly down the carpeted staircase into the restaurant none of the waiters looked up more than once, quickly, few of the guests turned, and the headwaiter came quietly and bowed agreeably before he turned to the room and the few vacant tables far in the back.

"Do you *mind* being so far away from everything, Alice?" Mrs. Wilkins, who was hostess, said to Mrs. Straw. "We can wait for a table, if you like. Or go somewhere else?"

"Of course not." Mrs. Straw was a rather large woman in a heavy flowered hat, and she looked affectionately at the substantial dinners set on near-by tables. "I don't mind where we sit; this is really lovely."

"Anywhere will do," Mrs. Wilkins said to the headwaiter. "Not *too* far back if you can help it."

The headwaiter listened carefully and nodded, stepping delicately off between the tables to one very far back, near the doorway where the entertainers came in and out, near the table where the lady who owned the restaurant was sitting drinking beer, near the kitchen doors. "Nothing nearer?" Mrs. Wilkins said, frowning at the headwaiter.

The headwaiter shrugged, gesturing at the other vacant tables. One was behind a post, another was set for a large party, a third was somehow behind the small orchestra.

"This will do beautifully, Jen," Mrs. Straw said. "We'll sit right down."

Mrs. Wilkins hesitated still, but Mrs. Straw pulled out the chair on one side of the table and sat down with a sigh, setting her gloves and pocketbook on the extra chair beside her, and reaching to unfasten the collar of her coat.

"I can't say I *like* this," Mrs. Wilkins said, sliding into the chair opposite. "I'm not sure we can see anything."

"Of course we can," Mrs. Straw said. "We can see all that's going on, and of course we'll be able to hear everything. Would you like to sit here instead?" she finished reluctantly.

"Of course not, Alice," Mrs. Wilkins said. She accepted the menu the waiter was offering her and set it down on the table, scanning it rapidly. "The food is quite good here," she said.

"Shrimp casserole," Mrs. Straw said. "Fried chicken." She sighed. "I certainly am hungry."

Mrs. Wilkins ordered quickly, with no debate, and then helped Mrs. Straw choose. When the waiter had gone Mrs. Straw leaned back comfortably and turned in her chair to see all of the restaurant. "This is a lovely place," she said.

"The people seem to be very nice," Mrs. Wilkins said. "The woman who owns it is sitting over there, in back of you. I've always thought she looked very clean and decent."

"She probably makes sure the glasses are washed," Mrs. Straw said. She turned back to the table and picked up her pocketbook, diving deep into it after a pack of cigarettes and a box of wooden safety matches, which she set on the table. "I like to see a place that serves food kept nice and clean," she said.

"They make a lot of money from this place," Mrs. Wilkins said. "Tom and I used to come here years ago before they enlarged it. It was very nice then, but it attracts a better class of people now."

Mrs. Straw regarded the crabmeat cocktail now in front of her with deep satisfaction. "Yes, indeed," she said.

Mrs. Wilkins picked up her fork indifferently, watching Mrs. Straw. "I had a letter from Walter yesterday," she said.

"What'd he have to say?" Mrs. Straw asked.

"He seems fine," Mrs. Wilkins said. "Seems like there's a lot he doesn't tell us."

"Walter's a good boy," Mrs. Straw said. "You worry too much."

The orchestra began to play suddenly and violently and the lights darkened to a spotlight on the stage.

"I hate to eat in the dark," Mrs. Wilkins said.

"We'll get plenty of light back here from those doors," Mrs. Straw said. She put down her fork and turned to watch the orchestra.

"They've made Walter a proctor," Mrs. Wilkins said.

"He'll be first in his class," Mrs. Straw said. "Look at the dress on that girl."

Mrs. Wilkins turned covertly, looking at the girl Mrs. Straw had indicated with her head. The girl had come out of the doorway that led to the entertainers' rooms; she was tall and very dark, with heavy black hair and thick eyebrows, and the dress was electric green satin, cut very low, with a flaming orange flower on one shoulder. "I never did see a dress like that," Mrs. Wilkins said. "She must be going to dance or something."

"She's not a very pretty girl," Mrs. Straw said. "And look at the fellow with her!"

Mrs. Wilkins turned again, and moved her head back quickly to smile at Mrs. Straw. "He looks like a monkey," she said.

"So little," Mrs. Straw said. "I hate those flabby little blond men."

"They used to have such a nice floor show here," Mrs. Wilkins said. "Music, and dancers, and sometimes a nice young man who would sing requests from the audience. Once they had an organist, I think."

"This is our dinner coming along now," Mrs. Straw said. The music had faded down, and the leader of the orchestra, who acted as master of ceremonies, introduced the first number, a pair of ballroom dancers. When the applause started, a tall young man and a tall young woman came out of the entertainers' door and made their way through the tables to the dance floor; on their way they both gave a nod of recognition to the girl in electric green and the man with her.

"Aren't they graceful?" Mrs. Wilkins said when the dance started. "They always look so pretty, that kind of dancers."

"They have to watch their weight," Mrs. Straw said critically. "Look at the figure on the girl in green."

Mrs. Wilkins turned again. "I hope they're not comedians."

"They don't look very funny right now," Mrs. Straw said. She estimated the butter left on her plate. "Every time I eat a good dinner," she said, "I think of Walter and the food we used to get in school."

"Walter writes that the food is quite good," Mrs. Wilkins said. "He's gained something like three pounds."

Mrs. Straw raised her eyes. "For heaven's sake!"

"What is it?"

"I think he's a ventriloquist," Mrs. Straw said. "I do believe he is."

"They're very popular right now," Mrs. Wilkins said.

"I haven't seen one since I was a kid," Mrs. Straw said. "He's got a little man—what do you call them?—in that box there." She continued to watch, her mouth a little open. "Look at it, Jen."

The girl in green and the man had sat down at a table near the entertainers' door. She was leaning forward, watching the dummy, which was sitting on the man's lap. It was a grotesque wooden copy of the man—where he was blond, the dummy was extravagantly yellow-haired, with sleek wooden curls and sideburns; where the man was small and ugly, the dummy was smaller and uglier, with the same wide mouth, the same staring eyes, the horrible parody of evening clothes, complete to tiny black shoes.

"I wonder how they happen to have a ventriloquist *here*," Mrs. Wilkins said.

The girl in green was leaning across the table to the dummy, straightening his tie, fastening one shoe, smoothing the shoulders of his coat. As she leaned back again the man spoke to her and she shrugged indifferently.

"I can't take my eyes off that green dress," Mrs. Straw said. She started as the waiter came softly up to her with the menu, waiting uneasily for their dessert orders, his eye on the stage where the orchestra was finishing a between-acts number. By the time Mrs. Straw had decided on apple pie with chocolate ice cream the master of ceremonies was introducing the ventriloquist ". . . and Marmaduke, a chip off the old block!"

"I hope it's not very long," Mrs. Wilkins said. "We can't hear from here anyway."

The ventriloquist and the dummy were sitting in the spotlight, both grinning widely, talking fast; the man's weak blond face was close to the dummy's staring grin, their black shoulders against one another. Their conversation was rapid; the audience was laughing affectionately, knowing most of the jokes before the dummy finished speaking, silent with interest for a minute and then laughing again before the words were out.

"I think he's terrible," Mrs. Wilkins said to Mrs. Straw during one roar of laughter. "They're always so coarse."

"Look at our friend in the green dress," Mrs. Straw said. The girl was leaning forward, following every word, tense and excited. For a minute the heavy sullenness of her face had vanished; she was laughing with everyone else, her eyes light. "*She* thinks it's funny," Mrs. Straw said.

Mrs. Wilkins drew her shoulders closer together and shivered. She attacked her dish of ice cream primly

"I always wonder," she began after a minute, "why places like this, you know, with really good food, never seem to think about desserts. It's always ice cream or something."

"Nothing better than ice cream," Mrs. Straw said.

"You'd think they'd have pastries, or some nice pudding," Mrs. Wilkins said. "They never seem to give any *thought* to it."

"I've never seen anything like that fig-and-date pudding you make, Jen," Mrs. Straw said.

"Walter always used to say that was the best—" Mrs. Wilkins began, and was cut short by a blare from the orchestra. The ventriloquist and the dummy were bowing, the man bowing deeply from the waist and the dummy bobbing his head courteously; the orchestra began quickly with a dance tune, and the man and the dummy turned and trotted off the stage.

"Thank heavens," Mrs. Wilkins said.

"I haven't seen one of those for years," Mrs. Straw said.

The girl in green had risen, waiting for the man and the dummy to come back to the table. The man sat down heavily, the dummy still on his knee, and the girl sat down again, on the edge of her chair, asking him something urgently.

"What do *you* think?" he said loudly, without looking at her. He waved to a waiter, who hesitated, looking in back of him at the table where the woman who owned the restaurant was sitting alone. After a minute the waiter approached the man, and the girl said, her voice clear over the soft waltz the orchestra was playing, "Don't drink anything more, Joey, we'll go somewhere and eat."

The man spoke to the waiter, ignoring the girl's hand on his arm. He turned to the dummy, speaking softly, and the dummy's face and broad grin looked at the girl and then back at the man. The girl sat back, looking out of the corners of her eyes at the owner of the restaurant.

"I'd hate to be married to a man like that," Mrs. Straw said.

"He's certainly not a very good comedian," Mrs. Wilkins said.

The girl was leaning forward again, arguing, and the man was talking to the dummy, making the dummy nod in agreement. When the girl put a hand on his shoulder the man shrugged it away without turning around. The girl's voice rose again. "Listen, Joey," she was saying.

"In a minute," the man said. "I just want to have this one drink."

"Yeah, leave him alone, can't you?" the dummy said.

"You don't need another drink now, Joey," the girl said. "You can get another drink later."

The man said, "Look, honey, I've got a drink ordered. I can't leave before it comes."

"Why don't you make old deadhead shut up?" the dummy said to the man, "always making a fuss when she sees someone having a good time. Why don't you tell her to shut up?"

"You shouldn't talk like that," the man said to the dummy. "It's not nice."

"*J* can talk if I want to," the dummy said. "She can't make *me* stop."

"Joey," the girl said, "I want to talk to you. Listen, let's go somewhere and talk."

"Shut up for a minute," the dummy said to the girl. "For God's sake will you shut up for a minute?"

People at nearby tables were beginning to turn, interested in the dummy's loud voice, and laughing already, hearing him talk. "*Please* be quiet," the girl said.

"Yeah, don't make such a fuss," the man said to the dummy. "I'm just going to have this one drink. She doesn't mind."

"He's not going to bring you any drink," the girl said impatiently. "They told him not to. They wouldn't give you a drink here, the way you're acting."

"I'm acting fine," the man said.

"*J'm* the one making the fuss," the dummy said. "It's time someone told you, sweetheart, you're going to get into trouble acting like a wet blanket all the time. A man won't stand for it forever."

"Be quiet," the girl said, looking around her anxiously. "Everyone can hear you."

"Let them hear me," the dummy said. He turned his grinning head around at his audience and raised his voice. "Just because a man wants to have a good time she has to freeze up like an icebag."

"Now, Marmaduke," the man said to the dummy, "you'd better talk nicer to your old mother."

"Why, I wouldn't tell that old bag the right time," the dummy said. "If she doesn't like it here, let her get back on the streets."

Mrs. Wilkins' mouth opened, and shut again; she put her napkin down on the table and stood up. While Mrs. Straw watched blankly she walked over to the other table and slapped the dummy sharply across the face.

By the time she had turned and come back to her own table Mrs. Straw had her coat on and was standing.

"We'll pay on the way out," Mrs. Wilkins said curtly.

She picked up her coat and the two of them walked with dignity to the door. For a moment the man and girl sat looking at the dummy slumped over sideways, its head awry. Then the girl reached over and straightened the wooden head.

‡

# SEVEN TYPES OF AMBIGUITY

THE BASEMENT ROOM of the bookstore seemed to be enormous; it stretched in long rows of books off into dimness at either end, with books lined in tall bookcases along the walls, and books standing in piles on the floor. At the foot of the spiral staircase winding down from the neat small store upstairs, Mr. Harris, owner and sales-clerk of the bookstore, had a small desk, cluttered with catalogues, lighted by one dirty overhead lamp. The same lamp served to light the shelves which crowded heavily around Mr. Harris' desk; farther away, along the lines of book tables, there were other dirty overhead lamps, to be lighted by pulling a string and turned off by the customer when he was ready to grope his way back to Mr. Harris' desk, pay for his purchases and have them wrapped. Mr. Harris, who knew the position of any author or any title in all the heavy shelves, had one customer at the moment, a boy of about eighteen, who was standing far down the long room directly under one of the lamps, leafing through a book he had selected from the shelves. It was cold in the big basement room; both Mr. Harris and the boy had their coats on. Occasionally Mr. Harris got up from his desk to put a meagre shovelful of coal on a small iron stove which stood in the curve of the staircase. Except when Mr. Harris got up, or the boy turned to put a book back into the shelves and take out another, the room was quiet, the books standing silent in the dim light.

Then the silence was broken by the sound of the door opening in the little upstairs bookshop where Mr. Harris kept his best-sellers and art books on display. There was the sound of voices, while both Mr. Harris and the boy listened, and then the girl who took care of the upstairs bookshop said, "Right on down the stairs. Mr. Harris will help you."

Mr. Harris got up and walked around to the foot of the stairs, turning on another of the overhead lamps so that his new customer would be able to see his way down. The boy put his book back in the shelves and stood with his hand on the back of it, still listening.

When Mr. Harris saw that it was a woman coming down the stairs he stood back politely and said, "Watch the bottom step. There's one more than people think." The woman stepped carefully down and stood looking around. While she stood there a man came carefully around the turn in the staircase, ducking his head so his hat would clear the low ceiling. "Watch the bottom step," the woman said in a soft clear voice. The man came down beside her and raised his head to look around as she had.

"Quite a lot of books you have here," he said.

Mr. Harris smiled his professional smile. "Can I help you?"

The woman looked at the man, and he hesitated a minute and then said, "We want to get some books. Quite a few of them." He waved his hand inclusively. "Sets of books."

"Well, if it's books you want," Mr. Harris said, and smiled again. "Maybe the lady would like to come over and sit down?" He led the way around to his desk, the woman following him and the man walking uneasily between the tables of books, his hands close to his sides as though he were afraid of breaking something. Mr. Harris gave the lady his desk chair and then sat down on the edge of his desk, shoving aside a pile of catalogues.

"This is a very interesting place," the lady said, in the same soft voice she had used when she spoke before. She was middle-aged and nicely dressed; all her clothes were fairly new, but quiet and well planned for her age and air of shyness. The man was big and hearty-looking, his face reddened by the cold air and his big hands holding a pair of wool gloves uneasily.

"We'd like to buy some of your books," the man said. "Some good books."

"Anything in particular?" Mr. Harris asked.

The man laughed loudly, but with embarrassment. "Tell the truth," he said, "I sound sort of foolish, now. But I don't know much about these things, like books." In the large quiet store his voice seemed to echo, after his wife's soft voice and Mr. Harris'. "We were sort of hoping you'd be able to tell *us*," he said. "None of this trash they turn out nowadays." He cleared his throat. "Something like Dickens," he said.

"Dickens," Mr. Harris said.

"I used to read Dickens when I was a kid," the man said. "Books like that, now, good books." He looked up as the boy who had been standing off among the books came over to them. "I'd like to read Dickens again," the big man said.

"Mr. Harris," the boy asked quietly.

Mr. Harris looked up. "Yes, Mr. Clark?" he said.

The boy came closer to the desk, as though unwilling to interrupt Mr. Harris with his customers. "I'd like to take another look at the Empson," he said.

Mr. Harris turned to the glass-doored bookcase immediately behind his desk and selected a book. "Here it is," he said, "you'll have it read through before you buy it at this rate." He smiled at the big man and his wife. "Some day he's going to come in and buy that book," he said, "and I'm going to go out of business from shock."

The boy turned away, holding the book, and the big man leaned forward to Mr. Harris. "I figure I'd like two good sets, big, like Dickens," he said, "and then a couple of smaller sets."

"And a copy of *Jane Eyre*," his wife said, in her soft voice. "I used to love that book," she said to Mr. Harris.

"I can let you have a very nice set of the Brontës," Mr. Harris said. "Beautiful binding."

"I want them to look nice," the man said, "but solid, for reading. I'm going to read through all of Dickens again."

The boy came back to the desk, holding the book out to Mr. Harris. "It still looks good," he said.

"It's right here when you want it," Mr. Harris said, turning back to the bookcase with the book. "It's pretty scarce, that book."

"I guess it'll be here a while longer," the boy said.

"What's the name of this book?" the big man asked curiously.

"*Seven Types of Ambiguity*," the boy said. "It's quite a good book."

"There's a fine name for a book," the big man said to Mr. Harris. "Pretty smart young fellow, reading books with names like that."

"It's a good book," the boy repeated.

"I'm trying to buy some books myself," the big man said to the boy. "I want to catch up on a few I've missed. Dickens, I've always liked his books."

"Meredith is good," the boy said. "You ever try reading Meredith?"

"Meredith," the big man said. "Let's see a few of your books," he said to Mr. Harris. "I'd sort of like to pick out a few I want."

"Can I take the gentleman down there?" the boy said to Mr. Harris. "I've got to go back anyway to get my hat."

"I'll go with the young man and look at the books, Mother," the big man said to his wife. "You stay here and keep warm."

"Fine," Mr. Harris said. "He knows where the books are as well as I do," he said to the big man.

The boy started off down the aisle between the book tables, and the big man followed, still walking carefully, trying not to touch anything. They went down past the lamp still burning where the boy had left his hat and gloves, and the boy turned on another lamp further down. "Mr. Harris keeps most of his sets around here," the boy said. "Let's see what we can find." He squatted down in front of the bookcases, touching the backs of the rows of books lightly with his fingers. "How do you feel about the prices?" he asked.

"I'm willing to pay a reasonable amount for the books I have in mind," the big man said. He touched the book in front of him experimentally, with one finger. "A hundred and fifty, two hundred dollars altogether."

The boy looked up at him and laughed. "That ought to get you some nice books," he said.

"Never saw so many books in my life," the big man said. "I never thought I'd see the day when I'd just walk into a bookstore and buy up all the books I always wanted to read."

"It's a good feeling."

"I never got a chance to read much," the man said. "Went right into the machine-shop where my father worked when I was much younger than you, and worked ever since. Now all of a sudden I find I have a little more money than I used to, and Mother and I decided we'd like to get ourselves a few things we always wanted."

"Your wife was interested in the Brontës," the boy said. "Here's a very good set."

The man leaned down to look at the books the boy pointed out. "I don't know much about these things," he said. "They look nice, all alike. What's the next set?"

"Carlyle," the boy said. "You can skip him. He's not quite what you're looking for. Meredith is good. And Thackeray. I think you'd want Thackeray; he's a great writer."

The man took one of the books the boy handed him and opened it carefully, using only two fingers from each of his big hands. "This looks fine," he said.

"I'll write them down," the boy said. He took a pencil and a pocket memorandum from his coat pocket. "Brontës," he said, "Dickens, Meredith, Thackeray." He ran his hand along each of the sets as he read them off.

The big man narrowed his eyes. "I ought to take one more," he said. "These won't quite fill up the bookcase I got for them."

"Jane Austen," the boy said. "Your wife would be pleased with that."

"You read all these books?" the man asked.

"Most of them," the boy said.

The man was quiet for a minute and then he went on, "I never got much of a chance to read anything, going to work so early. I've got a lot to catch up on."

"You're going to have a fine time," the boy said.

"That book you had a while back," the man said. "What was that book?"

"It's aesthetics," the boy said. "About literature. It's very scarce. I've been trying to buy it for quite a while and haven't had the money."

"You go to college?" the man asked.

"Yes."

"Here's one I ought to read again," the man said. "Mark Twain. I read a couple of his books when I was a kid. But I guess I have enough to start on." He stood up.

The boy rose too, smiling. "You're going to have to do a lot of reading."

"I like to read," the man said. "I really like to read."

He started back down the aisles, going straight for Mr. Harris' desk. The boy turned off the lamps and followed, stopping to get his hat and gloves. When the big man reached Mr. Harris' desk he said to his wife, "That's sure a smart kid. He knows those books right and left."

"Did you pick out what you want?" his wife asked.

"The kid has a fine list for me." He turned to Mr. Harris and went on, "It's quite an experience seeing a kid like that liking books the way he does. When I was his age I was working for four or five years."

The boy came up with the slip of paper in his hand. "These ought to hold him for a while," he said to Mr. Harris.

Mr. Harris glanced at the list and nodded. "That Thackeray's a nice set of books," he said.

The boy had put his hat on and was standing at the foot of the stairs. "Hope you enjoy them," he said. "I'll be back for another look at that Empson, Mr. Harris."

"I'll try to keep it around for you," Mr. Harris said. "I can't promise to hold it, you know."

"I'll just count on it's being here," the boy said.

"Thanks, son," the big man called out as the boy started up the stairs. "Appreciate your helping me."

"That's all right," the boy said.

"He's sure a smart kid," the man said to Mr. Harris. "He's got a great chance, with an education like that."

"He's a nice young fellow," Mr. Harris said, "and he sure wants that book."

"You think he'll ever buy it?" the big man asked.

"I doubt it," Mr. Harris said. "If you'll just write down your name and address, I'll add these prices."

Mr. Harris began to note down the prices of the books, copying from the boy's neat list. After the big man had written his name and address, he stood for a minute drumming his fingers on the desk, and then he said, "Can I have another look at that book?"

"The Empson?" Mr. Harris said, looking up.

"The one the boy was so interested in." Mr. Harris reached around to the bookcase in back of him and took out the book. The big man held it delicately, as he had held the others, and he frowned as he turned the pages. Then he put the book down on Mr. Harris' desk.

"If he isn't going to buy it, will it be all right if I put this in with the rest?" he asked.

Mr. Harris looked up from his figures for a minute, and then he made the entry on his list. He added quickly, wrote down the total, and then pushed the paper across the desk to the big man. While the man checked over the figures Mr. Harris turned to the woman and said, "Your husband has bought a lot of very pleasant reading."

"I'm glad to hear it," she said. "We've been looking forward to it for a long time."

The big man counted out the money carefully, handing the bills to Mr. Harris. Mr. Harris put the money in the top drawer of his desk and said, "We can have these delivered to you by the end of the week, if that will be all right."

"Fine," the big man said. "Ready, Mother?"

The woman rose, and the big man stood back to let her go

ahead of him. Mr. Harris followed, stopping near the stairs to say to the woman, "Watch the bottom step."

They started up the stairs and Mr. Harris stood watching them until they got to the turn. Then he switched off the dirty overhead lamp and went back to his desk.

‡

# COME DANCE WITH ME IN IRELAND

YOUNG MRS. ARCHER was sitting on the bed with Kathy Valentine and Mrs. Corn, playing with the baby and gossiping, when the doorbell rang. Mrs. Archer, saying, "Oh, dear!," went to push the buzzer that released the outside door of the apartment building. "We *had* to live on the ground floor," she called to Kathy and Mrs. Corn. "Everybody rings our bell for everything."

When the inner doorbell rang she opened the door of the apartment and saw an old man standing in the outer hall. He was wearing a long, shabby black overcoat and had a square white beard. He held out a handful of shoelaces.

"Oh," Mrs. Archer said. "Oh, I'm terribly sorry, but—"

"Madam," the old man said, "if you would be so kind. A nickel apiece."

Mrs. Archer shook her head and backed away. "I'm afraid not," she said.

"Thank you anyway, Madam," he said, "for speaking courteously. The first person on this block who has been decently polite to a poor old man."

Mrs. Archer turned the doorknob back and forth nervously. "I'm awfully sorry," she said. Then, as he turned to go, she said, "Wait a minute," and hurried into the bedroom. "Old man selling shoelaces," she whispered. She pulled open the top dresser drawer, took out her pocketbook, and fumbled in the change purse. "Quarter," she said. "Think it's all right?"

"Sure," Kathy said. "Probably more than he's gotten all day." She was Mrs. Archer's age, and unmarried. Mrs. Corn was a stout woman in her middle fifties. They both lived in the building and spent a good deal of time at Mrs. Archer's, on account of the baby.

Mrs. Archer returned to the front door. "Here," she said, holding out the quarter. "I think it's a shame everyone was so rude."

The old man started to offer her some shoelaces, but his hand shook and the shoelaces dropped to the floor. He leaned heavily against the wall. Mrs. Archer watched, horrified. "Good Lord," she said, and put out her hand. As her fingers touched the dirty old overcoat she hesitated and then, tightening her lips, she put her arm firmly through his and tried to help him through the doorway. "Girls," she called, "come help me, quick!"

Kathy came running out of the bedroom, saying, "Did you call, Jean?" and then stopped dead, staring.

"What'll I do?" Mrs. Archer said, standing with her arm through the old man's. His eyes were closed and he seemed barely able, with her help, to stand on his feet. "For heaven's sake, grab him on the other side."

"Get him to a chair or something," Kathy said. The hall was too narrow for all three of them to go down side by side, so Kathy took the old man's other arm and half-led Mrs. Archer and him into the living-room. "Not in the good chair," Mrs. Archer exclaimed. "In the old leather one." They dropped the old man into the leather chair and stood back. "What on earth do we do now?" Mrs. Archer said.

"Do you have any whiskey?" Kathy asked.

Mrs. Archer shook her head. "A little wine," she said doubtfully.

Mrs. Corn came into the living-room, holding the baby. "Gracious!" she said. "He's drunk!"

"Nonsense," Kathy said. "I wouldn't have let Jean bring him in if he were."

"Watch out for the baby, Blanche," Mrs. Archer said.

"Naturally," Mrs. Corn said. "We're going back into the bedroom, honey," she said to the baby, "and then we're going to get into our lovely crib and go beddy-bye."

The old man stirred and opened his eyes. He tried to get up.

"Now you stay right where you are," Kathy ordered, "and Mrs. Archer here is going to bring you a little bit of wine. You'd like that, wouldn't you?"

The old man raised his eyes to Kathy. "Thank you," he said.

Mrs. Archer went into the kitchen. After a moment's thought she took the glass from over the sink, rinsed it out, and poured some sherry into it. She took the glass of sherry back into the living-room and handed it to Kathy.

"Shall I hold it for you or can you drink by yourself?" Kathy asked the old man.

"You are much too kind," he said, and reached for the glass. Kathy steadied it for him as he sipped from it, and then he pushed it away.

"That's enough, thank you," he said. "Enough to revive me." He tried to rise. "Thank you," he said to Mrs. Archer, "and thank *you*," to Kathy. "I had better be going along."

"Not until you're quite firm on your feet," Kathy said. "Can't afford to take chances, you know."

The old man smiled. "*I* can afford to take chances," he said.

Mrs. Corn came back into the living-room. "Baby's in his crib," she said, "and just about asleep already. Does *he* feel better now? I'll bet he was just drunk or hungry or something."

"Of course he was," Kathy said, fired by the idea. "He was

hungry. That's what was wrong all the time, Jean. How silly we were. Poor old gentleman!" she said to the old man. "Mrs. Archer is certainly not going to let you leave here without a full meal inside of you."

Mrs. Archer looked doubtful. "I have some eggs," she said.

"Fine!" Kathy said. "Just the thing. They're easily digested," she said to the old man, "and especially good if you haven't eaten for"—she hesitated—"for a while."

"Black coffee," Mrs. Corn said, "if you ask me. Look at his hands shake."

"Nervous exhaustion," Kathy said firmly. "A nice hot cup of bouillon is all he needs to be good as ever, and he has to drink it very slowly until his stomach gets used to food again. The stomach," she told Mrs. Archer and Mrs. Corn, "shrinks when it remains empty for any great period of time."

"I would rather not trouble you," the old man said to Mrs. Archer.

"Nonsense," Kathy said. "We've got to see that you get a good hot meal to go on with." She took Mrs. Archer's arm and began to walk her out to the kitchen. "Just some eggs," she said. "Fry four or five. I'll get you half a dozen later. I don't suppose you have any bacon. I'll tell you, fry up a few potatoes too. He won't care if they're half-raw. These people eat things like heaps of fried potatoes and eggs and—"

"There's some canned figs left over from lunch," Mrs. Archer said. "I was wondering what to do with them."

"I've got to run back and keep an eye on him," Kathy said. "He might faint again or something. You just fry up those eggs and potatoes. I'll send Blanche out if she'll come."

Mrs. Archer measured out enough coffee for two cups and set the pot on the stove. Then she took out her frying pan. "Kathy," she said, "I'm just a little worried. If he really is drunk, I mean, and if Jim should hear about it, with the baby here and everything. . . ."

"Why, Jean!" Kathy said. "You should live in the country for a while, I guess. Women always give out meals to starving men. And you don't need to *tell* Jim. Blanche and I certainly won't say anything."

"Well," said Mrs. Archer, "you're sure he isn't drunk?"

"I know a starving man when I see one," Kathy said. "When an old man like that can't stand up and his hands shake and he looks so funny, that means he's starving to death. Literally starving."

"Oh, my!" said Mrs. Archer. She hurried to the cupboard under the sink and took out two potatoes. "Two enough, do you think? I guess we're really doing a good deed."

Kathy giggled. "Just a bunch of Girl Scouts," she said. She started out of the kitchen, and then she stopped and turned around. "You have any pie? They always eat pie."

"It was for dinner, though," Mrs. Archer said.

"Oh, give it to him," Kathy said. "We can run out and get some more after he goes."

While the potatoes were frying, Mrs. Archer put a plate, a cup and saucer, and a knife and fork and spoon on the dinette table. Then, as an afterthought, she picked up the dishes and, taking a paper bag out of a cupboard, tore it in half and spread it smoothly on the table and put the dishes back. She got a glass and filled it with water from the bottle in the refrigerator, cut three slices of bread and put them on a plate, and then cut a small square of butter and put it on the plate with the bread. Then she got a paper napkin from the box in the cupboard and put it beside the plate, took it up after a minute to fold it into a triangular shape, and put it back. Finally she put the pepper and salt shakers on the table and got out a box of eggs. She went to the door and called, "Kathy! Ask him how does he want his eggs fried?"

There was a murmur of conversation in the living-room and Kathy called back, "Sunny side up!"

Mrs. Archer took out four eggs and then another and broke them one by one into the frying-pan. When they were done she called out, "All right, girls! Bring him in!"

Mrs. Corn came into the kitchen, inspected the plate of potatoes and eggs, and looked at Mrs. Archer without speaking. Then Kathy came, leading the old man by the arm. She escorted him to the table and sat him down in a chair. "There," she said. "Now, Mrs. Archer's fixed you a lovely hot meal."

The old man looked at Mrs. Archer. "I'm very grateful," he said.

"Isn't that nice!" Kathy said. She nodded approvingly at Mrs. Archer. The old man regarded the plate of eggs and potatoes. "Now pitch right in," Kathy said. "Sit down, girls. I'll get a chair from the bedroom."

The old man picked up the salt and shook it gently over the eggs. "This looks delicious," he said finally.

"You just go right ahead and eat," Kathy said, reappearing with a chair. "We want to see you get filled up. Pour him some coffee, Jean."

Mrs. Archer went to the stove and took up the coffeepot. "Please don't bother," he said.

"That's all right," Mrs. Archer said, filling the old man's cup. She sat down at the table. The old man picked up the fork and then put it down again to take up the paper napkin and spread it carefully over his knees.

"What's your name?" Kathy asked.

"O'Flaherty, Madam. John O'Flaherty."

"Well, John," Kathy said, "I am Miss Valentine and this lady is Mrs. Archer and the other one is Mrs. Corn."

"How do you do?" the old man said.

"I gather you're from the old country," Kathy said.

"I beg your pardon?"

"Irish, aren't you?" Kathy said.

"I am, Madam." The old man plunged the fork into one of the eggs and watched the yoke run out onto the plate. "I knew Yeats," he said suddenly.

"Really?" Kathy said, leaning forward. "Let me see—he was the writer, wasn't he?"

" 'Come out of charity, come dance with me in Ireland,' " the old man said. He rose and, holding on to the chair back, bowed solemnly to Mrs. Archer, "Thank you again, Madam, for your generosity." He turned and started for the front door. The three women got up and followed him.

"But you didn't finish," Mrs. Corn said.

"The stomach," the old man said, "as this lady has pointed out, shrinks. Yes, indeed," he went on reminiscently, "I knew Yeats."

At the front door he turned and said to Mrs. Archer, "Your kindness should not go unrewarded." He gestured to the shoelaces lying on the floor. "These," he said, "are for you. For your kindness. Divide them with the other ladies."

"But I wouldn't dream—" Mrs. Archer began.

"I insist," the old man said, opening the door. "A small return, but all that I have to offer. Pick them up yourself," he added abruptly. Then he turned and thumbed his nose at Mrs. Corn. "I hate old women," he said.

"Well!" said Mrs. Corn faintly.

"I may have imbibed somewhat freely," the old man said

to Mrs. Archer, "but I never served bad sherry to my guests We are of two different worlds, Madam."

"Didn't I tell you?" Mrs. Corn was saying. "Haven't I kept telling you all along?"

Mrs. Archer, her eyes on Kathy, made a tentative motion of pushing the old man through the door, but he forestalled her.

" 'Come dance with me in Ireland,' " he said. Supporting himself against the wall, he reached the outer door and opened it. "And time runs on," he said.

# IV

We are never liable to be so betray'd and abused, till, by our vile *Dispositions* and *Tendencies*, we have forfeited the *tutelary* Care, and *Oversight* of the better Spirits; who, tho' generally they are our Guard and Defence against the Malice and Violence of evil *Angels*, yet it may well enough be thought, that some Time they may take their Leave of such as are swallow'd up by *Malice, Envy,* and *Desire* of *Revenge,* Qualities most contrary to their *Life* and *Nature;* and leave them exposed to the *Invasion* and *Solicitations* of those *wicked Spirits,* to whom such hateful *Attributes* make them very suitable.

Joseph Glanvil: *Sadducismus Triumphatus*

# ‡
## OF COURSE

MRS. TYLOR, in the middle of a busy morning, was far too polite to go out on the front porch and stare, but she saw no reason for avoiding the windows; when her vacuuming or her dishwashing, or even the upstairs bedmaking, took her near a window on the south side of the house she would lift the curtain slightly, or edge to one side and stir the shade. All she could see, actually, was the moving van in front of the house, and various small activities going on between the movers; the furniture, what she could see of it, looked fine.

Mrs. Tylor finished the beds and came downstairs to start lunch, and in the short space of time it took her to get from the front bedroom window to the kitchen window a taxi had stopped in front of the house next door and a small boy was dancing up and down on the sidewalk. Mrs. Taylor estimated him; about four, probably, unless he was small for his age; about right for her youngest girl. She turned her attention to the woman who was getting out of the taxi, and was further reassured. A nice-looking tan suit, a little worn and perhaps a *little* too light in color for moving day, but nicely cut, and Mrs. Tylor nodded appreciatively over the carrots she was scraping. *Nice* people, obviously.

Carol, Mrs. Tylor's youngest, was leaning on the fence in front of the Tylor house, watching the little boy next door. When the little boy stopped dancing up and down Carol said, "Hi." The little boy looked up, took a step backward, and said, "Hi." His mother looked at Carol, at the Tylor house, and down at her son. Then she said, "Hello there" to Carol. Mrs. Tylor smiled in the kitchen. Then, on a sudden impulse she dried her hands on a paper towel, took off her apron, and went to the front door. "Carol," she called lightly, "Carol, dear." Carol turned around, still leaning on the fence. "What?" she said uncoöperatively.

"Oh, hello," Mrs. Tylor said to the lady still standing on the sidewalk next to the little boy. "I heard Carol talking to someone. . . ."

"The children were making friends," the lady said shyly.

Mrs. Tylor came down the steps to stand near Carol at the fence. "Are you our new neighbor?"

"If we ever get moved in," the lady said. She laughed. "Moving day," she said expressively.

"I know. Our name's Tylor," Mrs. Tylor said. "This is Carol."

"*Our* name is Harris," the lady said. "This is James Junior."

"Say hello to James," Mrs. Tylor said.

"And *you* say hello to Carol," Mrs. Harris said.

Carol shut her mouth obstinately and the little boy edged behind his mother. Both ladies laughed. "Children!" one of them said, and the other said, "Isn't it the way!"

Then Mrs. Tylor said, gesturing at the moving van and the two men moving in and out with chairs and tables and beds and lamps, "Heavens, isn't it terrible?"

Mrs. Harris sighed. "I think I'll just go crazy."

"Is there anything we can do to help?" Mrs. Tylor asked. She smiled down at James. "Perhaps James would like to spend the afternoon with us?"

"That *would* be a relief," Mrs. Harris agreed. She twisted around to look at James behind her. "Would you like to play with Carol this afternoon, honey?" James shook his head mutely and Mrs. Tylor said to him brightly, "Carol's two older sisters might, just *might* take her to the movies, James. You'd like *that*, wouldn't you?"

"I'm afraid not," Mrs. Harris said flatly. "James does not go to movies."

"Oh, well, of course," Mrs. Tylor said, "lots of mothers *don't*, of course, but when a child has two older. . . ."

"It isn't that," Mrs. Harris said. "We do not go to movies, any of us."

Mrs. Tylor quickly registered the "any" as meaning there was probably a Mr. Harris somewhere around, and then her mind snapped back and she said blankly, "Don't go to movies?"

"Mr. Harris," Mrs. Harris said carefully, "feels that movies are intellectually retarding. We do not go to movies."

"Naturally," Mrs. Tylor said. "Well, I'm sure Carol wouldn't mind staying home this afternoon. She'd love to play with James. Mr. Harris," she added cautiously, "wouldn't object to a sandbox?"

"I want to go to the movies," Carol said.

Mrs. Tylor spoke quickly. "Why don't you and James come over and rest at our house for a while? You've probably been running around all morning."

Mrs. Harris hesitated, watching the movers. "Thank you," she said finally. With James following along behind her, she came through the Tylors' gate, and Mrs. Tylor said, "If we sit in the garden out back we can still keep an eye on your movers." She gave Carol a small push. "Show James the sandbox, dear," she said firmly.

Carol took James sullenly by the hand and led him over to the sandbox. "See?" she said, and went back to kick the fence pickets deliberately. Mrs. Tylor sat Mrs. Harris in one of the garden chairs and went over and found a shovel for James to dig with.

"It certainly feels good to sit down," Mrs. Harris said. She sighed. "Sometimes I feel that moving is the most terrible thing I have to do."

"You were lucky to get that house," Mrs. Tylor said, and Mrs. Harris nodded. "We'll be glad to get nice neighbors," Mrs. Tylor went on. "There's something so nice about congenial people right next door. I'll be running over to borrow cups of sugar," she finished roguishly.

"I certainly hope you will," Mrs. Harris said. "We had such disagreeable people next door to us in our old house. Small things, you know, and they do irritate you so." Mrs. Tylor sighed sympathetically. "The radio, for instance," Mrs. Harris continued, "all day long, and so *loud*."

Mrs. Tylor caught her breath for a minute. "You must be sure and tell us if ours is ever too loud."

"Mr. Harris cannot bear the radio," Mrs. Harris said. "We do not own one, of course."

"Of course," Mrs. Tylor said. "No radio."

Mrs. Harris looked at her and laughed uncomfortably. "You'll be thinking my husband is crazy."

"Of course not," Mrs. Tylor said. "After all, lots of people don't like radios; my oldest nephew, now, he's just the *other* way—"

"Well," Mrs. Harris said, "newspapers, too."

Mrs. Tylor recognized finally the faint nervous feeling that was tagging her; it was the way she felt when she was irrevocably connected with something dangerously out of control: her car, for instance, on an icy street, or the time on Virginia's roller skates. . . . Mrs. Harris was staring absent-mindedly at the movers going in and out, and she was saying, "It isn't as though we hadn't ever *seen* a newspaper, not like the movies at all; Mr. Harris just feels that the newspapers are a mass degradation of taste. You really never *need* to read a newspaper, you know," she said, looking around anxiously at Mrs. Tylor.

"I never read anything but the—"

"And we took *The New Republic* for a *number* of years," Mrs. Harris said. "When we were first married, of course. Before James was born."

"What is your husband's business?" Mrs. Tylor asked timidly.

Mrs. Harris lifted her head proudly. "He's a scholar," she said. "He writes monographs."

Mrs. Tylor opened her mouth to speak, but Mrs. Harris leaned over and put her hand out and said, "It's *terribly* hard for people to understand the desire for a really peaceful life."

"What," Mrs. Tylor said, "what does your husband do for relaxation?"

"He reads plays," Mrs. Harris said. She looked doubtfully over at James. "Pre-Elizabethan, of course."

"Of course," Mrs. Tylor said, and looked nervously at James, who was shoveling sand into a pail.

"People are really very unkind," Mrs. Harris said. "Those people I was telling you about, next door. It wasn't only the radio, you see. Three times they *deliberately* left their *New York Times* on our doorstep. Once James nearly got it."

"Good Lord," Mrs. Tylor said. She stood up. "Carol," she called emphatically, "don't go away. It's nearly time for lunch, dear."

"Well," Mrs. Harris said. "I must go and see if the movers have done anything right."

Feeling as though she had been rude, Mrs. Tylor said, "Where is Mr. Harris now?"

"At his mother's," Mrs. Harris said. "He always stays there when we move."

"Of course," Mrs. Tylor said, feeling as though she had been saying nothing else all morning.

"They don't turn the radio on while he's there," Mrs. Harris explained.

"Of course," Mrs. Tylor said.

Mrs. Harris held out her hand and Mrs. Tylor took it. "I do so hope we'll be friends," Mrs. Harris said. "As you said, it means such a lot to have really thoughtful neighbors. And we've been so unlucky."

"Of course," Mrs. Tylor said, and then came back to herself abruptly. "Perhaps one evening soon we can get together for a game of bridge?" She saw Mrs. Harris's face and said, "No. Well, anyway, we must all get together some evening soon." They both laughed.

"It does sound silly, doesn't it," Mrs. Harris said. "Thanks so much for all your kindness this morning."

"Anything we can do," Mrs. Tylor said. "If you want to send James over this afternoon."

"Perhaps I shall," Mrs. Harris said. "If you really don't mind."

"Of course," Mrs. Tylor said. "Carol, dear."

With her arm around Carol she walked out to the front of the house and stood watching Mrs. Harris and James go into their house. They both stopped in the doorway and waved, and Mrs. Tylor and Carol waved back.

"Can't I go to the movies," Carol said, "*please*, Mother?"

"I'll go with you, dear," Mrs. Tylor said.

‡

# PILLAR OF SALT

FOR SOME REASON a tune was running through her head when she and her husband got on the train in New Hampshire for their trip to New York; they had not been to New York for nearly a year, but the tune was from farther back than that. It was from the days when she was fifteen or sixteen, and had never seen New York except in movies, when the city was made up, to her, of penthouses filled with Noel Coward people; when the height and speed and luxury and gaiety that made up a city like New York were confused inextricably with the dullness of being fifteen, and beauty unreachable and far in the movies.

"What *is* that tune?" she said to her husband, and hummed it. "It's from some old movie, I think."

"I know it," he said, and hummed it himself. "Can't remember the words."

He sat back comfortably. He had hung up their coats, put the suitcases on the rack, and had taken his magazine out. "I'll think of it sooner or later," he said.

She looked out the window first, tasting it almost secretly, savoring the extreme pleasure of being on a moving train with nothing to do for six hours but read and nap and go into the dining-car, going farther and farther every minute from the children, from the kitchen floor, with even the hills being incredibly left behind, changing into fields and trees too far away from home to be daily. "I love trains," she said, and her husband nodded sympathetically into his magazine.

Two weeks ahead, two unbelievable weeks, with all arrangements made, no further planning to do, except perhaps what theatres or what restaurants. A friend with an apartment went on a convenient vacation, there was enough money in the bank to make a trip to New York compatible with new snow suits for the children; there was the smoothness of un-opposed arrangements, once the initial obstacles had been overcome, as though when they had really made up their minds, nothing dared stop them. The baby's sore throat cleared up. The plumber came, finished his work in two days, and left. The dresses had been altered in time; the hardware store could be left safely, once they had found the excuse of looking over new city products. New York had not burned down, had not been quarantined, their friend had gone away according to schedule, and Brad had the keys to the apartment in his pocket. Everyone knew where to reach everyone else; there was a list of plays not to miss and a list of items to look out for in the stores—diapers, dress materials, fancy canned goods, tarnish-proof silverware boxes. And, finally, the train was there, performing its function, pacing through the after-noon, carrying them legally and with determination to New York.

Margaret looked curiously at her husband, inactive in the middle of the afternoon on a train, at the other fortunate peo-ple traveling, at the sunny country outside, looked again to make sure, and then opened her book. The tune was still in her head, she hummed it and heard her husband take it up softly as he turned a page in his magazine.

In the dining-car she ate roast beef, as she would have done in a restaurant at home, reluctant to change over too quickly to the new, tantalizing food of a vacation. She had ice cream for dessert but became uneasy over her coffee because they were due in New York in an hour and she still had to put on her coat and hat, relishing every gesture, and Brad must take the suitcases down and put away the magazines. They stood at the end of the car for the interminable underground run, picking up their suitcases and putting them down again, moving restlessly inch by inch.

The station was a momentary shelter, moving visitors gradually into a world of people and sound and light to prepare them for the blasting reality of the street outside. She saw it for a minute from the sidewalk before she was in a taxi moving into the middle of it, and then they were bewilderingly caught and carried on uptown and whirled out on to another sidewalk and Brad paid the taxi driver and put his head back to look up at the apartment house. "This is it, all right," he said, as though he had doubted the driver's ability to find a number so simply given. Upstairs in the elevator, and the key fit the door. They had never seen their friend's apartment before, but it was reasonably familiar—a friend moving from New Hampshire to New York carries private pictures of a home not erasable in a few years, and the apartment had enough of home in it to settle Brad immediately in the right chair and comfort her with instinctive trust of the linen and blankets.

"This is home for two weeks," Brad said, and stretched. After the first few minutes they both went to the windows automatically; New York was below, as arranged, and the houses across the street were apartment houses filled with unknown people.

"It's wonderful," she said. There were cars down there, and people, and the noise was there. "I'm so happy," she said, and kissed her husband.

They went sight-seeing the first day; they had breakfast in an Automat and went to the top of the Empire State building.

"Got it all fixed up now," Brad said, at the top. "Wonder just where that plane hit."

They tried to peer down on all four sides, but were embarrassed about asking. "After all," she said reasonably, giggling in a corner, "if something of mine got broken I wouldn't want people poking around asking to see the pieces."

"If you owned the Empire State building you wouldn't care," Brad said.

They traveled only in taxis the first few days, and one taxi had a door held on with a piece of string; they pointed to it and laughed silently at each other, and on about the third day, the taxi they were riding in got a flat tire on Broadway and they had to get out and find another.

"We've only got eleven days left," she said one day, and then, seemingly minutes later, "we've already been here six days."

They had got in touch with the friends they had expected to get in touch with, they were going to a Long Island summer home for a week end. "It looks pretty dreadful right now," their hostess said cheerfully over the phone, "and we're leaving in a week ourselves, but I'd never *forgive* you if you didn't see it *once* while you were here." The weather had been fair but cool, with a definite autumn awareness, and the clothes in the store windows were dark and already hinting at furs and velvets. She wore her coat every day, and suits most of the time. The light dresses she had brought were hanging in the closet in the apartment, and she was thinking now of getting a sweater in one of the big stores, something impractical for New Hampshire, but probably good for Long Island.

"I have to do some shopping, at least one day," she said to Brad, and he groaned.

"Don't ask me to carry packages," he said.

"You aren't up to a good day's shopping," she told him, "not after all this walking around you've been doing. Why don't you go to a movie or something?"

"I want to do some shopping myself," he said mysteriously. Perhaps he was talking about her Christmas present; she had thought vaguely of getting such things done in New York; the children would be pleased with novelties from the city, toys not seen in their home stores. At any rate she said, "You'll probably be able to get to your wholesalers at last."

They were on their way to visit another friend, who had found a place to live by a miracle and warned them consequently not to quarrel with the appearance of the building, or the stairs, or the neighborhood. All three were bad, and the stairs were three flights, narrow and dark, but there was a place to live at the top. Their friend had not been in New York long, but he lived by himself in two rooms, and had easily caught the mania for slim tables and low bookcases which made his rooms look too large for the furniture in some places, too cramped and uncomfortable in others.

"What a lovely place," she said when she came in, and then was sorry when her host said, "Some day this damn situation will let up and I'll be able to settle down in a really decent place."

There were other people there; they sat and talked companionably about the same subjects then current in New Hampshire, but they drank more than they would have at home and it left them strangely unaffected; their voices were louder and their words more extravagant; their gestures, on the other hand, were smaller, and they moved a finger where in New Hampshire they would have waved an arm. Margaret said frequently, "We're just staying here for a couple of weeks, on a vacation," and she said, "It's wonderful, so *exciting*," and she said, "We were *terribly* lucky; this friend went out of town just at the right. . . ."

Finally the room was very full and noisy, and she went into a corner near a window to catch her breath. The window had been opened and shut all evening, depending on whether the person standing next to it had both hands free; and now it was shut, with the clear sky outside. Someone came and stood next to her, and she said, "Listen to the noise outside. It's as bad as it is inside."

He said, "In a neighborhood like this someone's always getting killed."

She frowned. "It sounds different than before. I mean, there's a different sound to it."

"Alcoholics," he said. "Drunks in the streets. Fighting going on across the way." He wandered away, carrying his drink.

She opened the window and leaned out, and there were people hanging out of the windows across the way shouting, and people standing in the street looking up and shouting, and from across the way she heard clearly, "Lady, lady." They must mean me, she thought, they're all looking this way. She leaned out farther and the voices shouted incoherently but somehow making an audible whole, "Lady, your house is on fire, lady, lady."

She closed the window firmly and turned around to the other people in the room, raising her voice a little. "Listen," she said, "they're saying the house is on fire." She was desperately afraid of their laughing at her, of looking like a fool while Brad across the room looked at her blushing. She said again, "The *house* is on *fire*," and added, "They say," for fear of sounding too vehement. The people nearest to her turned and someone said, "She says the house is on fire."

She wanted to get to Brad and couldn't see him; her host was not in sight either, and the people all around were strangers. They don't listen to me, she thought, I might as well not be here, and she went to the outside door and opened it. There was no smoke, no flame, but she was telling herself, I might as well not be here, so she abandoned Brad in panic and ran without her hat and coat down the stairs, carrying a glass in one hand and a package of matches in the other. The stairs were insanely long, but they were clear and safe, and she opened the street door and ran out. A man caught her arm and said, "Everyone out of the house?" and she said, "No, Brad's still there." The fire engines swept around the corner, with people leaning out of the windows watching them, and the man holding her arm said, "It's down here," and left her. The fire was two houses away; they could see flames behind the top windows, and smoke against the night sky, but in ten minutes it was finished and the fire engines pulled away with an air of martyrdom for hauling out all their equipment to put out a ten-minute fire.

She went back upstairs slowly and with embarrassment, and found Brad and took him home.

"I was so frightened," she said to him when they were safely in bed, "I lost my head completely."

"You should have tried to find someone," he said.

"They wouldn't listen," she insisted. "I kept telling them and they wouldn't listen and then I thought I must have been mistaken. I had some idea of going down to see what was going on."

"Lucky it was no worse," Brad said sleepily.

"I felt trapped," she said. "High up in that old building with a fire; it's like a nightmare. And in a strange city."

"Well, it's all over now," Brad said.

The same faint feeling of insecurity tagged her the next day; she went shopping alone and Brad went off to see hardware, after all. She got on a bus to go downtown and the bus was too full to move when it came time for her to get out. Wedged standing in the aisle she said, "Out, please," and, "Excuse me," and by the time she was loose and near the door the bus had started again and she got off a stop beyond. "No one *listens* to me," she said to herself. "Maybe it's because I'm too polite." In the stores the prices were all too high and the sweaters looked disarmingly like New Hampshire ones. The toys for the children filled her with dismay; they were so obviously for New York children: hideous little parodies of adult life, cash registers, tiny pushcarts with imitation fruit, telephones that really worked (as if there weren't enough phones in New York that really worked), miniature milk bottles in a carrying case. "We get our milk from cows," Margaret told the salesgirl. "My children wouldn't know what these were." She was exaggerating, and felt guilty for a minute, but no one was around to catch her.

She had a picture of small children in the city dressed like their parents, following along with a miniature mechanical civilization, toy cash registers in larger and larger sizes that eased them into the real thing, millions of clattering jerking small imitations that prepared them nicely for taking over the large useless toys their parents lived by. She bought a pair of skis for her son, which she knew would be inadequate for the New Hampshire snow, and a wagon for her daughter inferior to the one Brad could make at home in an hour. Ignoring the toy mailboxes, the small phonographs with special small records, the kiddie cosmetics, she left the store and started home.

She was frankly afraid by now to take a bus; she stood on the corner and waited for a taxi. Glancing down at her feet, she saw a dime on the sidewalk and tried to pick it up, but there were too many people for her to bend down, and she was afraid to shove to make room for fear of being stared at. She put her foot on the dime and then saw a quarter near it, and a nickel. Someone dropped a pocketbook, she thought, and put her other foot on the quarter, stepping quickly to make it look natural; then she saw another dime and another nickel, and a third dime in the gutter. People were passing her, back and forth, all the time, rushing, pushing against her, not looking at her, and she was afraid to get down and start gathering up the money. Other people saw it and went past, and she realized that no one was going to pick it up. They were all embarrassed, or in too much of a hurry, or too crowded. A taxi stopped to let someone off, and she hailed it. She lifted her feet off the dime and the quarter, and left them there when she got into the taxi. This taxi went slowly and bumped as it went; she had begun to notice that the gradual decay was not peculiar to the taxis. The buses were cracking open in unimportant seams, the leather seats broken and stained. The buildings were going, too—in one of the nicest stores there had been a great gaping hole in the tiled foyer, and you walked around it. Corners of the buildings seemed to be crumbling away into fine dust that drifted downward, the granite was eroding unnoticed. Every window she saw on her way uptown seemed to be broken; perhaps every street corner was peppered with small change. The people were moving faster than ever before; a girl in a red hat appeared at the upper side of the taxi window and was gone beyond the lower side before you could see the hat; store windows were so terribly bright because you only caught them for a fraction of a second. The people seemed hurled on in a frantic action that made every hour forty-five minutes long, every day nine hours, every year fourteen days.

Food was so elusively fast, eaten in such a hurry, that you were always hungry, always speeding to a new meal with new people. Everything was imperceptibly quicker every minute. She stepped into the taxi on one side and stepped out the other side at her home; she pressed the fifth-floor button on the elevator and was coming down again, bathed and dressed and ready for dinner with Brad. They went out for dinner and were coming in again, hungry and hurrying to bed in order to get to breakfast with lunch beyond. They had been in New York nine days; tomorrow was Saturday and they were going to Long Island, coming home Sunday, and then Wednesday they were going home, really home. By the time she had thought of it they were on the train to Long Island; the train was broken, the seats torn and the floor dirty; one of the doors wouldn't open and the windows wouldn't shut. Passing through the outskirts of the city, she thought, It's as though everything were traveling so fast that the solid stuff couldn't stand it and were going to pieces under the strain, cornices blowing off and windows caving in. She knew she was afraid to say it truly, afraid to face the knowledge that it was a voluntary neck-breaking speed, a deliberate whirling faster and faster to end in destruction.

On Long Island, their hostess led them into a new piece of New York, a house filled with New York furniture as though on rubber bands, pulled this far, stretched taut, and ready to snap back to the city, to an apartment, as soon as the door was opened and the lease, fully paid, had expired. "We've had this place every year for simply ages," their hostess said. "Otherwise we couldn't have gotten it *possibly* this year."

"It's an awfully nice place," Brad said. "I'm surprised you don't live here all year round."

"Got to get back to the city *some* time," their hostess said, and laughed.

"Not much like New Hampshire," Brad said. He was beginning to be a little homesick, Margaret thought; he wants to yell, just once. Since the fire scare she was apprehensive about large groups of people gathering together; when friends began to drop in after dinner she waited for a while, telling herself they were on the ground floor, she could run right outside, all the windows were open; then she excused herself and went to bed. When Brad came to bed much later she woke up and he said irritably, "We've been playing anagrams. Such crazy people." She said sleepily, "Did you win?" and fell asleep before he told her.

The next morning she and Brad went for a walk while their host and hostess read the Sunday papers. "If you turn to the right outside the door," their hostess said encouragingly, "and walk about three blocks down, you'll come to our beach."

"What do they want with our beach?" their host said. "It's too damn cold to do anything down there."

"They can look at the *water*," their hostess said.

They walked down to the beach; at this time of year it was bare and windswept, yet still nodding hideously under traces of its summer plumage, as though it thought itself warmly inviting. There were occupied houses on the way there, for instance, and a lonely lunchstand was open, bravely advertising hot dogs and root beer. The man in the lunchstand watched them go by, his face cold and unsympathetic. They walked far past him, out of sight of houses, on to a stretch of grey pebbled sand that lay between the grey water on one side and the grey pebbled sand dunes on the other.

"Imagine going swimming here," she said with a shiver. The beach pleased her; it was oddly familiar and reassuring and at the same time that she realized this, the little tune came back to her, bringing a double recollection. The beach was the one where she had lived in imagination, writing for herself dreary love-broken stories where the heroine walked beside the wild waves; the little tune was the symbol of the golden world she escaped into to avoid the everyday dreariness that drove her into writing depressing stories about the beach. She laughed out loud and Brad said, "What on earth's so funny about his Godforsaken landscape?"

"I was just thinking how far away from the city it seems," she said falsely.

The sky and the water and the sand were grey enough to make it feel like late afternoon instead of midmorning; she was tired and wanted to go back, but Brad said suddenly, "Look at that," and she turned and saw a girl running down over the dunes, carrying her hat, and her hair flying behind her.

"Only way to get warm on a day like this," Brad remarked, but Margaret said, "She looks frightened."

The girl saw them and came toward them, slowing down as she approached them. She was eager to reach them but when she came within speaking distance the familiar embarrassment, the not wanting to look like a fool, made her hesitate and look from one to the other of them uncomfortably.

"Do you know where I can find a policeman?" she asked finally.

Brad looked up and down the bare rocky beach and said solemnly, "There don't seem to be any around. Is there something we can do?"

"I don't think so," the girl said. "I really need a policeman."

They go to the police for everything, Margaret thought, these people, these New York people, it's as though they had selected a section of the population to act as problem-solvers, and so no matter what they want they look for a policeman.

"Be glad to help you if we can," Brad said.

The girl hesitated again. "Well, if you *must* know," she said crossly, "there's a leg up there."

They waited politely for the girl to explain, but she only said, "Come *on*, then," and waved to them to follow her. She led them over the dunes to a spot near a small inlet, where the dunes gave way abruptly to an intruding head of water. A leg was lying on the sand near the water, and the girl gestured at it and said, "There," as though it were her own property and they had insisted on having a share.

They walked over to it and Brad bent down gingerly. "It's a leg all right," he said. It looked like part of a wax dummy, a death-white wax leg neatly cut off at top-thigh and again just above the ankle, bent comfortably at the knee and resting on the sand. "It's real," Brad said, his voice slightly different. "You're right about that policeman."

They walked together to the lunchstand and the man listened unenthusiastically while Brad called the police. When the police came they all walked out again to where the leg was lying and Brad gave the police their names and addresses, and then said, "Is it all right to go on home?"

"What the hell you want to hang around for?" the policeman inquired with heavy humor. "You waiting for the rest of him?"

They went back to their host and hostess, talking about the leg, and their host apologized, as though he had been guilty of a breach of taste in allowing his guests to come on a human leg; their hostess said with interest, "There was an arm washed up in Bensonhurst, I've been reading about it."

"One of these killings," the host said.

Upstairs Margaret said abruptly, "I suppose it starts to happen first in the suburbs," and when Brad said, "What starts to happen?" she said hysterically, "People starting to come apart."

In order to reassure their host and hostess about their minding the leg, they stayed until the last afternoon train to New York. Back in their apartment again it seemed to Margaret that the marble in the house lobby had begun to age a little; even in two days there were new perceptible cracks. The elevator seemed a little rusty, and there was a fine film of dust over everything in the apartment. They went to bed feeling uncomfortable, and the next morning Margaret said immediately, "I'm going to stay in today."

"You're not upset about yesterday, are you?"

"Not a bit," Margaret said. "I just want to stay in and rest."

After some discussion Brad decided to go off again by himself; he still had people it was important to see and places he must go in the few days they had left. After breakfast in the Automat Margaret came back alone to the apartment, carrying the mystery story she had bought on the way. She hung up her coat and hat and sat down by the window with the noise and the people far below, looking out at the sky where it was grey beyond the houses across the street.

I'm not going to worry about it, she said to herself, no sense thinking all the time about things like that, spoil your vacation and Brad's too. No sense worrying, people get ideas like that and then worry about them.

The nasty little tune was running through her head again, with its burden of suavity and expensive perfume. The houses across the street were silent and perhaps unoccupied at this time of day; she let her eyes move with the rhythm of the tune, from window to window along one floor. By gliding quickly across two windows, she could make one line of the tune fit one floor of windows, and then a quick breath and a drop down to the next floor; it had the same number of windows and the tune had the same number of beats, and then the next floor and the next. She stopped suddenly when it seemed to her that the windowsill she had just passed had soundlessly crumpled and fallen into fine sand; when she looked back it was there as before but then it seemed to be the windowsill above and to the right, and finally a corner of the roof.

No sense worrying, she told herself, forcing her eyes down to the street, stop thinking about things all the time. Looking down at the street for long made her dizzy and she stood up and went into the small bedroom of the apartment. She had made the bed before going out to breakfast, like any good housewife, but now she deliberately took it apart, stripping the blankets and sheets off one by one, and then she made it again, taking a long time over the corners and smoothing out every wrinkle. "*That*'s done," she said when she was through, and went back to the window. When she looked across the street the tune started again, window to window, sills dissolving and falling downward. She leaned forward and looked down at her own window, something she had never thought of before, down to the sill. It was partly eaten away; when she touched the stone a few crumbs rolled off and fell.

It was eleven o'clock; Brad was looking at blowtorches by now and would not be back before one, if even then. She thought of writing a letter home, but the impulse left her before she found paper and pen. Then it occurred to her that she might take a nap, a thing she had never done in the morning in her life, and she went in and lay down on the bed. Lying down, she felt the building shaking.

No sense worrying, she told herself again, as though it were a charm against witches, and got up and found her coat and hat and put them on. I'll just get some cigarettes and some letter paper, she thought, just run down to the corner. Panic caught her going down in the elevator; it went too fast, and when she stepped out in the lobby it was only the people standing around who kept her from running. As it was, she went quickly out of the building and into the street. For a minute she hesitated, wanting to go back. The cars were going past so rapidly, the people hurrying as always, but the panic of the elevator drove her on finally. She went to the corner, and, following the people flying along ahead, ran out into the street, to hear a horn almost overhead and a shout from behind her, and the noise of brakes. She ran blindly on and reached the other side where she stopped and looked around. The truck was going on its appointed way around the corner, the people going past on either side of her, parting to go around her where she stood.

No one even noticed me, she thought with reassurance, everyone who saw me has gone by long ago. She went into the drugstore ahead of her and asked the man for cigarettes; the apartment now seemed safer to her than the street—she could walk up the stairs. Coming out of the store and walking to the corner, she kept as close to the buildings as possible, refusing to give way to the rightful traffic coming out of the doorways. On the corner she looked carefully at the light; it was green, but it looked as though it were going to change. Always safer to wait, she thought, don't want to walk into another truck.

People pushed past her and some were caught in the middle of the street when the light changed. One woman, more cowardly than the rest, turned and ran back to the curb, but the others stood in the middle of the street, leaning forward and then backward according to the traffic moving past them on both sides. One got to the farther curb in a brief break in the line of cars, the others were a fraction of a second too late and waited. Then the light changed again and as the cars slowed down Margaret put a foot on the street to go, but a taxi swinging wildly around her corner frightened her back and she stood on the curb again. By the time the taxi had gone the light was due to change again and she thought, I can wait once more, no sense getting caught out in the middle. A man beside her tapped his foot impatiently for the light to change back; two girls came past her and walked out into the street a few steps to wait, moving back a little when cars came too close, talking busily all the time. I ought to stay right with them, Margaret thought, but then they moved back against her and the light changed and the man next to her charged into the street and the two girls in front waited a minute and then moved slowly on, still talking, and Margaret started to follow and then decided to wait. A crowd of people formed around her suddenly; they had come off a bus and were crossing here, and she had a sudden feeling of being jammed in the center and forced out into the street when all of them moved as one with the light changing, and she elbowed her way desperately out of the crowd and went off to lean against a building and wait. It seemed to her that people passing were beginning to look at her. What do they think of me, she wondered, and stood up straight as though she were waiting for someone. She looked at her watch and frowned, and then thought, What a fool I must look like, no one here ever saw me before, they all go by too fast. She went back to the curb again but the green light was just changing to red and she thought, I'll go back to the drugstore and have a coke, no sense going back to that apartment.

The man looked at her unsurprised in the drugstore and she sat and ordered a coke but suddenly as she was drinking it the panic caught her again and she thought of the people who had been with her when she first started to cross the street, blocks away by now, having tried and made perhaps a dozen lights while she had hesitated at the first; people by now a mile or so downtown, because they had been going steadily while she had been trying to gather her courage. She paid the man quickly, restrained an impulse to say that there was nothing wrong with the coke, she just had to get back, that was all, and she hurried down to the corner again.

The minute the light changes, she told herself firmly; there's no sense. The light changed before she was ready and in the minute before she collected herself traffic turning the corner overwhelmed her and she shrank back against the curb. She looked longingly at the cigar store on the opposite corner, with her apartment house beyond; she wondered, How do people ever manage to get there, and knew that by wondering, by admitting a doubt, she was lost. The light changed and she looked at it with hatred, a dumb thing, turning back and forth, back and forth, with no purpose and no meaning. Looking to either side of her slyly, to see if anyone were watching, she stepped quietly backward, one step, two, until she was well away from the curb. Back in the drugstore again she waited for some sign of recognition from the clerk and saw none; he regarded her with the same apathy as he had the first time. He gestured without interest at the telephone; he doesn't care, she thought, it doesn't matter to him who I call.

She had no time to feel like a fool, because they answered the phone immediately and agreeably and found him right away. When he answered the phone, his voice sounding surprised and matter-of-fact, she could only say miserably, "I'm in the drugstore on the corner. Come and get me."

"What's the matter?" He was not anxious to come.

"Please come and get me," she said into the black mouthpiece that might or might not tell him, "please come and get me, Brad. *Please.*"

‡

# MEN WITH THEIR BIG SHOES

It was young Mrs. Hart's first summer living in the country, and her first year being married and the mistress of a house; she was going to have her first baby soon, and it was the first time she had ever had anyone, or thought of having anyone, who could remotely be described as a maid. Young Mrs. Hart spent almost hours every day, while she was resting as the doctor told her to, in peacefully congratulating herself. When she was sitting in the rocking chair on the front porch she could look down the quiet street with the trees and gardens and kind people who smiled at her as they passed; or she could turn her head and look through the wide windows in her own house, into the pretty living-room with the chintz curtains and matching slip-covers and maple furniture; she could raise her eyes a little and look at the ruffled white curtains on the bedroom windows. It was a real house: the milkman left milk there every morning, the brightly painted pots in a row along the porch railing held real plants which grew and needed regular watering; you could cook on the real stove in the kitchen, and Mrs. Anderson was always complaining about the shoe marks on the clean floors, just like a real maid.

"It's the men who make dirt on the floor," Mrs. Anderson would say, regarding the print of a heel. "A woman, you watch them, she always puts her feet down quiet. Men with their big shoes." And she would flick carelessly at the mark with the dustcloth.

Although Mrs. Hart was unreasonably afraid of Mrs. Anderson, she had heard and read so much about how all housewives these days were intimidated by their domestic help that she was never surprised at first by her own timid uneasiness; Mrs. Anderson's belligerent authority, moreover, seemed to follow naturally from a knowledge of canning and burnt-sugar gravy and setting yeast rolls out to rise. When Mrs. Anderson, all elbows and red face, her hair pulled disagreeably tight, had presented herself first at the back door with an offer to help, Mrs. Hart had accepted blindly, caught between unwashed windows in a litter of unpacking and dust; Mrs. Anderson had started correctly with the kitchen, and made Mrs. Hart a hot cup of tea first thing; "You can't afford to get too tired," she said, eyeing Mrs. Hart's waist, "you got to be careful right along."

By the time Mrs. Hart discovered that Mrs. Anderson never got anything quite clean, never completely managed to get anything back where it belonged, it was incredible to think of doing anything about it. Mrs. Anderson's thumbprints were on all the windows and Mrs. Hart's morning cup of tea was a regular institution; Mrs. Hart put the water on to boil directly after breakfast and Mrs. Anderson made them each a cup of tea when she came at nine. "You need a hot cup of tea to start your day off right," she said amiably every morning, "it settles your stomach for the day."

Mrs. Hart never allowed herself to think further about Mrs. Anderson than to feel comfortably proud of having all the housework done for her ("a regular *treasure*," she wrote to her girl friends in New York, "and she fusses over me like I was actually *her* baby!"); it was not until Mrs. Anderson had been coming dutifully every morning for over a month that Mrs. Hart recognized with sickening conviction that the faint small uneasiness was justified.

It was a warm sunny morning, the first after a week of rain, and Mrs. Hart put on an especially pretty house dress—washed and ironed by Mrs. Anderson—and made her husband a soft-boiled egg for his breakfast, and went down the front walk with him to wave good-bye till he got to the corner and the bus which took him to his job at the bank in the neighboring town. Coming back up the walk to her house, Mrs. Hart admired the sunlight on the green shutters, and spoke affectionately to her next-door neighbor, who was out already sweeping her porch. Pretty soon I'll have my baby out in the garden in his play pen, Mrs. Hart thought, and left the front door open behind her for the sun to come in and soak into the floor. When she came into the kitchen, Mrs. Anderson was sitting at the table and the tea was poured.

"Good morning," Mrs. Hart said. "Isn't it a beautiful day?"

"Morning," Mrs. Anderson said. She waved at the tea. "I knew you was just out front so I got everything all ready. Can't start the day off without your cup of tea."

"I was beginning to think the sun would never come out again," Mrs. Hart said. She sat down and pulled her cup toward her. "It's so lovely to be dry and warm again."

"It settles your stomach, tea does," Mrs. Anderson said. "I already put the sugar in. You'll be having trouble with your stomach right along now."

"You know," Mrs. Hart said happily, "last summer about this time I was still working in New York and I didn't think Bill and I were *ever* going to get married. And *now* look at me," she added, and laughed.

"You never know what's going to happen to you," Mrs. Anderson said. "When things look worst, you'll either die or get better. I used to have a neighbor was always saying that." She sighed and rose, taking her cup with her to the sink. "Of course some of us never get much good coming along," she said.

"And then everything happened in about two weeks," Mrs. Hart said. "Bill got this job up here and the girls at the office gave us a waffle iron."

"It's up on the shelf," Mrs. Anderson said. She reached out for Mrs. Hart's cup. "You sit still," she said. "You'll never have another chance to take it easy like this."

"I can't remember to sit still all the time," Mrs. Hart said. "Everything's too exciting."

"It's for your own good," Mrs. Anderson said. "I'm only thinking of you."

"You've been very nice already," Mrs. Hart said dutifully, "coming to help every morning like this. And taking such good care of me."

"I don't want thanks," Mrs. Anderson said. "You just come through all right, that's all I want to see."

"But I really don't know what to do without you," Mrs. Hart said. That ought to be enough for today, she thought suddenly, and laughed aloud at the idea of a portion of gratitude doled out every morning to Mrs. Anderson, like a bonus on her hourly wage. It's true, though, she thought; I have to say it every day, sooner or later.

"You laughing about something?" Mrs. Anderson said, half-turning with her hard red wrists braced against the sink. "I say something funny?"

"I was just thinking," Mrs. Hart said quickly, "thinking about the girls I used to be in the office with. They'd be so jealous if they could see me now."

"Never know when they're well off," Mrs. Anderson said.

Mrs. Hart reached out and touched the yellow curtain at the window beside her, thinking of the one-room apartments in New York and the dark office. "I wish *I* could be cheerful these days," Mrs. Anderson went on.

Mrs. Hart dropped her hand quickly from the curtain and turned to smile sympathetically at Mrs. Anderson. "I know," she murmured.

"You never know how bad it can be," Mrs. Anderson said. She jerked her head toward the back door. "*He* was at it again. All night long." By now Mrs. Hart knew how to tell whether "*he*" meant Mr. Anderson or Mr. Hart; a gesture of Mrs. Anderson's head toward the back door and the path she took home every day meant Mr. Anderson; the same gesture toward the front door where every night Mrs. Hart met her husband meant Mr. Hart. "Not a minute's sleep for *me*," Mrs. Anderson was saying.

"Isn't that a shame," Mrs. Hart said. She stood up quickly and started for the back door. "Dish towels on the line," she explained.

"I'll do it, later," Mrs. Anderson said. "Cursing and yelling," she went on, "I thought I was going crazy. 'Why don't you go on and get out?' he says to me. Went over and opened the door wide as it would go and yelled so's all the neighbors could hear him. 'Why don't you get out?' he says."

"Terrible," Mrs. Hart said, her hand on the back door knob.

"Thirty-seven years," Mrs. Anderson said. She shook her head. "And he wants me to get out." She watched Mrs. Hart light a cigarette and said, "You shouldn't smoke. You'll likely be sorry if you go on smoking like that. That's why I never had any children," she went on. "What would I do, him acting like that with children around listening?"

Mrs. Hart walked across to the stove and looked into the teapot. "Believe I'll have another cup," she said. "Will you have another, Mrs. Anderson?"

"Gives me heartburn," Mrs. Anderson said. She put the

freshly washed cup back on the table. "I just washed this," she said, "but it's your cup. And your house. I guess you can do what you want to."

Mrs. Hart laughed and brought the teapot over to the table. Mrs. Anderson watched her pour the tea and then took the teapot away. "I'll just wash this," she said, "before you decide to drink any more." She dropped her voice. "Too much liquid spoils the kidneys."

"I always drink a lot of tea and coffee," Mrs. Hart said.

Mrs. Anderson looked at the dried dishes standing on the drain of the sink, and then picked up three glasses in each great hand. "You sure had a lot of dirty glasses around this morning."

"I was just too tired last night to clean up," Mrs. Hart said. Besides, she thought, cleaning up is what I pay *her* for; and she added, making her voice light, "So I just left everything for you."

"It's my job to clean up after people," Mrs. Anderson said. "Someone always has to do the dirty work for the rest. You have a lot of company?"

"Some people my husband knows in town," Mrs. Hart said. "About six altogether."

"He shouldn't bring his friends home with you like *that*," Mrs. Anderson said.

Mrs. Hart thought of the pleasant chatter about the New York theatre and the local roadhouse where they all might go dancing soon, and the pretty compliments on her house, and showing the baby things to the two other young wives, and sighed. She had lost track of what Mrs. Anderson was saying.

"—Right in front of his own wife," Mrs. Anderson finished,

and moved her head significantly toward the front door. "He do much drinking?"

"No, not much," Mrs. Hart said.

Mrs. Anderson nodded. "I know what you mean," she said. "You watch them taking one drink after another and you can't think of any way to tell them to stop. And then something makes them mad and first thing you know they're telling you to go on and get out." She nodded again. "There's nothing any woman can do but make sure when she does have to get out she sure has some place to go."

Mrs. Hart said carefully, "Now, Mrs. Anderson, I don't really think that all husbands—"

"You only been married a year," Mrs. Anderson said dismally, "and no one that's older around to tell you."

Mrs. Hart lit a second cigarette from the end of the first. "I'm really not at all worried about my husband's drinking," she said formally.

Mrs. Anderson stopped, holding a pile of clean plates. "Other women?" she asked. "Is *that* what it is?"

"What on *earth* makes you say that?" Mrs. Hart demanded. "Bill would no more *look*—"

"You need someone to be looking after you, times like this," Mrs. Anderson said. "Don't think I don't know; you just want to tell someone about it all. I guess all men treat their wives the same, only some of them are drinkers and some of them throw their money away on gambling and some of them chase every young girl they see." She laughed her abrupt laugh. "And some not so young, if you ask the wives," she said. "If most women knew how their husbands were going to turn out, there'd be less marrying going on."

"I think a successful marriage is the woman's responsibility," Mrs. Hart said.

"Mrs. Martin now, down at the grocery, she was telling me, the other day, some of the things *her* husband used to do before he died," Mrs. Anderson said. "You'd never suspect what some men do." She looked thoughtfully at the back door. "Some's worse than others, though. She thinks you're real sweet, Mrs. Martin does."

"That's nice of her," Mrs. Hart said.

"I didn't say nothing about *him*," Mrs. Anderson said, her head moving toward the front door. "I don't mention any names, not where anybody'd think I know the people."

Mrs. Hart thought of Mrs. Martin, keen-eyed and shrill, watching other people's groceries ("Two loaves of whole wheat today, Mrs. Hart? Company tonight, maybe?") "I think she's such a nice person," Mrs. Hart said, wanting to add, You tell her I said so.

"I'm not saying she isn't," Mrs. Anderson said grimly. "You just don't want to let her figure out anything's wrong."

"I'm sure—" Mrs. Hart began.

"I *told* her," Mrs. Anderson said, "I said I was sure Mr. Hart never did any running around's far as I knew. Nor drinking like some. I said I felt like you might be my own daughter sometimes and no man was going to mistreat you while I was around."

"I wish," Mrs. Hart began again, a quick fear touching her; her kind neighbors watching her beneath their friendliness, looking out quietly from behind curtains, watching Bill, perhaps? "I don't think people ought to talk about other people," she said desperately, "I mean, I don't think it's fair to say things when you can't *know* for sure."

Mrs. Anderson laughed again suddenly and went over to open the mop closet. "You don't want to let anything scare you," she said, "not right now. Will I do the living-room this morning? I could get the little rugs out to air in the sun. It's just that *he*—" the back door "—got me all upset. You know."

"I'm sorry," Mrs. Hart said. "Isn't that a shame."

"Mrs. Martin said why didn't I come live with you folks," Mrs. Anderson said, searching violently in the mop closet, her voice sounding muffled and dusty. "Mrs. Martin was saying a young woman like you, just starting out, always needs a friend around."

Mrs. Hart looked down at her fingers twisting the handle of the cup; she had only drunk half her tea. It's too late now for me to walk into another room, she thought; I can always say Bill would never allow it. "I met Mrs. Martin in town a few days ago," she said. "She was wearing an awfully good-looking blue coat." She smoothed her house dress with her hand, and added irritably, "I wish I could get into a decent dress again."

" 'Why don't you get out?' he says to me." Mrs. Anderson backed out of the mop closet with a dustpan in one hand and a cleaning cloth in the other. "Drunk and cursing so's all the neighbors could hear. 'Why don't you get out?' I thought sure you'd hear him even up here."

"I'm sure he couldn't mean it," Mrs. Hart said, trying to make her voice sound final.

"*You* wouldn't stand for it," Mrs. Anderson said. She put the dustpan and cloth down and came over and sat down at the table opposite Mrs. Hart. "Mrs. Martin was thinking if you wanted me to I could come right into your spare room. Do all the cooking."

"You could," Mrs. Hart said amiably, "except that I'm going to put the baby in there."

"We'd put the baby in your room," Mrs. Anderson said. She laughed and gave Mrs. Hart's hand a push. "Don't worry," she said, "I'd keep out of your way. Well, and if you wanted to put the baby in with me then I could get up at night to feed it for you. Guess I could take care of a baby all right."

Mrs. Hart smiled cheerfully back at Mrs. Anderson. "I'd love to, of course," she said. "Some day. Right now of *course* Bill would never let me do it."

"Of course not," Mrs. Anderson said. "The men never do, do they? I told Mrs. Martin down at the grocery, she's the nicest little thing in the world, I said, but her husband wouldn't let the scrubwoman come live with them."

"Why, Mrs. Anderson," Mrs. Hart said, looking horrified, "saying things like that about yourself!"

"And another woman, one who's older and knows a little more," Mrs. Anderson said. "She might see a little more, too, maybe."

Mrs. Hart, her fingers tight on the teacup, caught a quick picture of Mrs. Martin, leaning comfortably across the counter ("I see you've got a new star boarder, Mrs. Hart. Mrs. Anderson'll see that you're taken good care of!"). And her neighbors, their frozen faces regarding her as she walked down to meet Bill at the bus; the girls in New York, reading her letters together and envying her ("Such a perfect *jewel*— she's going to live with us and do *all* the work!"). Looking up at Mrs. Anderson's knowing smile across the table, Mrs. Hart realized with a sudden unalterable conviction that she was lost.

‡

# THE TOOTH

THE BUS was waiting, panting heavily at the curb in front
of the small bus station, its great blue-and-silver bulk glittering
in the moonlight. There were only a few people interested in
the bus, and at that time of night no one passing on the sidewalk: the one movie theatre in town had finished its show
and closed its doors an hour before, and all the movie patrons
had been to the drugstore for ice cream and gone on home;
now the drugstore was closed and dark, another silent doorway in the long midnight street. The only town lights were
the street lights, the lights in the all-night lunchstand across
the street, and the one remaining counter lamp in the bus
station where the girl sat in the ticket office with her hat and
coat on, only waiting for the New York bus to leave before
she went home to bed.

Standing on the sidewalk next to the open door of the bus,
Clara Spencer held her husband's arm nervously. "I feel so
funny," she said.

"Are you all right?" he asked. "Do you think I ought to
go with you?"

"No, of course not," she said. "I'll be all right." It was hard
for her to talk because of her swollen jaw; she kept a handkerchief pressed to her face and held hard to her husband.
"Are you sure *you*'ll be all right?" she asked. "I'll be back
tomorrow night at the latest. Or else I'll call."

"Everything will be fine," he said heartily. "By tomorrow
noon it'll all be gone. Tell the dentist if there's anything
wrong I can come right down."

"I feel so funny," she said. "Light-headed, and sort of dizzy."

"That's because of the dope," he said. "All that codeine, and the whisky, and nothing to eat all day."

She giggled nervously. "I couldn't comb my hair, my hand shook so. I'm glad it's dark."

"Try to sleep in the bus," he said. "Did you take a sleeping pill?"

"Yes," she said. They were waiting for the bus driver to finish his cup of coffee in the lunchstand; they could see him through the glass window, sitting at the counter, taking his time. "I feel so *funny*," she said.

"You know, Clara," he made his voice very weighty, as though if he spoke more seriously his words would carry more conviction and be therefore more comforting, "you know, I'm glad you're going down to New York to have Zimmerman take care of this. I'd never forgive myself if it turned out to be something serious and I let you go to this butcher up here."

"It's just a *toothache*," Clara said uneasily, "nothing very serious about a *toothache*."

"You can't tell," he said. "It might be abscessed or something; I'm sure he'll have to pull it."

"Don't even talk like that," she said, and shivered.

"Well, it looks pretty bad," he said soberly, as before. "Your face so swollen, and all. Don't you worry."

"I'm not worrying," she said. "I just feel as if I were all tooth. Nothing else."

The bus driver got up from the stool and walked over to pay his check. Clara moved toward the bus, and her husband said, "Take your time, you've got plenty of time."

"I just feel funny," Clara said.

"Listen," her husband said, "that tooth's been bothering

you off and on for years; at least six or seven times since I've known you you've had trouble with that tooth. It's about time something was done. You had a toothache on our honeymoon," he finished accusingly.

"Did I?" Clara said. "You know," she went on, and laughed, "I was in such a hurry I didn't dress properly. I have on old stockings and I just dumped everything into my good pocketbook."

"Are you sure you have enough money?" he said.

"Almost twenty-five dollars," Clara said. "I'll be home tomorrow."

"Wire if you need more," he said. The bus driver appeared in the doorway of the lunchroom. "Don't worry," he said.

"Listen," Clara said suddenly, "are you *sure* you'll be all right? Mrs. Lang will be over in the morning in time to make breakfast, and Johnny doesn't need to go to school if things are too mixed up."

"I know," he said.

"Mrs. Lang," she said, checking on her fingers. "I called Mrs. Lang, I left the grocery order on the kitchen table, you can have the cold tongue for lunch and in case I don't get back Mrs. Lang will give you dinner. The cleaner ought to come about four o'clock, I won't be back so give him your brown suit and it doesn't matter if you forget but be sure to empty the pockets."

"Wire if you need more money," he said. "Or call. I'll stay home tomorrow so you can call at home."

"Mrs. Lang will take care of the baby," she said.

"Or you can wire," he said.

The bus driver came across the street and stood by the entrance to the bus.

"Okay?" the bus driver said.

"Good-bye," Clara said to her husband.

"You'll feel all right tomorrow," her husband said. "It's only a toothache."

"I'm fine," Clara said. "Don't you worry." She got on the bus and then stopped, with the bus driver waiting behind her. "Milkman," she said to her husband. "Leave a note telling him we want eggs."

"I will," her husband said. "Good-bye."

"Good-bye," Clara said. She moved on into the bus and behind her the driver swung into his seat. The bus was nearly empty and she went far back and sat down at the window outside which her husband waited. "Good-bye," she said to him through the glass, "take care of yourself."

"Good-bye," he said, waving violently.

The bus stirred, groaned, and pulled itself forward. Clara turned her head to wave good-bye once more and then lay back against the heavy soft seat. Good Lord, she thought, what a thing to do! Outside, the familiar street slipped past, strange and dark and seen, unexpectedly, from the unique station of a person leaving town, going away on a bus. It isn't as though it's the first time I've ever been to New York, Clara thought indignantly, it's the whisky and the codeine and the sleeping pill and the toothache. She checked hastily to see if her codeine tablets were in her pocketbook; they had been standing, along with the aspirin and a glass of water, on the dining-room sideboard, but somewhere in the lunatic flight from her home she must have picked them up, because they were in her pocketbook now, along with the twenty-odd dollars and her compact and comb and lipstick. She could tell from the feel of the lipstick that she had brought the old, nearly finished one, not the new one that was a darker shade and had cost two-fifty. There was a run in her stocking and a hole in the toe that she never noticed at home wearing her old comfortable shoes, but which was now suddenly and disagreeably apparent inside her best walking shoes. Well, she thought, I can buy new stockings in New York tomorrow, after the tooth is fixed, after everything's all right. She put her tongue cautiously on the tooth and was rewarded with a split-second crash of pain.

The bus stopped at a red light and the driver got out of his seat and came back toward her. "Forgot to get your ticket before," he said.

"I guess I was a little rushed at the last minute," she said. She found the ticket in her coat pocket and gave it to him. "When do we get to New York?" she asked.

"Five-fifteen," he said. "Plenty of time for breakfast. One-way ticket?"

"I'm coming back by train," she said, without seeing why she had to tell him, except that it was late at night and people isolated together in some strange prison like a bus had to be more friendly and communicative than at other times.

"Me, I'm coming back by bus," he said, and they both laughed, she painfully because of her swollen face. When he went back to his seat far away at the front of the bus she lay back peacefully against the seat. She could feel the sleeping pill pulling at her; the throb of the toothache was distant now, and mingled with the movement of the bus, a steady beat like her heartbeat which she could hear louder and louder, going on through the night. She put her head back and her feet up, discreetly covered with her skirt, and fell asleep without saying good-bye to the town.

She opened her eyes once and they were moving almost silently through the darkness. Her tooth was pulsing steadily

and she turned her cheek against the cool back of the seat
in weary resignation. There was a thin line of lights along the
ceiling of the bus and no other light. Far ahead of her in the
bus she could see the other people sitting; the driver, so far
away as to be only a tiny figure at the end of a telescope,
was straight at the wheel, seemingly awake. She fell back
into her fantastic sleep.

She woke up later because the bus had stopped, the end of
that silent motion through the darkness so positive a shock
that it woke her stunned, and it was a minute before the ache
began again. People were moving along the aisle of the bus
and the driver, turning around, said, "Fifteen minutes." She
got up and followed everyone else out, all but her eyes still
asleep, her feet moving without awareness. They were stopped
beside an all-night restaurant, lonely and lighted on the vacant
road. Inside, it was warm and busy and full of people. She saw
a seat at the end of the counter and sat down, not aware that
she had fallen asleep again when someone sat down next to
her and touched her arm. When she looked around foggily he
said, "Traveling far?"

"Yes," she said.

He was wearing a blue suit and he looked tall; she could
not focus her eyes to see any more.

"You want coffee?" he asked.

She nodded and he pointed to the counter in front of her
where a cup of coffee sat steaming.

"Drink it quickly," he said.

She sipped at it delicately; she may have put her face down
and tasted it without lifting the cup. The strange man was
talking.

"Even farther than Samarkand," he was saying, "and the
waves ringing on the shore like bells."

"Okay, folks," the bus driver said, and she gulped quickly at the coffee, drank enough to get her back into the bus.

When she sat down in her seat again the strange man sat down beside her. It was so dark in the bus that the lights from the restaurant were unbearably glaring and she closed her eyes. When her eyes were shut, before she fell asleep, she was closed in alone with the toothache.

"The flutes play all night," the strange man said, "and the stars are as big as the moon and the moon is as big as a lake."

As the bus started up again they slipped back into the darkness and only the thin thread of lights along the ceiling of the bus held them together, brought the back of the bus where she sat along with the front of the bus where the driver sat and the people sitting there so far away from her. The lights tied them together and the strange man next to her was saying, "Nothing to do all day but lie under the trees."

Inside the bus, traveling on, she was nothing; she was passing the trees and the occasional sleeping houses, and she was in the bus but she was between here and there, joined tenuously to the bus driver by a thread of lights, being carried along without effort of her own.

"My name is Jim," the strange man said.

She was so deeply asleep that she stirred uneasily without knowledge, her forehead against the window, the darkness moving along beside her.

Then again that numbing shock, and, driven awake, she said, frightened, "What's happened?"

"It's all right," the strange man—Jim—said immediately. "Come along."

She followed him out of the bus, into the same restaurant, seemingly, but when she started to sit down at the same seat at the end of the counter he took her hand and led her to a table. "Go and wash your face," he said. "Come back here afterward."

She went into the ladies' room and there was a girl standing there powdering her nose. Without turning around the girl said, "Cost's a nickel. Leave the door fixed so's the next one won't have to pay."

The door was wedged so it would not close, with half a match folder in the lock. She left it the same way and went back to the table where Jim was sitting.

"What do you want?" she said, and he pointed to another cup of coffee and a sandwich. "Go ahead," he said.

While she was eating her sandwich she heard his voice, musical and soft, "And while we were sailing past the island we heard a voice calling us. . . ."

Back in the bus Jim said, "Put your head on my shoulder now, and go to sleep."

"I'm all right," she said.

"No," Jim said. "Before, your head was rattling against the window."

Once more she slept, and once more the bus stopped and she woke frightened, and Jim brought her again to a restaurant and more coffee. Her tooth came alive then, and with one hand pressing her cheek she searched through the pockets of her coat and then through her pocketbook until she found the little bottle of codeine pills and she took two while Jim watched her.

She was finishing her coffee when she heard the sound of the bus motor and she started up suddenly, hurrying, and with Jim holding her arm she fled back into the dark shelter of her seat. The bus was moving forward when she realized that she had left her bottle of codeine pills sitting on the table in the restaurant and now she was at the mercy of her tooth. For a minute she stared back at the lights of the restaurant through the bus window and then she put her head on Jim's shoulder and he was saying as she fell asleep, "The sand is so white it looks like snow, but it's hot, even at night it's hot under your feet."

Then they stopped for the last time, and Jim brought her out of the bus and they stood for a minute in New York together. A woman passing them in the station said to the man following her with suitcases, "We're just on time, it's five-fifteen."

"I'm going to the dentist," she said to Jim.

"I know," he said. "I'll watch out for you."

He went away, although she did not see him go. She thought to watch for his blue suit going through the door, but there was nothing.

I ought to have thanked him, she thought stupidly, and went slowly into the station restaurant, where she ordered coffee again. The counter man looked at her with the worn sympathy of one who has spent a long night watching people get off and on buses. "Sleepy?" he asked.

"Yes," she said.

She discovered after a while that the bus station joined Pennsylvania Terminal and she was able to get into the main waiting-room and find a seat on one of the benches by the time she fell asleep again.

Then someone shook her rudely by the shoulder and said, "What train you taking, lady, it's nearly seven." She sat up and saw her pocketbook on her lap, her feet neatly crossed, a clock glaring into her face. She said, "Thank you," and got up and walked blindly past the benches and got on to the escalator. Someone got on immediately behind her and touched her arm; she turned and it was Jim. "The grass is so green and so soft," he said, smiling, "and the water of the river is so cool."

She stared at him tiredly. When the escalator reached the top she stepped off and started to walk to the street she saw ahead. Jim came along beside her and his voice went on, "The sky is bluer than anything you've ever seen, and the songs. . . ."

She stepped quickly away from him and thought that people were looking at her as they passed. She stood on the corner waiting for the light to change and Jim came swiftly up to her and then away. "Look," he said as he passed, and he held out a handful of pearls.

Across the street there was a restaurant, just opening. She went in and sat down at a table, and a waitress was standing beside her frowning. "You was asleep," the waitress said accusingly.

"I'm very sorry," she said. It was morning. "Poached eggs and coffee, please."

It was a quarter to eight when she left the restaurant, and she thought, if I take a bus, and go straight downtown now, I can sit in the drugstore across the street from the dentist's office and have more coffee until about eight-thirty and then go into the dentist's when it opens and he can take me first.

The buses were beginning to fill up; she got into the first bus that came along and could not find a seat. She wanted to go to Twenty-third Street, and got a seat just as they were passing Twenty-sixth Street; when she woke she was so far downtown that it took her nearly half-an-hour to find a bus and get back to Twenty-third.

At the corner of Twenty-third Street, while she was waiting

for the light to change, she was caught up in a crowd of people, and when they crossed the street and separated to go different directions someone fell into step beside her. For a minute she walked on without looking up, staring resentfully at the sidewalk, her tooth burning her, and then she looked up, but there was no blue suit among the people pressing by on either side.

When she turned into the office building where her dentist was, it was still very early morning. The doorman in the office building was freshly shaven and his hair was combed; he held the door open briskly, as at five o'clock he would be sluggish, his hair faintly out of place. She went in through the door with a feeling of achievement; she had come successfully from one place to another, and this was the end of her journey and her objective.

The clean white nurse sat at the desk in the office; her eyes took in the swollen cheek, the tired shoulders, and she said, "You poor thing, you look worn out."

"I have a toothache." The nurse half-smiled, as though she were still waiting for the day when someone would come in and say, "My feet hurt." She stood up into the professional sunlight. "Come right in," she said. "We won't make you wait."

There was sunlight on the headrest of the dentist's chair, on the round white table, on the drill bending its smooth chromium head. The dentist smiled with the same tolerance as the nurse; perhaps all human ailments were contained in the teeth, and he could fix them if people would only come to him in time. The nurse said smoothly, "I'll get her file, doctor. We thought we'd better bring her right in."

She felt, while they were taking an X-ray, that there was nothing in her head to stop the malicious eye of the camera, as though the camera would look through her and photograph the nails in the wall next to her, or the dentist's cuff buttons, or the small thin bones of the dentist's instruments; the dentist said, "Extraction," regretfully to the nurse, and the nurse said, "Yes, doctor, I'll call them right away."

Her tooth, which had brought her here unerringly, seemed now the only part of her to have any identity. It seemed to have had its picture taken without her; it was the important creature which must be recorded and examined and gratified; she was only its unwilling vehicle, and only as such was she of interest to the dentist and the nurse, only as the bearer of her tooth was she worth their immediate and practised attention. The dentist handed her a slip of paper with the picture of a full set of teeth drawn on it; her living tooth was checked with a black mark, and across the top of the paper was written "Lower molar; extraction."

"Take this slip," the dentist said, "and go right up to the address on this card; it's a surgeon dentist. They'll take care of you there."

"What will they do?" she said. Not the question she wanted to ask, not: What about me? or, How far down do the roots go?

"They'll take that tooth out," the dentist said testily, turning away. "Should have been done years ago."

I've stayed too long, she thought, he's tired of my tooth. She got up out of the dentist chair and said, "Thank you. Good-bye."

"Good-bye," the dentist said. At the last minute he smiled at her, showing her his full white teeth, all in perfect control.

"Are you all right? Does it bother you too much?" the nurse asked.

"I'm all right."

"I can give you some codeine tablets," the nurse said. "We'd rather you didn't take anything right now, of course, but I think I could let you have them if the tooth is really bad."

"No," she said, remembering her little bottle of codeine pills on the table of a restaurant between here and there. "No, it doesn't bother me too much."

"Well," the nurse said, "good luck."

She went down the stairs and out past the doorman; in the fifteen minutes she had been upstairs he had lost a little of his pristine morningness, and his bow was just a fraction smaller than before.

"Taxi?" he asked, and, remembering the bus down to Twenty-third Street, she said, "Yes."

Just as the doorman came back from the curb, bowing to the taxi he seemed to believe he had invented, she thought a hand waved to her from the crowd across the street.

She read the address on the card the dentist had given her and repeated it carefully to the taxi driver. With the card and the little slip of paper with "Lower molar" written on it and her tooth identified so clearly, she sat without moving, her hands still around the papers, her eyes almost closed. She thought she must have been asleep again when the taxi stopped suddenly, and the driver, reaching around to open the door, said, "Here we are, lady." He looked at her curiously.

"I'm going to have a tooth pulled," she said.

"Jesus," the taxi driver said. She paid him and he said, "Good luck," as he slammed the door.

This was a strange building, the entrance flanked by medical signs carved in stone; the doorman here was faintly professional, as though he were competent to prescribe if she did not care to go any farther. She went past him, going straight ahead until an elevator opened its door to her. In the elevator she showed the elevator man the card and he said, "Seventh floor."

She had to back up in the elevator for a nurse to wheel in an old lady in a wheel chair. The old lady was calm and restful, sitting there in the elevator with a rug over her knees; she said, "Nice day" to the elevator operator and he said, "Good to see the sun," and then the old lady lay back in her chair and the nurse straightened the rug around her knees and said, "Now we're not going to worry," and the old lady said irritably, "Who's worrying?"

They got out at the fourth floor. The elevator went on up and then the operator said, "Seven," and the elevator stopped and the door opened.

"Straight down the hall and to your left," the operator said.

There were closed doors on either side of the hall. Some of them said "DDS," some of them said "Clinic," some of them said "X-Ray." One of them, looking wholesome and friendly and somehow most comprehensible, said "Ladies." Then she turned to the left and found a door with the name on the card and she opened it and went in. There was a nurse sitting behind a glass window, almost as in a bank, and potted palms in tubs in the corners of the waiting room, and new magazines and comfortable chairs. The nurse behind the glass window said, "Yes?" as though you had overdrawn your account with the dentist and were two teeth in arrears.

She handed her slip of paper through the glass window and the nurse looked at it and said, "Lower molar, yes. They

called about you. Will you come right in, please? Through
the door to your left."

Into the vault? she almost said, and then silently opened
the door and went in. Another nurse was waiting, and she
smiled and turned, expecting to be followed, with no visible
doubt about her right to lead.

There was another X-ray, and the nurse told another nurse:
"Lower molar," and the other nurse said, "Come this way,
please."

There were labyrinths and passages, seeming to lead into
the heart of the office building, and she was put, finally, in
a cubicle where there was a couch with a pillow and a wash-
basin and a chair.

"Wait here," the nurse said. "Relax if you can."

"I'll probably go to sleep," she said.

"Fine," the nurse said. "You won't have to wait long."

She waited probably, for over an hour, although she spent
the time half-sleeping, waking only when someone passed
the door; occasionally the nurse looked in and smiled, once
she said, "Won't have to wait much longer." Then, suddenly,
the nurse was back, no longer smiling, no longer the good
hostess, but efficient and hurried. "Come along," she said,
and moved purposefully out of the little room into the hall-
ways again.

Then, quickly, more quickly than she was able to see, she
was sitting in the chair and there was a towel around her head
and a towel under her chin and the nurse was leaning a hand
on her shoulder.

"Will it hurt?" she asked.

"No," the nurse said, smiling. "You know it won't hurt,
don't you?"

"Yes," she said.

The dentist came in and smiled down on her from over her head. "Well," he said.

"Will it hurt?" she said.

"Now," he said cheerfully, "we couldn't stay in business if we hurt people." All the time he talked he was busying himself with metal hidden under a towel, and great machinery being wheeled in almost silently behind her. "We couldn't stay in business at all," he said. "All you've got to worry about is telling us all your secrets while you're asleep. Want to watch out for that, you know. Lower molar?" he said to the nurse.

"Lower molar, doctor," she said.

Then they put the metal-tasting rubber mask over her face and the dentist said, "You know," two or three times absent-mindedly while she could still see him over the mask. The nurse said "Relax your hands, dear," and after a long time she felt her fingers relaxing.

First of all things get so far away, she thought, remember this. And remember the metallic sound and taste of all of it. And the outrage.

And then the whirling music, the ringing confusedly loud music that went on and on, around and around, and she was running as fast as she could down a long horribly clear hall-way with doors on both sides and at the end of the hallway was Jim, holding out his hands and laughing, and calling something she could never hear because of the loud music, and she was running and then she said, "I'm not afraid," and someone from the door next to her took her arm and pulled her through and the world widened alarmingly until it would never stop and then it stopped with the head of the dentist looking down at her and the window dropped into place in front of her and the nurse was holding her arm.

"Why did you pull me back?" she said, and her mouth was full of blood. "I wanted to go on."

"I didn't pull you," the nurse said, but the dentist said, "She's not out of it yet."

She began to cry without moving and felt the tears rolling down her face and the nurse wiped them off with a towel. There was no blood anywhere around except in her mouth; everything was as clean as before. The dentist was gone, suddenly, and the nurse put out her arm and helped her out of the chair. "Did I talk?" she asked suddenly, anxiously. "Did I say anything?"

"You said, 'I'm not afraid,'" the nurse said soothingly. "Just as you were coming out of it."

"No," she said, stopping to pull at the arm around her. "Did I *say* anything? Did I say where he is?"

"You didn't say *anything*," the nurse said. "The doctor was only teasing you."

"Where's my tooth?" she asked suddenly, and the nurse laughed and said, "All gone. Never bother you again."

She was back in the cubicle, and she lay down on the couch and cried, and the nurse brought her whisky in a paper cup and set it on the edge of the wash-basin.

"God has given me blood to drink," she said to the nurse, and the nurse said, "Don't rinse your mouth or it won't clot."

After a long time the nurse came back and said to her from the doorway, smiling, "I see you're awake again."

"Why?" she said.

"You've been asleep," the nurse said. "I didn't want to wake you."

She sat up; she was dizzy and it seemed that she had been in the cubicle all her life.

"Do you want to come along now?" the nurse said, all kindness again. She held out the same arm, strong enough to guide any wavering footstep; this time they went back through the long corridor to where the nurse sat behind the bank window.

"All through?" this nurse said brightly. "Sit down a minute, then." She indicated a chair next to the glass window, and turned away to write busily. "Do not rinse your mouth for two hours," she said, without turning around. "Take a laxative tonight, take two aspirin if there is any pain. If there is much pain or excessive bleeding, notify this office at once. All right?" she said, and smiled brightly again.

There was a new little slip of paper; this one said, "Extraction," and underneath, "Do not rinse mouth. Take mild laxative. Two aspirin for pain. If pain is excessive or any hemorrhage occurs, notify office."

"Good-bye," the nurse said pleasantly.

"Good-bye," she said.

With the little slip of paper in her hand, she went out through the glass door and, still almost asleep, turned the corner and started down the hall. When she opened her eyes a little and saw that it was a long hall with doorways on either side, she stopped and then saw the door marked "Ladies" and went in. Inside there was a vast room with windows and wicker chairs and glaring white tiles and glittering silver faucets; there were four or five women around the wash-basins, combing their hair, putting on lipstick. She went directly to the nearest of the three wash-basins, took a paper towel, dropped her pocketbook and the little slip of paper on the floor next to her, and fumbled with the faucets, soaking the towel until it was dripping. Then she slapped it against her face violently. Her eyes cleared and she felt fresher, so she soaked the paper again and rubbed her face with it. She felt out blindly for another paper towel, and the woman next to her handed her one, with a laugh she could hear, although she could not see for the water in her eyes. She heard one of the women say, "Where we going for lunch?" and another one say, "Just downstairs, prob'ly. Old fool says I gotta be back in half-an-hour."

Then she realized that at the wash-basin she was in the way of the women in a hurry so she dried her face quickly. It was when she stepped a little aside to let someone else get to the basin and stood up and glanced into the mirror that she realized with a slight stinging shock that she had no idea which face was hers!

She looked into the mirror as though into a group of strangers, all staring at her or around her; no one was familiar in the group, no one smiled at her or looked at her with recognition; you'd think my own face would know me, she thought, with a queer numbness in her throat. There was a creamy chinless face with bright blond hair, and a sharp-looking face under a red veiled hat, and a colorless anxious face with brown hair pulled straight back, and a square rosy face under a square haircut, and two or three more faces pushing close to the mirror, moving, regarding themselves. Perhaps it's not a mirror, she thought, maybe it's a window and I'm looking straight through at women washing on the other side. But there were women combing their hair and consulting the mirror; the group was on her side, and she thought, I hope I'm not the blonde, and lifted her hand and put it on her cheek.

She was the pale anxious one with the hair pulled back and when she realized it she was indignant and moved hurriedly back through the crowd of women, thinking, It isn't fair, why don't I have any color in my face? There were some pretty faces there, why didn't I take one of those? I didn't have time, she told herself sullenly, they didn't give me time to think, I could have had one of the nice faces, even the blonde would be better.

She backed up and sat down in one of the wicker chairs. It's mean, she was thinking. She put her hand up and felt her hair; it was loosened after her sleep but that was definitely the way she wore it, pulled straight back all around and fastened at the back of her neck with a wide tight barrette. Like a schoolgirl, she thought, only—remembering the pale face in the mirror—only I'm older than that. She unfastened the barrette with difficulty and brought it around where she could look at it. Her hair fell softly around her face; it was warm and reached to her shoulders. The barrette was silver; engraved on it was the name, "Clara."

"Clara," she said aloud. "*Clara?*" Two of the women leaving the room smiled back at her over their shoulders; almost all the women were leaving now, correctly combed and lipsticked, hurrying out talking together. In the space of a second, like birds leaving a tree, they all were gone and she sat alone in the room. She dropped the barrette into the ashstand next to her chair; the ashstand was deep and metal, and the barrette made a satisfactory clang falling down. Her hair down on her shoulders, she opened her pocketbook, and began to take things out, setting them on her lap as she did so. Handkerchief, plain, white, uninitialled. Compact, square and brown tortoise-shell plastic, with a powder compartment and a rouge compartment; the rouge compartment had obviously never been used, although the powder cake was half-gone. That's why I'm so pale, she thought, and set the compact down. Lipstick, a rose shade, almost finished. A comb, an opened package of cigarettes and a package of matches, a change purse,

and a wallet. The change purse was red imitation leather
with a zipper across the top; she opened it and dumped the
money out into her hand. Nickels, dimes, pennies, a quarter.
Ninety-seven cents. Can't go far on that, she thought, and
opened the brown leather wallet; there was money in it but
she looked first for papers and found nothing. The only thing
in the wallet was money. She counted it; there were nineteen
dollars. I can go a little farther on *that*, she thought.

There was nothing else in the pocketbook. No keys—
shouldn't I have keys? she wondered—no papers, no address
book, no identification. The pocketbook itself was imitation
leather, light grey, and she looked down and discovered that
she was wearing a dark grey flannel suit and a salmon pink
blouse with a ruffle around the neck. Her shoes were black and
stout with moderate heels and they had laces, one of which
was untied. She was wearing beige stockings and there was
a ragged tear in the right knee and a great ragged run going
down her leg and ending in a hole in the toe which she could
feel inside her shoe. She was wearing a pin on the lapel of
her suit which, when she turned it around to look at it, was
a blue plastic letter C. She took the pin off and dropped it into
the ashstand, and it made a sort of clatter at the bottom, with
a metallic clang when it landed on the barrette. Her hands
were small, with stubby fingers and no nail polish; she wore
a thin gold wedding ring on her left hand and no other
jewelry.

Sitting alone in the ladies' room in the wicker chair, she
thought, The least I can do is get rid of these stockings. Since
no one was around she took off her shoes and stripped away
the stockings with a feeling of relief when her toe was released
from the hole. Hide them, she thought: the paper towel wastebasket. When she stood up she got a better sight of herself

in the mirror; it was worse than she had thought: the grey suit bagged in the seat, her legs were bony, and her shoulders sagged. I look fifty, she thought; and then, consulting the face, but I can't be more than thirty. Her hair hung down untidily around the pale face and with sudden anger she fumbled in the pocketbook and found the lipstick; she drew an emphatic rosy mouth on the pale face, realizing as she did so that she was not very expert at it, and with the red mouth the face looking at her seemed somehow better to her, so she opened the compact and put on pink cheeks with the rouge. The cheeks were uneven and patent, and the red mouth glaring, but at least the face was no longer pale and anxious.

She put the stockings into the wastebasket and went bare-legged out into the hall again, and purposefully to the elevator. The elevator operator said, "Down?" when he saw her and she stepped in and the elevator carried her silently downstairs. She went back past the grave professional doorman and out into the street where people were passing, and she stood in front of the building and waited. After a few minutes Jim came out of a crowd of people passing and came over to her and took her hand.

Somewhere between here and there was her bottle of codeine pills, upstairs on the floor of the ladies' room she had left a little slip of paper headed "Extraction"; seven floors below, oblivious of the people who stepped sharply along the sidewalk, not noticing their occasional curious glances, her hand in Jim's and her hair down on her shoulders, she ran barefoot through hot sand.

‡

## GOT A LETTER FROM JIMMY

SOMETIMES, she thought, stacking the dishes in the kitchen, sometimes I wonder if men are quite sane, any of them. Maybe they're all just crazy and every other woman knows it but me, and my mother never told me and my roommate just didn't mention it and all the other wives think I know. . . .

"Got a letter from Jimmy today," he said, when he was unfolding his napkin.

So you got it at last, she thought, so he finally broke down and wrote you, maybe now it will be all right, everything settled and friendly again. . . . "What did he have to say?" she asked casually.

"Don't know," he said, "didn't open it."

My God, she thought, seeing it clearly all the way through right then. She waited.

"Going to send it back to him tomorrow unopened."

I could have figured that one out by myself, she thought. I couldn't have kept that letter closed for five minutes. I would have figured out something nasty like tearing it up and sending it back in little pieces, or getting someone to write a sharp answer for me, but I couldn't have kept it around for five minutes.

"Had lunch with Tom today," he said, as though the subject were closed, just exactly as though the subject were closed, she thought, just exactly as though he never expected to think about it again. Maybe he doesn't, she thought, my God.

"I think you ought to open Jimmy's letter," she said. Maybe

it will all be just as easy as that, she thought, maybe he'll say all right and go open it, maybe he'll go home and live with his mother for a while.

"Why?" he said.

Start easy, she thought. You'll kill yourself if you don't. "Oh, I guess because I'm curious and I'll just die if I don't see what's in it," she said.

"Open it," he said.

Just watch me make a move for it, she thought. "Seriously," she said, "it's so silly to hold a grudge against a letter. Against Jimmy, all right. But not to read a letter out of spite is silly." Oh God, she thought, I said silly. I said silly twice. That finishes it. If he hears me say he's silly I'm through, I can talk all night.

"Why should I read it?" he said, "I wouldn't be interested in anything he had to say."

"I would."

"Open it," he said.

Oh God, she thought, oh God oh God, I'll steal it out of his brief case, I'll scramble it up with his eggs tomorrow, but I won't take a dare like that, he'd break my arm.

"Okay," she said, "so I'm not interested." Make him think you're through, let him get nicely settled in his chair, let him get to the lemon pie, get him off on some other subject.

"Had lunch with Tom today," he said.

Stacking the dishes in the kitchen, she thought, Maybe he means it, maybe he could kill himself first, maybe he really wasn't curious and even if he were he'd drive himself into a hysterical state trying to read through the envelope, locked in the bathroom. Or maybe he just got it and said, Oh, from Jimmy, and threw it in his brief case and forgot it. I'll murder him if he did, she thought, I'll bury him in the cellar.

Later, when he was drinking his coffee, she said, "Going to show it to John?" John will die too, she thought, John will edge around it just like I'm doing.

"Show what to John?" he said.

"Jimmy's letter."

"Oh," he said. "Sure."

A tremendous triumph captured her. So he really wants to show it to John, she thought, so he just wants to see for himself that he's still mad, he wants John to say, Really, are you still mad at Jimmy? And he wants to be able to say yes. Out of her great triumph she thought, He really has been thinking about it all this time, too; and she said, before she could stop herself:

"Thought you were going to send it back unopened?"

He looked up. "I forgot," he said. "Guess I will."

I had to open my mouth, she thought. He forgot. The trouble is, she thought, he really did forget. It slipped his mind completely, he never gave it a second thought, if it was a snake it would have bit him. Under the cellar steps, she thought, with his head bashed in and his goddam letter under his folded hands, and it's worth it, she thought, oh it's worth it.

‡

# THE LOTTERY

THE MORNING of June 27th was clear and sunny, with the fresh warmth of a full-summer day; the flowers were blossoming profusely and the grass was richly green. The people of the village began to gather in the square, between the post office and the bank, around ten o'clock; in some towns there were so many people that the lottery took two days and had to be started on June 26th, but in this village, where there were only about three hundred people, the whole lottery took less than two hours, so it could begin at ten o'clock in the morning and still be through in time to allow the villagers to get home for noon dinner.

The children assembled first, of course. School was recently over for the summer, and the feeling of liberty sat uneasily on most of them; they tended to gather together quietly for a while before they broke into boisterous play, and their talk was still of the classroom and the teacher, of books and reprimands. Bobby Martin had already stuffed his pockets full of stones, and the other boys soon followed his example, selecting the smoothest and roundest stones; Bobby and Harry Jones and Dickie Delacroix—the villagers pronounced this name "Dellacroy"— eventually made a great pile of stones in one corner of the square and guarded it against the raids of the other boys. The girls stood aside, talking among themselves, looking over their shoulders at the boys, and the very small children rolled in the dust or clung to the hands of their older brothers or sisters.

Soon the men began to gather, surveying their own children, speaking of planting and rain, tractors and taxes. They stood together, away from the pile of stones in the corner, and their jokes were quiet and they smiled rather than laughed. The women, wearing faded house dresses and sweaters, came shortly after their menfolk. They greeted one another and exchanged bits of gossip as they went to join their husbands. Soon the women, standing by their husbands, began to call to their children, and the children came reluctantly, having to be called four or five times. Bobby Martin ducked under his mother's grasping hand and ran, laughing, back to the pile of stones. His father spoke up sharply, and Bobby came quickly and took his place between his father and his oldest brother.

The lottery was conducted—as were the square dances, the teen-age club, the Halloween program—by Mr. Summers, who had time and energy to devote to civic activities. He was a round-faced, jovial man and he ran the coal business, and people were sorry for him, because he had no children and his wife was a scold. When he arrived in the square, carrying the black wooden box, there was a murmur of conversation among the villagers, and he waved and called, "Little late today, folks." The postmaster, Mr. Graves, followed him, carrying a three-legged stool, and the stool was put in the center of the square and Mr. Summers set the black box down on it. The villagers kept their distance, leaving a space between themselves and the stool, and when Mr. Summers said, "Some of you fellows want to give me a hand?" there was a hesitation before two men, Mr. Martin and his oldest son, Baxter, came forward to hold the box steady on the stool while Mr. Summers stirred up the papers inside it.

The original paraphernalia for the lottery had been lost long ago, and the black box now resting on the stool had been put into use even before Old Man Warner, the oldest man in town, was born. Mr. Summers spoke frequently to the villagers about making a new box, but no one liked to upset even as much tradition as was represented by the black box. There was a story that the present box had been made with some pieces of the box that had preceded it, the one that had been constructed when the first people settled down to make a village here. Every year, after the lottery, Mr. Summers began talking again about a new box, but every year the subject was allowed to fade off without anything's being done. The black box grew shabbier each year; by now it was no longer completely black but splintered badly along one side to show the original wood color, and in some places faded or stained.

Mr. Martin and his oldest son, Baxter, held the black box securely on the stool until Mr. Summers had stirred the papers thoroughly with his hand. Because so much of the ritual had been forgotten or discarded, Mr. Summers had been successful in having slips of paper substituted for the chips of wood that had been used for generations. Chips of wood, Mr. Summers had argued, had been all very well when the village was tiny, but now that the population was more than three hundred and likely to keep on growing, it was necessary to use something that would fit more easily into the black box. The night before the lottery, Mr. Summers and Mr. Graves made up the slips of paper and put them in the box, and it was then taken to the safe of Mr. Summers' coal company and locked up until Mr. Summers was ready to take it to the square next morning. The rest of the year, the box was put away, sometimes one place, sometimes another; it had spent one year in Mr. Graves's barn and another year underfoot in the post office, and sometimes it was set on a shelf in the Martin grocery and left there.

There was a great deal of fussing to be done before Mr. Summers declared the lottery open. There were the lists to make up—of heads of families, heads of households in each family, members of each household in each family. There was the proper swearing-in of Mr. Summers by the postmaster, as the official of the lottery; at one time, some people remembered, there had been a recital of some sort, performed by the official of the lottery, a perfunctory, tuneless chant that had been rattled off duly each year; some people believed that the official of the lottery used to stand just so when he said or sang it, others believed that he was supposed to walk among the people, but years and years ago this part of the ritual had been allowed to lapse. There had been, also, a ritual salute, which the official of the lottery had had to use in addressing each person who came up to draw from the box, but this also had changed with time, until now it was felt necessary only for the official to speak to each person approaching. Mr. Summers was very good at all this; in his clean white shirt and blue jeans, with one hand resting carelessly on the black box, he seemed very proper and important as he talked interminably to Mr. Graves and the Martins.

Just as Mr. Summers finally left off talking and turned to the assembled villagers, Mrs. Hutchinson came hurriedly along the path to the square, her sweater thrown over her shoulders, and slid into place in the back of the crowd. "Clean forgot what day it was," she said to Mrs. Delacroix, who stood next to her, and they both laughed softly. "Thought my old man was out back stacking wood," Mrs. Hutchinson went on, "and then I looked out the window and the kids was gone, and then I remembered it was the twenty-seventh and came a-running." She dried her hands on her apron, and Mrs. Delacroix said, "You're in time, though. They're still talking away up there."

Mrs. Hutchinson craned her neck to see through the crowd and found her husband and children standing near the front.

She tapped Mrs. Delacroix on the arm as a farewell and began to make her way through the crowd. The people separated good-humoredly to let her through; two or three people said, in voices just loud enough to be heard across the crowd, "Here comes your Missus Hutchinson," and "Bill, she made it after all." Mrs. Hutchinson reached her husband, and Mr. Summers, who had been waiting, said cheerfully, "Thought we were going to have to get on without you, Tessie." Mrs. Hutchinson said, grinning, "Wouldn't have me leave m'dishes in the sink, now, would you, Joe?," and soft laughter ran through the crowd as the people stirred back into position after Mrs. Hutchinson's arrival.

"Well, now," Mr. Summers said soberly, "guess we better get started, get this over with, so's we can go back to work. Anybody ain't here?"

"Dunbar," several people said. "Dunbar, Dunbar."

Mr. Summers consulted his list. "Clyde Dunbar," he said. "That's right. He's broke his leg, hasn't he? Who's drawing for him?"

"Me, I guess," a woman said, and Mr. Summers turned to look at her. "Wife draws for her husband," Mr. Summers said. "Don't you have a grown boy to do it for you, Janey?" Although Mr. Summers and everyone else in the village knew the answer perfectly well, it was the business of the official of the lottery to ask such questions formally. Mr. Summers waited with an expression of polite interest while Mrs. Dunbar answered.

"Horace's not but sixteen yet," Mrs. Dunbar said regretfully. "Guess I gotta fill in for the old man this year."

"Right," Mr. Summers said. He made a note on the list he was holding. Then he asked, "Watson boy drawing this year?"

A tall boy in the crowd raised his hand. "Here," he said. "I'm drawing for m'mother and me." He blinked his eyes nervously and ducked his head as several voices in the crowd said things like "Good fellow, Jack," and "Glad to see your mother's got a man to do it."

"Well," Mr. Summers said, "guess that's everyone. Old Man Warner make it?"

"Here," a voice said, and Mr. Summers nodded.

A sudden hush fell on the crowd as Mr. Summers cleared his throat and looked at the list. "All ready?" he called. "Now, I'll read the names—heads of families first—and the men come up and take a paper out of the box. Keep the paper folded in your hand without looking at it until everyone has had a turn. Everything clear?"

The people had done it so many times that they only half listened to the directions; most of them were quiet, wetting their lips, not looking around. Then Mr. Summers raised one hand high and said, "Adams." A man disengaged himself from the crowd and came forward. "Hi, Steve," Mr. Summers said, and Mr. Adams said, "Hi, Joe." They grinned at one another humorlessly and nervously. Then Mr. Adams reached into the black box and took out a folded paper. He held it firmly by one corner as he turned and went hastily back to his place in the crowd, where he stood a little apart from his family, not looking down at his hand.

"Allen," Mr. Summers said. "Anderson. . . . Bentham."

"Seems like there's no time at all between lotteries any more," Mrs. Delacroix said to Mrs. Graves in the back row. "Seems like we got through with the last one only last week."

"Time sure goes fast," Mrs. Graves said.

"Clark. . . . Delacroix."

"There goes my old man," Mrs. Delacroix said. She held her breath while her husband went forward.

"Dunbar," Mr. Summers said, and Mrs. Dunbar went steadily to the box while one of the women said, "Go on, Janey," and another said, "There she goes."

"We're next," Mrs. Graves said. She watched while Mr. Graves came around from the side of the box, greeted Mr. Summers gravely, and selected a slip of paper from the box. By now, all through the crowd there were men holding the small folded papers in their large hands, turning them over and over nervously. Mrs. Dunbar and her two sons stood together, Mrs. Dunbar holding the slip of paper.

"Harburt. . . . Hutchinson."

"Get up there, Bill," Mrs. Hutchinson said, and the people near her laughed.

"Jones."

"They do say," Mr. Adams said to Old Man Warner, who stood next to him, "that over in the north village they're talking of giving up the lottery."

Old Man Warner snorted. "Pack of crazy fools," he said. "Listening to the young folks, nothing's good enough for *them*. Next thing you know, they'll be wanting to go back to living in caves, nobody work any more, live *that* way for a while. Used to be a saying about 'Lottery in June, corn be heavy soon.' First thing you know, we'd all be eating stewed chickweed and acorns. There's *always* been a lottery," he added petulantly. "Bad enough to see young Joe Summers up there joking with everybody."

"Some places have already quit lotteries," Mrs. Adams said.

"Nothing but trouble in *that*," Old Man Warner said stoutly. "Pack of young fools."

"Martin." And Bobby Martin watched his father go forward. "Overdyke. . . . Percy."

"I wish they'd hurry," Mrs. Dunbar said to her older son. "I wish they'd hurry."

"They're almost through," her son said.

"You get ready to run tell Dad," Mrs. Dunbar said.

Mr. Summers called his own name and then stepped forward precisely and selected a slip from the box. Then he called, "Warner."

"Seventy-seventh year I been in the lottery," Old Man Warner said as he went through the crowd. "Seventy-seventh time."

"Watson." The tall boy came awkwardly through the crowd. Someone said, "Don't be nervous, Jack," and Mr. Summers said, "Take your time, son."

"Zanini."

After that, there was a long pause, a breathless pause, until Mr. Summers, holding his slip of paper in the air, said, "All right, fellows." For a minute, no one moved, and then all the slips of paper were opened. Suddenly, all the women began to speak at once, saying, "Who is it?," "Who's got it?," "Is it the Dunbars?," "Is it the Watsons?" Then the voices began to say, "It's Hutchinson. It's Bill," "Bill Hutchinson's got it."

"Go tell your father," Mrs. Dunbar said to her older son.

People began to look around to see the Hutchinsons. Bill Hutchinson was standing quiet, staring down at the paper in his hand. Suddenly, Tessie Hutchinson shouted to Mr. Summers, "You didn't give him time enough to take any paper he wanted. I saw you. It wasn't fair!"

"Be a good sport, Tessie," Mrs. Delacroix called, and Mrs. Graves said, "All of us took the same chance."

"Shut up, Tessie," Bill Hutchinson said.

"Well, everyone," Mr. Summers said, "that was done pretty fast, and now we've got to be hurrying a little more to get done in time." He consulted his next list. "Bill," he said, "you draw for the Hutchinson family. You got any other households in the Hutchinsons?"

"There's Don and Eva," Mrs. Hutchinson yelled. "Make *them* take their chance!"

"Daughters draw with their husbands' families, Tessie," Mr. Summers said gently. "You know that as well as anyone else."

"It wasn't *fair*," Tessie said.

"I guess not, Joe," Bill Hutchinson said regretfully. "My daughter draws with her husband's family, that's only fair. And I've got no other family except the kids."

"Then, as far as drawing for families is concerned, it's you," Mr. Summers said in explanation, "and as far as drawing for households is concerned, that's you, too. Right?"

"Right," Bill Hutchinson said.

"How many kids, Bill?" Mr. Summers asked formally.

"Three," Bill Hutchinson said. "There's Bill, Jr., and Nancy, and little Dave. And Tessie and me."

"All right, then," Mr. Summers said. "Harry, you got their tickets back?"

Mr. Graves nodded and held up the slips of paper. "Put them in the box, then," Mr. Summers directed. "Take Bill's and put it in."

"I think we ought to start over," Mrs. Hutchinson said, as quietly as she could. "I tell you it wasn't *fair*. You didn't give him time enough to choose. *Every*body saw that."

Mr. Graves had selected the five slips and put them in the box, and he dropped all the papers but those onto the ground, where the breeze caught them and lifted them off.

"Listen, everybody," Mrs. Hutchinson was saying to the people around her.

"Ready, Bill?" Mr. Summers asked, and Bill Hutchinson, with one quick glance around at his wife and children, nodded.

"Remember," Mr. Summers said, "take the slips and keep them folded until each person has taken one. Harry, you help little Dave." Mr. Graves took the hand of the little boy, who came willingly with him up to the box. "Take a paper out of the box, Davy," Mr. Summers said. Davy put his hand into the box and laughed. "Take just *one* paper," Mr. Summers said. "Harry, you hold it for him." Mr. Graves took the child's hand and removed the folded paper from the tight fist and held it while little Dave stood next to him and looked up at him wonderingly.

"Nancy next," Mr. Summers said. Nancy was twelve, and her school friends breathed heavily as she went forward, switching her skirt, and took a slip daintily from the box. "Bill, Jr.," Mr. Summers said, and Billy, his face red and his feet overlarge, nearly knocked the box over as he got a paper out. "Tessie," Mr. Summers said. She hesitated for a minute, looking around defiantly, and then set her lips and went up to the box. She snatched a paper out and held it behind her.

"Bill," Mr. Summers said, and Bill Hutchinson reached into the box and felt around, bringing his hand out at last with the slip of paper in it.

The crowd was quiet. A girl whispered, "I hope it's not Nancy," and the sound of the whisper reached the edges of the crowd.

"It's not the way it used to be," Old Man Warner said clearly. "People ain't the way they used to be."

"All right," Mr. Summers said. "Open the papers. Harry, you open little Dave's."

Mr. Graves opened the slip of paper and there was a general sigh through the crowd as he held it up and everyone could see that it was blank. Nancy and Bill, Jr., opened theirs at the same time, and both beamed and laughed, turning around to the crowd and holding their slips of paper above their heads.

"Tessie," Mr. Summers said. There was a pause, and then Mr. Summers looked at Bill Hutchinson, and Bill unfolded his paper and showed it. It was blank.

"It's Tessie," Mr. Summers said, and his voice was hushed. "Show us her paper, Bill."

Bill Hutchinson went over to his wife and forced the slip of paper out of her hand. It had a black spot on it, the black spot Mr. Summers had made the night before with the heavy pencil in the coal-company office. Bill Hutchinson held it up, and there was a stir in the crowd.

"All right, folks," Mr. Summers said. "Let's finish quickly."

Although the villagers had forgotten the ritual and lost the original black box, they still remembered to use stones. The pile of stones the boys had made earlier was ready; there were stones on the ground with the blowing scraps of paper that had come out of the box. Mrs. Delacroix selected a stone so large she had to pick it up with both hands and turned to Mrs. Dunbar. "Come on," she said. "Hurry up.'

Mrs. Dunbar had small stones in both hands, and she said, gasping for breath, "I can't run at all. You'll have to go ahead and I'll catch up with you."

The children had stones already, and someone gave little Davy Hutchinson a few pebbles.

Tessie Hutchinson was in the center of a cleared space by now, and she held her hands out desperately as the villagers moved in on her. "It isn't fair," she said. A stone hit her on the side of the head.

Old Man Warner was saying, "Come on, come on, every-one." Steve Adams was in the front of the crowd of villagers, with Mrs. Graves beside him.

"It isn't fair, it isn't right," Mrs. Hutchinson screamed, and then they were upon her.

# V

*Epilogue*

. . . She set her foot upon the ship,
    No mariners could she behold,
But the sails were o the taffetie,
    And the masts o the beaten gold.

She had not sailed a league, a league,
    A league but barely three,
When dismal grew his countenance,
    And drumlie grew his ee.

They had not sailed a league, a league,
    A league but barely three,
Until she espied his cloven foot,
    And she wept right bitterlie.

'O hold your tongue of your weeping,' says he,
    'Of your weeping now let me be,
I will shew you how the lilies grow
    On the banks of Italy.'

'O what hills are yon, yon pleasant hills,
    That the sun shines sweetly on?'
'O yon are the hills of heaven,' he said,
    'Where you will never win.'

'O whaten a mountain is yon,' she said,
    'All so dreary wi frost and snow?'
'O yon is the mountain of hell,' he cried,
    'Where you and I will go.'

He strack the tap-mast wi his hand,
  The fore-mast wi his knee,
And he brake that gallant ship in twain,
  And sank her in the sea.

from James Harris, The Daemon Lover

(Child Ballad No. 243)